A MOMENT IN TIME is dedicated to my mum, Judy.
Without her continued support & guidance,
many things I do would be impossible.

A MOMENT IN TIME is also dedicated to the
many Emergency Services & Public Safety workers
in Australia & across the world who dedicate
their lives to serving their communities in many ways.
Sadly, some of them do not make it home at the end
of their shifts.

Thank you to the many people who have supported me
during the creation of A MOMENT IN TIME. It certainly has
been a very interesting ride as a first time author! There are more
acknowledgements at the end of the story.

A MOMENT IN TIME

written by

Eric Brook

http://www.amomentintimenovel.com

A MOMENT IN TIME by Eric Brook

First published in 2010
© 2010 Erk Communications

National Library of Australia Cataloguing-in-Publication entry
Author: Brook, Eric.
Title: A Moment In Time / Eric Brook.
Edition: 1st ed.
ISBN: 9780980865905 (pbk.)
Dewey Number: A823.4

A MOMENT IN TIME was mostly written on an iPhone using the
My Writing Nook application http://www.mywritingnook.com

For more information about this book and the author, visit
http://www.amomentintime.com

A MOMENT IN TIME is presented by Channel Erk. A podcast version
will debut in 2011. http://www.channelerk.com

Covers by Thorium Girl http://www.thoriumgirl.com

http://www.amomentintimenovel.com

A MOMENT IN TIME by Eric Brook

http://www.amomentintimenovel.com

Chapter 1 – Rise & Shine, Caroline!

12 noon, Thursday April 1 2010

The small inner-city apartment was in darkness. The woman sleeping in the bed had no idea what was happening in the outside world. The weather had been unpredictable over the last few days in Sydney, mainly in terms of being dry or wet. It was not cold in the apartment but she felt comfortable with the blankets up to her shoulders. For some reason, she felt better about sleeping with a sheet or a blanket covering her as she slept. Despite summer officially being over, it was not uncommon for hot weather to continue well into April. There was a ceiling fan and an air conditioner in the apartment. The ceiling fan was on low, circulating air around the bedroom.

There was a large digital clock in the room on the bedside table that was pointed away from the bed. If the clock with the big red numbers on it was pointed towards the woman, it might keep her awake if she was in a light sleep. In the past, she had found that with the clock pointed towards her, she would continually look towards it and wonder how long it would be before she was due to wake up. This was very annoying. It happened more often to her if she had to be awake early in the morning.

http://www.amomentintimenovel.com

A MOMENT IN TIME by Eric Brook

Caroline was in a deep sleep. She had been awaiting this day for months but she was not sure how she would sleep the night before. She did not take any sleeping tablets but she was tempted. It would have been totally understandable had she not been able to sleep as she had been looking forward to this day since she was a small child. Unlike many people that she knew, she was about to achieve her life-long dream. It was a dream that many people had tried to warn her against pursuing. They said that it was dangerous and that it was no place for a woman. Comments like that made Caroline more determined to do it. This afternoon was the start of a new part of her life. She would soon find out if all of the doubters were right or not. She wanted to prove them wrong.

The small bedroom had heavy curtains to try and block out the noise of the outside world as she needed to sleep when most of her surrounding world was awake. As a shift worker, she needed to be able to sleep when other people were awake. Living in an apartment was not ideal for this but it was all she could afford in the inner city. Because she was renting, she could not sound proof the apartment as much as she wanted. Ideally, she would love to have a roller shutter on every window. This would mean, however, that the remaining windows on other apartments on the block would also need them. Caroline would be quite happy to pay for her own shutters but not the shutters of the remaining apartments. There was a lot of compromises that Caroline had to make in order to be able to live where she did and be comfortable.

A MOMENT IN TIME by Eric Brook

Suddenly, she heard a really loud buzzing noise. Despite being in a deep sleep, it was enough to jolt her out of her slumber. Groggily opening her eyes, she looked at the calendar attached to a cupboard door. It was the 1st of April but the calendar was still showing March with all 31 days crossed out. Looking at the calendar, she knew her day had arrived. Throwing the blankets back, Caroline slowly got out of bed. Her room was tidy so she did not trip over anything as she went to the bathroom. She thought to herself "I need a shower to wake myself up."

She lived alone so she did not find it strange to find a quiet apartment when she woke up. With her job, she preferred to live alone, even though she did have a steady boyfriend. It was easier for the moment for Caroline to live in her apartment and for Dave to live in his. Luckily for them, Dave and Caroline lived close to each other. They often alternated between each other's apartment and spent a lot of time together when they were not working. She was not the type of woman who needed to see Dave every day which suited both of their lifestyles. Not bothering to take a dressing gown to the bathroom, Caroline walked the short distance in her red satin pyjamas. She looked into the mirror and rubbed the sleep out of her eyes.

A MOMENT IN TIME by Eric Brook

She stretched her arms above her head and smiled at the reflection in the mirror. "I am placing you under arrest for being awesome" she said to the reflection. "You are not obliged to say or do anything but anything you say or do may be used as evidence against you. Do you understand?" With a comical tone and a strange look on her face, the reflection replied "Anything you say, Officer."

After having a long shower, the bathroom was full of steam. A long shower was great after waking up. It was a bonus on a cool day. She was not a morning person. She hated going to bed like a little kid and hated waking up early. Sleeping in until lunchtime was heaven in her eyes, especially if she was working until 3am. A 3am finish meant she would go to sleep by around 5am. If she was doing a few 12 hour shifts in a row, she wanted to get at least 8 hours sleep. Caroline returned to her bedroom. Living alone and comfortable with her slim but curvy body, Caroline did not need to worry about using a towel for the short distance back to the bedroom. Even if Dave was around, she would have walked naked for that short distance.

Reaching into a drawer, she selected a matching lacy bra and pantie set and then shook her head. "Caroline, you numpty" she said out loud to no one, "You are going to work". Placing the lacy underwear back in the drawer, she went to the next drawer down and selected a sports bra and comfortable undies. After all, she did not know how far she would have to run today.

A MOMENT IN TIME by Eric Brook

After putting her underwear on, Caroline reached to her dressing table and selected a black spray can. She firstly sprayed her underarms and then her back with deodorant and opened the big cupboard door. She selected a clothes hanger that had a sky blue shirt and navy blue cargo pants on the same hanger. She put the shirt on first, briefly looking at the shoulder patch and smiling. She especially liked the way she looked in the newer cargo pants female constables could wear now compared to the traditional policewoman's pants which added kilos to even the smallest bottom. Doing up the buttons, she walked over to her dressing table and picked up a name badge that said "Constable Caroline Clarke". She pinned the badge to her shirt, even though it was likely that soon, she'd have a new badge reading "City Central" and a number.

After making sure the badge was on straight, she sat down on the bed and put her navy blue pants and socks on. Reaching down to the bottom of her cupboard, she selected her army-style boots and placed them on her feet. Her boots were heavy but she was now used to them, having worn the same shoes throughout the majority of her course. With the long shifts, it was important that the shoes fit correctly, that they were comfortable and that she was able to run in them when required. It was likely that she might spend the majority of the shift on her feet so comfort was very important. Safety, of course, was an important consideration as well. The shoes needed to be tough.

A MOMENT IN TIME by Eric Brook

"Almost ready", Caroline thought. She placed her new wallet complete with shiny new police badge in her pants pocket. Standing up, she walked to the coat rack in a corner of the room. She reached for the smaller of the two belts first and placed it around her waist. She needed to do this to make sure that her pants stayed up. The larger belt she reached for next was not to keep her pants up but contained most of the equipment she needed. She put the larger belt (called a duty belt) around her, attaching it to the smaller belt. The various pouches were empty because the contents (also called appointments) were waiting for her at the police station.

While the two belt arrangement might have been overkill at that moment, once all of her equipment was secured to the belt, two belts were essential. The larger belt would hold things like her gun, handcuffs, batons and assorted other items. Some officers called their duty belt their "hell belt". It had been proven that the design of the belt and the ever increasing amount of things being attached to it was not good for an officer's health. Many people had stress related injuries due to their hell belts.

If she was on a station-based shift (for instance working on the station's enquiry counter) or at court, she would not be able to wear her duty belt so the inner belt was essential. The practice had been tried and tested over many years and worked well. At the end of the shift, Caroline would be able to take her hell belt off without being worried about her pants falling around her ankles.

A MOMENT IN TIME by Eric Brook

Satisfied that she was completely dressed, she pulled the blankets up and made the bed quickly. Looking at the clock, she saw that it was now approaching 1pm. She lived a short drive from the police station and still had 2 hours before her 12 hour shift started at 3pm. But because this was her first day as a Police Officer and her first day at her new Police Station, she wanted to give herself extra time. Walking to the bathroom again, Caroline combed her medium length hair into a functional ponytail. She did not believe in wearing make-up to work because it would be next to useless if she sweated.

She did not want to known as a woman who was always looking at herself in the mirror or was powdering her nose while the local crooks were using her partner as a punching bag. Hopefully, the other women at her station felt the same way. Once someone had that sort of reputation, it was very hard to shake it. Many careers had been ruined by reputations and rumours, even if they were untrue. Mud stuck, even if it was thrown towards the wrong person for the wrong reasons. It was something that was stressed during her training, the importance of each person having trust in the rest of their team.

A MOMENT IN TIME by Eric Brook

The noise of a ringing telephone filled the apartment. Running to her cordless phone on the kitchen table, she lifted the handset and held it to her ear. She was only expecting one call this morning and a quick glance at the phone's display confirmed the identity of the caller. It was clearly someone she wanted to talk to and not a telemarketer.

"Hey babe! What's doing?"

Luckily for Caroline, she knew that the person on the other end of the phone was her boyfriend, Dave. "I'm just calling to wish you good luck for your first day. I didn't wake you up, did I? Are you nervous about today?", he asked.

Dave and Caroline had met a few years ago. Like so many people in the current day, they met on the internet. It was a mere coincidence at the time that he was a police officer. Now, they were both cops. Luckily, they were working at different stations. Dave worked at the North Shore command based at Chatswood. It was very handy, though. Not many people understood what it was like to be a shift worker and fewer still understood what it was like to be in law enforcement. Cop on cop action might be a Hollywood cliche but in many cases, it worked fine.

A MOMENT IN TIME by Eric Brook

Now that Caroline had finished her training, it would be interesting to see if their relationship changed. She had deliberately chosen not to work at Dave's station. During her training, she was able to choose a list of stations for her first posting. She did not tempt fate by selecting North Shore.

"Nah, I'm fine. I'm all dressed and ready to go. Can't wait to get started. I hope my partner is cool. I just want to get on the truck and pitch in. Gotta go, babe. I'm getting ready to head off. Talk later. Enjoy your day off. I'll be fine.", Caroline spoke into the phone. After a few moments of kissing noises, Caroline hung up the phone. She hoped to see Dave sometime over the weekend. If that was not possible, a few phone calls would have to do. As much as she wanted to talk to Dave, she had to cut the conversation short. Knowing her routine, he understood this.

Grooming complete, she walked into the bedroom again and went to the big cupboard again. She removed all her work uniforms from the cupboard and took them out to her living room, carefully placing them onto her lounge. Going back into her bedroom, she went back into her cupboard and grabbed a blue backpack. She placed some toiletries into the bag as well as what she called her street policing cap. It was important to her to make sure that she had spare uniforms and toiletries in her locker at work. It was not as if she was an office worker and one application of perfume was enough for the entire day.

A MOMENT IN TIME by Eric Brook

She put on her official police hat that in the current day was used more for court appearances than anything else and went to the bathroom again. Caroline checked herself in the mirror and smiled. She gave herself a once-over look to make sure that she looked presentable and professional. Satisfied that she was looking smart and that she had not forgotten anything, she returned to the bedroom, picked up her backpack and walked back to the lounge room. Her excitement was building because she knew that she had to leave for work very soon.

The lounge room was small but it was home to Caroline. Devoid to photos and paintings, the only thing on the wall was the clock that now read 1.15pm. "I've still got enough time", she thought. Walking to the refrigerator, she opened it and looked inside briefly. She knew that she should probably eat something before she went to work. Reaching inside, she grabbed a large bottle of orange juice and poured herself a glass. "Do I eat something now?" she thought. "I don't want to get any food on my uniform" she said aloud to herself. "Mental note to self" saying to no one in particular, "Have breakfast then get dressed." Knowing there was no one in the apartment but her, she knew that it was pointless talking out loud but sometimes did that anyway for her own amusement.

The orange juice refreshed her somewhat but she knew that one glass was not going to be enough for the whole day. She also knew that drinking too much juice could mean too many visits to the toilet. Washing and drying her glass, she placed the backpack on her back and her coat hangered uniforms over one extended arm. After a quick search, she grabbed her small bunch of keys from the table, she looked around the room for a final time and left the apartment. She was doubly sure to lock the door, even though she lived in a quiet neighbourhood. She now knew through her training that criminals would often target quieter neighbourhoods some distance from their own.

Now outside, Caroline could see the outside world for the first time today. It was a bright and sunny day and she had no need for a jacket. The previous night, she had loaded her various work jackets into the boot of the car. She did not want to wear her uniform to and from work every day. She knew that even though she was close to work, the weather conditions could be different. Also, some types of assignments meant that she had to wear different items of clothing. It was not a good move to try to explain to her supervisor that she could not wear her high visibility gear because it was sitting at home in her cupboard in her bedroom.

For the first day at least, she took all she needed with her to place in her locker at the police station. She knew from her training that is what most people did. After all, a change of uniform at the station could be very handy if her uniform was damaged in any way mid shift. She knew that at least for one day a week, she would need to drive to work in order to bring her used uniforms home and wash them.

A MOMENT IN TIME by Eric Brook

Looking around from her 4th floor vantage point, she could see a few local landmarks. She loved her local community but did not want to police there. She would much rather walk down the street as citizen Caroline Clarke in her local neighbourhood. Of course, she had been warned at the Police Academy that a Police Officer is truly never off-duty and that one day, you might have to enforce the law in your own street.

Caroline was happy with her posting at the City Central command rather than her local Harbourside command because it was busier. She had put in some hard yards during the last 6 months of training and study and wanted to put that to good use. She liked the vibe of the area that she was going to be policing as she was a true city girl.

Despite the stereotype, it was not common for new police officers to be sent out to the middle of beyond. Working in the metro area was an ideal learning environment. Some of her classmates had selected commands close to their homes so they would not have to drive long distances, especially at the end of a hard shift. With only 12 hours between shifts at times, it was very important to spend as little time travelling as possible to and from the police station.

Loading her car with her uniforms and backpack, she felt strange getting into her own car in uniform. Her car was an older model Toyota sedan and not the newer models that the police used for driving around in. She loved her car but she was undecided at this point about driving to work every day. She knew that parking was not going to be easy around the City Central Police Station. She had not been there as a part of her training so she did not know about things like parking, special entrances and places to eat around the station. During her training, she had (not by choice) spent time at quieter commands in the suburbs. This was one of the reasons that she preferred a busier command such as City Central.

It was an easy drive at the times she would be driving. She had not yet studied her public transport options but knew it would be a limited option, especially considering she was due to finish at 3am. She knew that getting a taxi at that time of the morning would be difficult. While it might be ok for the occasional trip, to do it every day would be very expensive.

Caroline started her car and reversed out of her underground parking spot. She reached out of her window and pushed a button for the car park door to open. The door opened and she drove out. The time on her stereo told her it was now 1.35pm. Knowing the traffic the way she did, she would be happy if she was at work at about 2.15pm. She had driven to the city from her apartment many times so she knew the best way to get there.

A MOMENT IN TIME by Eric Brook

Before joining the police, Caroline had worked in a range of service industry jobs in the city. She had done some waitressing and bar work, often late at night. This often meant working when many people were out having fun. This would be no different in her new job. While in the past she had reason to call the police to deal with drunks, now she was the police. Her police training would have been very handy in her previous professions, especially with her bar work. She enjoyed the work but policing was her childhood dream. Besides, a government job paid better and policing was a recession proof industry.

With the radio on a rock music station, she was singing along to the music that she loved. Occasionally she was stopped at the traffic lights and someone in another car would give her a strange look. She thought it was because of her singing but then realised that it could be because of the uniform that she was wearing. Fortunately, she had remembered to take her police hat off while driving. The old style police hat was not one that you could wear driving as it would add an inch or two to your height and was uncomfortable to wear from long periods.

While heading towards the city, Caroline saw that there was a lot of traffic heading out of the city. She then remembered that many people in Sydney would be taking a long weekend for Easter. She was one of the unlucky ones that was rostered to work every day over Easter but she thought of the extra money she would get. Yes, even

A MOMENT IN TIME by Eric Brook

Police Officers think of their wages from time to time. Many people had seemingly got an early start to their long weekend as they headed out of Sydney in the general direction of the North Shore and the Central Coast.

She was not religious and if she had to work, she had to work. Policing did not observe public holidays where everything shuts down like happens in other industries. In fact, public holidays often added to the workload as many people took advantage of having a 3 day weekend. This also included treating tonight's Thursday shift like a Friday night because that is what many of the punters would do. They just saw tonight as an extra night to party.

Suddenly, her phone started to ring. It took her by surprise because she had already spoken to Dave and he knew she was going to work. It should not have been the police station calling because she was not due in yet to start her shift. Reaching over to the phone which was in a cradle in near the car stereo, an excited voice filled Caroline's car. For the moment, though, the excited female voice was competing with the music from the radio.

"Hang on, babe!" Caroline shouted, trying to get her voice heard over that of the singer of Guns n Roses, Axl Rose. Quite appropriately for today, he was singing one of her favourite songs, "Welcome To The Jungle".

A MOMENT IN TIME by Eric Brook

"Hey! How you doing?" Caroline asked the female caller. It was her best friend of the last six months, Megan Dean. Out of all of the women that Caroline met during her 6 months of training, Megan was the one who she got on best with in both a professional and a social way. It was handy that they lived in the same part of the city. The course was a weekday residential course however people did have the option to return home on weekends. Caroline wanted to return home to see Dave and Megan was a good study buddy and friend.

Megan sounded very excited. Today was also her first day on the beat however she was stationed at Manly. Reasonably close to Caroline's house in a opposite direction, Manly is a busy command, mostly in a tourist area. Once described as 7 miles away from the city but a million miles away from care, Manly was an anti-social hotspot especially late at night. Even though it was relatively close to the city, the layout of the area meant that transport was not ideal. To get to the city, there was the choice of a long bus ride or a ferry ride across Sydney Harbour. The police station was close to Megan's home which is what she wanted. She loved the beach and coastal lifestyle after many years of working in the western suburbs.

A MOMENT IN TIME by Eric Brook

"Guess what, Clarkey?", Megan squealed down the phone. Without waiting for Caroline to answer, Megan continued the conversation. "I got my first arrest this morning!" All of the students in the class wanted to get straight into action. Caroline knew that Megan was excited and with good reason.

"What happened? Tell me all about it!"

"We got called to a shoppie (police slang for shoplifter – someone who steals from shops) and the Senior let me do the arrest. Young mother decided to use her baby's stroller as a shopping trolley and not pay for the stuff. She turned it on, too. What about you? Are you on the scoreboard yet?"

"Nah, not yet. I'm just heading to Central now for day 1. I'm on at 3. Shouldn't be too long, though. I can't see us going too long without taking someone back. If I can't do it there, I can't do it anywhere. I guess it depends on if I'm just licking the windows or not. You know me! I'll be fine! Catch you soon for a drink, yeah? I'm nearly at work. I'll text you when I get my first body."

"I'll look out for you on TV! Stay safe, babe!"

"See ya later! Congrats on the collar!"

http://www.amomentintimenovel.com

A MOMENT IN TIME by Eric Brook

Concentrating on the road once more, Caroline always enjoyed driving her car over the Sydney Harbour Bridge. Regularly, she would see the trains cross the bridge while she was stuck in traffic and thought that the train driver had better luck with the traffic than her. Sometimes she wondered what it would be like to be a train driver. Were there many female train drivers working? How did the male drivers treat the female drivers? How did the female drivers cope with the shift work? Was the shift work better or worse there than with her job?

Caroline knew that in the event of a major accident on the Bridge, the traffic would be screwed for hours. She presumed that police from Harbourside command would come from the north while The Rocks command would come from the south. She also knew that depending on the workload, the size of the accident and the location of a car from her command, City Central, might go there as well.

The Coathanger (as the Sydney Harbour Bridge was often called) was a Sydney landmark known the world over. It consisted of 2 train tracks and 8 lanes of road traffic. The direction of some lanes varied depending on the time of the day. Partly for this reason, there was no centre divider. When Caroline drove over the bridge, she tried to keep away from the centre lanes as much as possible. Surprisingly though, there not many head on accidents.

A MOMENT IN TIME by Eric Brook

Apart from accidents, breakdowns were a huge problem on the Harbour Bridge. There were traffic cameras and dedicated breakdown crews on hand to try to keep the traffic moving. There was an alternative route in the form of the Sydney Harbour Tunnel which ran parallel to the Harbour Bridge but the usefulness of the tunnel was limited. It was a great alternative if you were heading to the eastern suburbs or some parts of the city but if you were looking to head to the western parts of the city, it was useless. There were other ways to cross the harbour to avoid the city altogether which required someone to head to the west before selecting the required southbound route. For many people, though, the Sydney Harbour Bridge was the way to get into the city.

With the traffic lighter than she thought it would be, it was a pleasant surprise to be earlier than her prediction of 2.15pm. It was 2.06pm when she drove past her new home away from home for the first time. Turning into a side street, she saw a few spaces vacant with a sign saying "Police Vehicles Only". She knew she was a Police Officer but still did not want to park there. There was a car parked in a space with the usual police stripes that had CI35 on the doors. She knew that car was known on the radio as City 35 and wondered if that was the car she would be riding in shortly. "Hi, City 35", she said out loud to herself as she went by.

Turning a couple of corners into a street parallel to the police station, she was lucky to find a 30 minute parking spot. Hopefully that would be all she would need. Her plan was to park the car and walk to the station and introduce herself to her boss. He hopefully would tell her where to park so she could go back to the car and unload her uniforms. She parked the car and went to the parking meter. The sign said it would cost $3 for 30 minutes at the time of the day she was parking. Reaching into her pocket, she grabbed some gold coins and placed it into the machine. The machine printed out a ticket which she placed onto the dashboard of the car.

Remembering to grab her hat off the passenger's seat, she locked the car and walked down the hill to the station. The parking gods were looking after Caroline today. She recalled going to a party in nearby Surry Hills on a Saturday night and spending 60 minutes looking for a legal car parking space. If for some strange reason that she was not able to park at the station, she was prepared to park in a long term parking station for tonight before working on a Plan B for the future. All day on street parking was impossible in the city centre. During the morning and afternoon peak hours, every available lane would be needed to get everyone to where they needed to be.

Clearways, Transit Lanes and Bus Lanes were important tools that were needed to keep traffic moving as much as possible. Many people did not consider this when parking their vehicles. Depending on the location, each parking spot could have several different parking restrictions each day. Sometimes, it would be essential to spend 30 seconds looking at the sign and looking at the time to see if it was legal to park in that space.

Chapter 2 – Welcome to Central, Caroline!

2.30pm, Thursday 01 April 2010

Approaching the City Central Police Station, she could see the size of the building. At the time, she did not know how much of the building was used by the police and how much was leased out to other companies. She knew that this station was the most important station in the city apart from the nearby Sydney Police Centre. The front door of the station was not very inviting. It was not bright and cheery at all. Black tiles surrounded the front door with "City Central Police" in silver letters to one side.

Apart from the glass door itself, the most noticeable feature was the blue and white checker board sticker that had been placed to one side of the door from the ground to the height of the door. It was almost as if the sticker had been placed their as an afterthought. For the casual passer-by, the biggest clue to the building was the surrounding police vehicles. There was a dedicated parking area for police vehicles outside the front of the station on Day Street as well as in a side alley.

Taking one last breath, Caroline walked towards the front door which opened automatically for her. In what looked like a doctor's waiting room, she saw a few people waiting for service. Some were sitting down, some were standing still. Others paced around like an expectant father at a maternity hospital. She saw a counter with a sign above it that said "Welcome" in white writing on a dark blue background with the traditional blue and white checker board at the bottom. She walked to the counter and after taking a deep breath, she said her first word in the station.

"G'day."

At the counter was a male uniformed Police Officer. Somehow, that did surprise her somewhat even though she was in a police station and she was a uniformed Police Officer herself. She did not exactly know who she would see at the counter when she arrived. During her training, she had been in other stations and knew that they all had the same basic structure. The male police officer was also shocked to see her approach the counter. All of the local officers just walked straight into the restricted area behind the counter.

"I'm Caroline Clarke", she said. "It's my first day here today. I need to see the Shift Supervisor, please".

The middle aged Senior Constable looked at her and smiled. "I'm Senior Constable David Jones but you can call me DJ. I'll see if James is available for you. Go to the door on your left and I'll buzz you in".

A MOMENT IN TIME by Eric Brook

Caroline looked to her left and saw a door just as DJ had described. She heard a click and took that as her cue to pull the handle. DJ was waiting for her at the door and the pair shook hands firmly.

"First day? Where were you stationed at before?"

Caroline took this to mean that he thought that she was transferring from one station to another. The few months of wearing the uniform at the Police Academy meant that the uniform was still fresh but did not have that first day look about it. "This is my first day out of the Academy." Caroline said. "I'm really looking forward to working here. I did some time at Gladesville and Sutherland during the course but I came here because I like the city. Those two areas were too quiet for me!"

DJ walked down a corridor with many doors on either side. Caroline followed him, glancing at the names on the doors. She knew she would get a station tour at some point. DJ stopped at a door marked "Shift Supervisor" and knocked on the door in the traditional policeman knock.

"Come in" said an older voice that Caroline could hear but not see. DJ walked in first and Caroline stayed behind, not knowing if she should enter or not. DJ turned around and did not see Caroline next to or behind him. Maybe she had not heard the older man over the constant din of the Police Radio that was playing on all the speakers in the station. DJ stuck his head outside and whispered "You can come in, Caroline". Nervously, she walked into the door with a half grin on her face.

"Good afternoon, sir", Caroline said to the older man behind the desk. Looking at his shoulder insignia, she knew he was a Senior Sergeant. Knowing someone's rank by simply looking at them was an important skill, especially as a new officer. Different ranks demanded different protocol when speaking with them. A junior officer needed to know who they were dealing with in the chain of command. Caroline was desperate to make a good first impression with the first person of supervisor rank that she met. "I'm Probationary Constable Caroline Clarke. It's my first day here."

The Senior Sergeant extended his hand to Caroline and they shook hands. "Hi, Caroline. I've been expecting you. Good to see you here early. I'm James Thomas, one of the Shift Supervisors here. You don't have to call me sir unless you get in trouble." How a supervisor addressed a junior officer was often an indication of their management style. Some were very formal while others were very relaxed. At the moment, James seemed to be heading towards relaxed rather than super formal.

James turned his attention to DJ. "Thanks, DJ. I'll get Caroline started here and get her to come and see you shortly to show her around." Obviously, DJ had been at

Central for a long time and had James' respect and trust. Otherwise, he might have called him "David" or "Senior Constable Jones". DJ turned and left the room to return to his counter.

Returning his attention to his new officer, he quizzed her. "So, what brings you to City Central?"

Caroline looked around the room and saw that it was fairly typical of a Shift Supervisor's office. It was devoid of personality because all of the Shift Supervisors used the same office. "I like the city" she stated with a higher pitched voice than she normally would. "I thought that I'd like to be placed in the suburbs but the course changed that for me. I want to get right into the action. I don't want to be sitting around doing nothing. I'm eager to get out onto the truck and get the job done with the crew."

"Okie dokie" James said. "But before we turn you loose on the very unsuspecting citizens of Sydney, let's get the paperwork sorted." He knew that Caroline was coming so he had what she needed in a large plastic bag. "You don't have your appointments and firearm with you, do you?".

She shook her head. He got up out of his chair and for the first time, she could see how tall James really was. He was a man-mountain. He walked over to the filing cabinet and unlocked it. He reached into a drawer and found a large yellow courier style plastic envelope marked "P/Cst

Clarke" which he lifted out and placed on the table. He sat back down and reached for the large plastic bag. He handed the bag to Caroline and said "Take all the stuff out and place it onto the table here". She did so and her eyes widened when she saw her new name badge and official police identification badge. James could see her eyes looking at the badge and said "Put it on if you like".

Caroline replaced her generic badge with one that read "Constable Caroline Clarke" on one line and "City Central LAC" on the next. She grabbed the ID and placed it into her police wallet which was now complete once it had the ID in it. Anyone could steal a police badge and while many people did not ask to see ID, they could if they wanted to. She knew that was usually not necessary, especially if she was in uniform. James handed her another card which was a proximity card which allowed her to access various parts of the station. He handed her various other bits and pieces including a box of business cards to give to victims and witnesses, a locker key and various forms.

She placed these on the table and saw James reach over to the yellow bag. He ripped it open and handed her some handcuffs, pepper spray, ammunition and her gun. It was the same gun that she used at the academy but the Police Force did not want their students taking their guns home any more. Now that she was at City Central, she could keep her gear at the station in her locker. A small part of each locker was specifically for their weapon and ammunition.

A MOMENT IN TIME by Eric Brook

James looked at Caroline and said "Have you got all your bits and pieces now?" meaning her handcuffs, gun, bullets, extendible baton & gloves. She nodded. "I need you to sign this paperwork for all that stuff. Once you've done that, we can get you settled in before your briefing."

Each form looked the same to Caroline but she knew that they were for different purposes. She would soon learn how much time that an officer would spend on paperwork. One form was for her timekeeper so he would know that she had graduated and was at City Central. She signed for her appointments, her ID and proximity cards and also filled him her personal details. "Did you drive today?" James asked. Caroline nodded. "Go grab your car and park it in the Van Dock. On your way out, grab DJ to give you a hand."

She shook James' hand and said "Thank you sir....I mean James". James smiled. He was used to seeing people on their first day at work. He knew they would be a little nervous. It was his job to ease their nerves.

Caroline turned and left the office and headed back to the counter. She bumped into DJ in the corridor and asked him "Are you busy, DJ? I'm ready for the tour now. James asked me to ask you to give me a hand and show me where to park." The two cops left the station through the front door. DJ enjoyed mentoring new police to the station and he also enjoyed the sun as he had not been outside for a few hours.

http://www.amomentintimenovel.com

A MOMENT IN TIME by Eric Brook

Caroline led DJ to her car and luckily, she had a couple of minutes remaining on the meter. A parking fine would have been the last thing Caroline needed on her first day. Years ago, Police solely enforced the parking rules so if the cop knew Caroline's car, he might have ignored it. But today, the Sydney City Council's Rangers would be writing the ticket quicker than Caroline could introduce herself. Nor did she fancy taking the Infringement Notice to her Commander. More than likely, he would tell her just to pay the fine.

After a short walk, the two police officers climbed into Caroline's car. To the outsider, it might have looked like the old cop and the new cop were going out on patrol. DJ directed Caroline around the corner to a dead end street with a huge garage door at the end. Caroline stopped at the boom gate before the door not knowing what to do. DJ told her the combination for the keypad and she punched it in. The boom gate opened and the garage door copied. DJ pointed out where the entrance to the charge room and holding cells were adding "Don't park anywhere near there. We park our own cars on the other side. The crooks sometimes hit the cars as we bring them in."

Caroline saw the assortment of other cars and knew that this where she should park. She found a spot and parked the car. DJ told her not to worry about her spare uniforms straight away. "They'll be right here for the moment. You don't want to be late for the briefing on your first day, do you?" He laughed. She wanted to laugh back but was not sure if she should or not. She was deadly serious about turning up on time and being ready to go on time. The last thing that her supervisors wanted was an officer to be running late for work.

Caroline looked at the clock in the car and saw that it was 2.50pm. She was glad she came in early. She grabbed her backpack and one set of uniforms and followed DJ to a separate door away from the Charge Room door near her parking spot. "Don't go through the Charge Room door unless you have a prisoner" DJ said. "The Custody Sergeants don't like that. And this way is shorter."

She swiped her card next to the reader and heard the tell-tale click. She pulled the door and her and DJ entered. DJ motioned to the left and they walked. "I want to give you the full tour, Caroline, but we have to be at the briefing in a sec." They walked past the Briefing Room door, which DJ pointed out. A bit further down, there was a door marked Break Room. Behind this door was where the cops wound down. It was very noisy behind that door.

Many war stories and the solutions to every problem known to man were usually hot discussion topics in this room. While they could not usually spend the whole shift in the room, it was important that there was a space for them to be able to relax with each other out of public view. The supervisors somewhat encouraged this.

A MOMENT IN TIME by Eric Brook

DJ and Caroline continued down the corridor, the Police Radio constantly blaring in the background. None of the voices were familiar to Caroline. Over time, she would get to know the various voices at both ends of the radio. At the end of the corridor, there were two doors. One was marked Male Locker Room and the other was marked Female Locker Room. DJ motioned to the Female Locker Room and said "Your locker is in there. I don't think I need to show you where it is in there, do I? Dump your stuff then come to the briefing room. I'll see you there in a minute or two."

Caroline swiped her card again and the door was unlocked. She reached into her pocket where she had placed her locker key. She saw the locker key was marked 42. She found locker 42 and placed her belongings in the locker. She looked forward to being able to personalise it a bit later. There was another door in the room where Caroline could hear female voices. "Time to get social later" she thought, "I have to get to the briefing room."

She closed her locker and placed the locker key on her keyring with her house and car keys before thinking twice about that. She did not want to take her keys on patrol with her. She attached her locker key to her handcuff keys instead, locking the house and car keys in the locker.

Turning around, she left the locker room and headed back to the briefing room. It was 2.59pm. She had made it. Now she was going to meet her crew and find out what she was going to do for the day. She fully expected to be put onto the counter with DJ until his shift ended in 3 hours but preferred to be on patrol. At the very least, she wanted to know where everything in the station was. Naturally, it would take more than a short moment in time to fully get her bearings around the station and around the city.

Caroline held her police issue baseball cap nervously in her left hand. She took a deep breath and pushed the briefing room door with her right hand. Thankfully, she thought, the room was empty. This did surprise her a little because at the Academy, she was always told that 3pm was 3pm, not 3.01pm or 3.05pm. Being on time was something that Caroline had always taken seriously.

She noticed that the chairs were lined up in rows but there were no tables. The chairs were facing a wall which featured a large map of City Central's command area. She could see on the map that The Rocks command was to the north. Surry Hills and Kings Cross were to the east and Redfern was to the south. To the west was Glebe but she was not expecting to cross Darling Harbour too often to be in Glebe's area. Out of her neighbours, Glebe was the quietest command, especially compared to the others.

Soon enough, several Police Officers entered the room at the last possible second. Most of them were younger officers as City Central was often seen as a transit lounge between the Academy and the suburbs. More experienced officers such as DJ loved policing the city and mentoring younger police. One such example of an experienced female officer stood in front of her now.

"Hi, Caroline" said Sergeant Sabrina Simpson. "I'm Sabrina, I'll be your Shift Supervisor this afternoon. Are you settled in? Do you have everything you need?" Sabrina looked up and down at Caroline and said "You look ready."

Sabrina was one of the few female Shift Supervisors in the Inner Metropolitan Region. She had been a Police Officer for 20 years and had seen major changes in the police force over that time. Times had changed for Sabrina and unlike many (but not all) of her male colleagues of a similar age, she was able to embrace change. To her, it did not matter that she was a shorter woman and that she was not as strong as her fellow male officers.

She learnt early on that it was not how quick you were to punch on with an offender but how you spoke to people. She was empathetic towards people and was able to talk her way out of problems while other people were talking themselves into trouble. She could have chosen to take on the easier day shift but she enjoyed being where the action is. At City Central there was always action but it was often a lot busier in the afternoon and nights.

A MOMENT IN TIME by Eric Brook

"I just need to check and load my gun", Caroline said. "Otherwise, I'm good. I still don't know exactly where everything in the station is yet but I'll be fine. It's a lot bigger than it looks from the outside!"

The room suddenly got a lot louder as it started to fill up as the afternoon shift gathered for their daily briefing. Sometimes it was a simple briefing but considering it was Caroline's first day, today's briefing would not be short. Sabrina ignored the noisy bunch as she was still talking with Caroline.

"I'll tell you shortly what car you are on. Once the brief is finished, get your stuff together. Bring your high vis vest. Welcome to City Central, Caroline. If you need anything, let me or one of the other supervisors know. You'll be fine."

"Thanks, Sergeant. It's nice to meet you." Caroline said, somewhat formally. It was good manners to be polite to the more senior officers using their title until they said otherwise.

"Let's keep the formal stuff to around the public. Call me Sabrina." Caroline smiled. Having a female supervisor on shift was not something that Caroline had experienced during her training. It was a pleasant surprise. It would take her some time to get to know all of the officers at the station across all the shifts. In time, she might be able to stay on the same shifts all the time however it was usual practice to alternate between shifts. Caroline hoped that she could stay on afternoon shifts but knew that this might not be possible, especially initially.

Moving to address the whole group gathered before her, Sabrina said "Good afternoon, team. First things first, we have a new probie (police shorthand for a Probationary Constable). Please make Caroline feel welcome. It's her first day out of Goulburn."

A murmur filled the room as most people said hi to Caroline all at once. Some of the male officers seemed to be very happy to see her. Caroline looked around the room, not exactly sure where to focus her attention. She scanned the room quickly before returning her attention to Sabrina at the front of the room.

"As you all know, it is the day before the Easter weekend", Sabrina continued. "Every man and his dog is going to be out there drinking tonight and they don't care about tomorrow. So expect tonight to be like a Friday or Saturday night. You all know the usual trouble spots."

Caroline must have had a strange expression on her face because Sabrina amended her previous statement after looking in Caroline's direction.

A MOMENT IN TIME by Eric Brook

"OK then, everyone except for Caroline knows all the usual trouble spots. And I'm sure that by the end of the long weekend, she'll know them as well."

Caroline looked at the map behind Sabrina. There was a blue star for each of the local commands and out stations. While City Central was a big station, smaller satellite stations under the station's control were located at Town Hall and Central. The various railway station were marked with a gold circle. Various red triangles were seemingly randomly placed on the map. "Maybe someone will explain the map to me later", Caroline thought.

"As most of you know, the media have been all over late night alcohol related violence here in the inner city, especially the Terrorgraph."

This was as close to humour in a briefing that Sabrina got, giving the biggest newspaper in the city a nickname. Sabrina did not wait for someone to laugh at her joke. She was not known for her humour in briefings but already had said two things that could have been considered funny.

"The public will expect to see us out there tonight. Remember officer safety. Look out for each other." A couple of officers behind Caroline coughed. "Because if we don't look after each other, don't expect Joe Public to!"

A MOMENT IN TIME by Eric Brook

Caroline looked around the room at her new work mates while Sabrina was talking. She was wondering who she could or could not trust on the street. They were probably doing exactly the same thing about her. She was merely the latest newest officer to work through the doors. Her mind drifted over to visualising classmate Megan's first arrest. Caroline hoped that it would go smoothly as she had heard many stories from various officers about their first arrest.

"F-Y-I", Sabrina spelt out, "the Commuter Crime Unit or whatever they call themselves this week are doing a high vis operation with a drug dog at Central Railway. If you get called there by Radio, please wear your high vis vest if you can."

If anyone was counting, that was the third non serious thing that Sabrina had said in the few minutes that she had been talking. There was an element of truth to her statement, though. Older specialist areas such as the Water Police were now known as the Marine Area Command and new specialists such as the Public Order & Riot Squad were coming into the police vernacular on a regular basis. The Commuter Crime Unit used to be known as the Transit Police.

The Commuter Crime Unit were police dedicated to working on the crime on the city's various transport systems. Mainly concentrating on the city's railway stations and trains, they could also travel on buses and ferries. They were trained to the same standards as all of the officers that were sitting in Sabrina's foreground and could be called to assist her officers at any time. Some people decided to move out of General Duties policing as quick as they could into specialist areas while others were quite happy to stay. Caroline had not thought about a specialist area yet which was a wish decision at the early stage of her career.

Sabrina continued her briefing. "In addition, Highway are doing RBT outside the Town Hall later tonight. We might need 35 and 36 to give them a hand with the tests. I'll know more when the operation briefing happens a little later at 8pm. I'll let you know if you are needed later, 35 & 36."

Usually, Highway Patrol officers from around the region would conduct an operation on long weekends such as the Easter weekend which was about to start. Random Breath Testing (RBT) was something that had to be done if there was time to do it. Emergency calls had to come first however RBT statistics were important to higher ranking people than Sabrina. It then became Sabrina's problem which meant that it became City 35 & City 36's problem.

"Unless radio or I tell you otherwise, all medium and high range charges from that operation will go to Surry Hills, Trucks. I think we'll be busy enough here. They'll handle the low range people themselves because they should have the big booze bus with them. We'll only have to take the ones who need to dry out for a while."

She looked at a sheet of paper in her hand. "Alright guys, here's your assignments. It's pretty much the same as yesterday's." Caroline's ears pricked up. She had not had a chance to meet anyone else yet because she had been talking to Sabrina, DJ & James. "For Caroline's benefit, wave when I call you, please. I don't need to remind everyone what it was like for them on their first day here, do I?" In a roll call style fashion, Sabrina read the assignments. She knew that they were there and they did not have to answer their name.

Each vehicle usually had 2 people listed. One was the driver of the vehicle and the other was the passenger and radio operator. Normally if both officers had the same driving classification, they would decide between them who drove the vehicle. As long as they followed the rules, Sabrina personally did not mind who drove. But on other shifts with other supervisors, the first person name for a vehicle was the person who drove and was responsible for the car. The driver drove the car and the other officer would be responsible for using the radio, doing pursuit commentaries, doing person and vehicle checks. It was usually the passenger who was the first person out of the vehicle in case of a traffic stop or a foot pursuit.

A MOMENT IN TIME by Eric Brook

City 1 – Tom

City 14 – Sabrina

City 15 – Justin & Wayne

City 16 - Colin & Dave

City 17 – Matt & Brad

City 18 - Andrew & Lee

City 35 - Sarah & Scott

City 36 - Nicole, Leila & Caroline

City 45 – Simon & Scott

City 300 – Tony & Martin

Tom was the Commander of the station, the big boss. You knew it was serious when you heard "City 1" over the radio. Unlike anyone else in the station, there was only the one person who could use the radio call sign of City 1 and that was Tom. He would be going home soon but would be on call overnight for critical incidents. You also knew you had something to worry about when Tom wanted to see you.

Unless he had a meeting to go to or there was a a major incident, Tom spent most of his time at the station. He had a team of civilian administration staff to assist him in the running of the station, writing letters, doing rosters, compiling statistics, answering complaints and a lot more. You knew that you were old in the job if you could remember when City 1 was a Caged Truck for prisoner transport.

City 14 was the call sign of the Shift Supervisor. They were usually a Sergeant or a Senior Sergeant. They usually stayed at the station unless needed. Caroline was firstly greeted by James who was the morning shift's supervisor. James would be going home very shortly. By doing the afternoon briefing, Sabrina had taken control of the afternoon shift. If you had any problem that you could not solve with the help of your partner, the Shift Supervisor was the first person that you should see. Some people made the mistake of running straight to the Commander, bypassing the Shift Supervisor. The Shift Supervisor did not always like being bypassed.

Most commands had 2 prisoner transport vehicles, usually called a Caged Truck. Called a truck for short, the trucks had to be fully crewed first before using cars. A truck was usually the busiest vehicle at the station. Because City Central was a busier station, they had 4 caged trucks, City 15, 16, 17 & 18. While the designs varied, the rear of the truck was designed for prisoner transport. Because of this, they were not the preferred vehicle to lead a pursuit. Some models of truck could become unstable at high speed and on several embarrassing occasions, the truck had rolled over.

A MOMENT IN TIME by Eric Brook

Unless it was unavoidable, the sedans (City 35, 36 & 45) were not to be used for prisoner transports. These sedans were very similar in design to a taxi. Some officers even referred to their cars as a Blue Light Taxi as drunks expected the police to drive them around. Some people were so drunk they genuinely thought that the police car was a taxi. Somehow, Sydney's police had not followed the lead of bigger police forces such as New York's where the NYPD regularly transported offenders in the American version of a sedan.

Even though the shift changeover was at 3pm and the plan each day was for the cars to start coming in from 2pm so officers can do paperwork, that was not always possible. Sabrina told the room that 18 & 36 were still out on a job. So until the morning crew in City 36 came back to the station, Caroline was not going anywhere.

This gave Nicole, Leila & Caroline a chance to get to know each other. Sabrina dismissed the briefing with the usual "Stay safe out there" message. Unless there was a special operation being conducted, the crews did most of their work by listening to the radio and responding to calls. After seeing their waves, Caroline walked across the room to meet her shift partners. Nicole was the senior of the two and was the second highest ranking woman on shift.

Sabrina walked over and met the all female crew of City 36. "Caroline, meet Nicole and Leila. They are good eggs. They'll look after you." Looking to her experienced officers, Sabrina smiled. "Please look after Caroline. I have heard good things about her. We don't want to repeat what happened last time we had a newbie here. That was a bit messy if you know what I mean."

Nicole and Leila knew exactly what Sabrina was talking about. They were used to seeing new officers come and go. Some people could handle it, some could not. Which category Caroline fell into was partly up to the team and partly up to Caroline and how she applied herself.

The three women shook hands. Caroline looked blankly at Sabrina who reassured her. "You'll be fine, Caroline."

Caroline knew that it was in everyone's interest - including her own - to help her ease into the job. This did not mean that Caroline was to be treated as a mere passenger in the rear seat of City 36. She had to get used to working with a variety of people across the command. Not everyone on the staff were as good with new police officers as Nicole and Leila were. As much as training had improved, there was no substitute for time on the street.

Even though she was now officially a Police Officer, many people did not make it to the levels of experience that Nicole and Leila had. Policing was not a job for everyone. Some people found this out during the training but others took longer to come to the same conclusion.

A MOMENT IN TIME by Eric Brook

Senior Constable Nicole Webb loved the city and while most women would leave City Central after a couple of years, she had been there for 10 years. Nicole was a perfect female mentor for Caroline. She was a trusted member of the team. Sabrina wanted Nicole to apply for a Sergeant's position but Nicole was quite happy to remain walking the beat. She enjoyed mentoring staff such as Caroline. From time to time, she thought about moving to Highway Patrol as she really enjoyed driving and making sure other people obeyed the road rules. There was not a lot of Highway Patrol cars in the inner city area, however. While she could drive fast, Nicole was not prepared to move to the suburbs to do move into Highway Patrol just yet.

Nicole was tall like Caroline. Her body still looked young but her brain had aged beyond her years. She was street-smart and knew many of the local crooks and how they operated. She had many stories to tell about working the beat in Australia's busiest city and the darker sides that the many tourists thankfully never got to see. Sabrina wanted to ensure that Caroline had the best start at Central possible. Teaming Nicole and Leila together with Caroline was a planned move.

First Class Constable Leila Harrison had been at Central for a couple of years straight out of the Academy. She knew all too well what it was like to be the new girl on the beat and could understand what Caroline was going through today. Sometimes she enjoyed working in the city but she did not suffer fools gladly, including her colleagues. She was highly focused on her career and wanted to be a valuable member of the team and not someone to be wheeled in when a victim was upset and needed to be calmed down. While she had compassion for her victims, traditionally female officers often were placed on victim support roles while the men were chasing the crooks.

Leila loved outsmarting the crooks and would rather work out which corner to hid behind rather than chasing them for 10 minutes on foot. She was cool and calm under pressure normally but if you were the target of her anger, she had a sharp tongue. She might be smaller than Nicole but often technique meant that Leila could do things that you would not think she could do by looking at her. Leila was very good at calming difficult situations down and was better at this than Nicole. Even though she only had a couple of years service, a lot had happened to the flame haired officer and she had come out of it a better officer. Others could have quit like many before her but not Leila. Leila was not a quitter.

Unlike some previous female officers there, Nicole and Leila had proven themselves to their superiors and their fellow workers. Now it was Caroline's turn to do the same. City Central was an ideal environment to learn from a variety of people in a variety of situations. The three women exchanged greetings. Nicole started to walk so Leila & Caroline joined her. They walked out of the briefing room and towards the break room. The break room was an ideal place to sit and wait for their car to arrive after the morning shift. Neither woman had any idea about how much Caroline did or did not know about her new home away from home.

"Seeing as though our ride isn't here, do you need to do anything before you go, girls?" Nicole asked. Leila said that she was fine while Caroline said she needed to sort her appointments out. "Caroline, go and do that quickly and Leila and I will meet you in the break room. Do you know where that is?"

"Yes", Caroline confirmed. There was many rooms that she did know know about yet but the break room was one room that she did know all about. In some ways, it was ideal that the car was not available yet. It gave Caroline a little bit of time to calm the nerves a little and to be really sure that she was ready to hit the street.

Caroline went to her locker and prepared her Glock 9mm semi-auto pistol for service. She grabbed her hi-visibilty yellow vest and locked her locker. She walked back to the break room and found her partners. The room was large. There were several groups of tables on one side of the room with a food servery just like at the Academy.

Central was one of the few police stations to have an in-station eatery where the food was prepared on site. There were enough people on shift to be able to justify the expense. The kitchen also prepared the food for the prisoners being held at City Central, Surry Hills & the Sydney Police Centre. It was often easier for the officers to choose their own food, especially at the suburban stations. Despite the station having food available, Leila especially knew where all the good food was in the city within walking distance from the station.

"Have we got time to eat?" Leila asked Nicole. Despite her slender frame, Leila enjoyed eating. If she recommended a particular place to eat, you could rely on the food being great. That was the first time Caroline had heard Leila speak apart from her brief introduction. Nicole nodded and held one finger to her ear, indicating to both women to keep an ear open for the call sign of their car, City 36. Leila knew that she was not the senior officer on the team and showed Nicole the respect that her rank deserved.

This was not usual for their vehicle to be late back to the station. Normally, the sedans were always back for their changeover. Leila knew what she had to do but the signal was more for Caroline's benefit. It was easy to sit back and ignore the radio but they had to get on patrol as soon as they could do so. There would be plenty of things to do once they had their car available, even if they did not have a keen probationary constable in the vehicle.

A MOMENT IN TIME by Eric Brook

The three women went to the eatery and selected small portions in case they got called out. Caroline looked at the clock in the room and it read 1610. It did not seem like over an hour since the briefing at started. Their car was still out which was really unusual. The morning crew of City 36 were due to finish work at 3pm and by still being out were accumulating some serious overtime. They would be eagerly awaiting to be released from their task because they had been working now for more than the standard 12 hour shift.

Eating some pasta, Caroline was enjoying her first meal of her day. "Don't get used to this, Caroline!", Nicole warned. "This doesn't happen every day. I'm not sure what they are at but it must be bad for them still to be there now. Normally we'd be on the road straight after the briefing. You look hungry."

Caroline was very hungry. She did not want to eat too much, nor did she want to spill food on her uniform. In between bites, a small conversation started. "Are you married, Caroline?" Leila asked. Caroline had a mouth full of pasta so she shook her head. Caroline thought that was a strange topic to start a discussion about while eating. Maybe this was Leila's way of breaking the ice with the young officer. Many women did not wear wedding rings while at work so an absence of a wedding ring did not mean that Caroline was automatically single.

A MOMENT IN TIME by Eric Brook

When she finished her current mouthful of food, Caroline said "My boyfriend Dave's on the job at Chatswood".

There was no real need to explain any more. This sort of talk was very common when someone new arrived at a station. Remembering that it was not all about her, Caroline returned the question. "How about you? Anything happening in that department?"

"Nah, I'm currently enjoying being single. It's hard enough to find a decent guy as it is. Then when they ask about what I do for a living and I tell them, they either run or want me to handcuff them. In that case, I run.", Leila explained. "Maybe I should tell them that I'm in the public service. That feels like lying to me although I do know that some people do it. And technically speaking, we are public servants as they continually remind us, right?"

"Oh I hear you! I was single for a while there but now I'm lucky that I have Dave but I knew him before I was on the job. But now I'm on the job too, it's sweet. Is there any talent here? Any guys I need to be careful of?" Caroline asked. "Not that I'm looking, of course!"

A MOMENT IN TIME by Eric Brook

"I'd prefer not to get my meat where I get my potatoes if you know what I mean. Sure the guys here are good to get along with but I don't want to get the reputation as the station bike. Could be a career limiting move.", Leila pointed out. "I'm here to arrest the bad guys, not to shag the good guys. Be strong and the guys know not to mess with you. Being one of the boys isn't always a bad thing."

Suddenly, a slightly comical male voice announced over the station's internal Public Address system. "36! 36! Your meal is ready at the bistro." Caroline looked at Nicole and Leila but like her, they were eating. Caroline gave Nicole a strange look.

Nicole said "That's DJ being a smart arse. He means that the car is ready. Don't forget, the public can hear those announcements as well. We'll often get called by our call sign. It's a good habit to get into. We'll grab the keys from him at the front counter. He'll tell us if it is out the front or in the dock. If you can, park out the front if you don't have a crook on board. Witnesses and victims do not come through the dock. Stay here and finish up while I get the keys." Nicole left.

Leila and Caroline quietly finished their food (it was lucky that they purposely selected small portions) and washed their hands. While wiping their hands, Caroline heard DJ over the PA again.

"Constable Caroline, your limo is at the front door."

Even though it was her first day, Caroline knew that Nicole was waiting at the front for her and Leila. Caroline laughed, she had obviously made a good impression on DJ.

There was a time and a place for humour. That time was usually during downtime at the station or in the car between jobs. DJ was taking full advantage of having a captive audience. Unlike 99 percent of the station, DJ had not used all of his usual jokes, one liners and other war stories (he had a few to choose from) on Caroline just yet. She felt good as she laughed at the joke that she had only heard for the first time. It might help to get rid of some of the nervous tension that she must have felt, even if she was not showing it to the outside world.

Walking through the station, Caroline walked behind the tiny Leila. Caroline was roughly as tall as Nicole but she could see over Leila's head quite easily. Even during her training, Caroline was among the taller officers (male and female) in her class. Judging by some of the men she had quickly looked at during the briefing, sometime in the future she would be the taller of the two police officers on a vehicle. Height was not always an automatic advantage, though. Walking past DJ, Caroline said "Thanks, DJ." DJ looked at both officers and said "Stay safe, 36."

Nicole was waiting in the white Holden Commodore sedan marked CI36. Apart from anything else, the number let each cop know who was who on the road. From above, the Police helicopter could also see who was who. Each command or section had a 2 or 3 letter code on the bonnet of the car, City Central's was CI. The roof of the vehicle had the number of the vehicle on the roof, in this case 36. For many years, all of the vehicles only had bonnet and roof markings. A few years ago, a few commands marked each front quarter panel and the rear of the car in smaller letters. Eventually, it became a state standard.

Caroline would soon get used to seeing vehicles from her surrounding commands including SH (Surry Hills), RX (The Rocks), KX (Kings Cross) around the area as well as possibly RF (Redfern), HS (Harbourside), NS (North Shore – she had seen that a lot thanks to visiting Dave at his station) and EB (Eastern Beaches). The latter commands could sometimes be seen at the local court complex or while visiting the Sydney Police Centre at Surry Hills.

Leila took the front passenger seat beside Nicole. Caroline could not drive under lights and sirens (code red) as she was a new officer. In time, she could become a proceed only driver (no lights and sirens) and then a urgent duty driver (lights and sirens). It was not practical to switch drivers just in case they got an urgent job needing lights and/or sirens. Besides, you did not know when a simple traffic stop could turn into a city-wide pursuit.

A MOMENT IN TIME by Eric Brook

Leila had her pursuit ranking just like Nicole. Leila could have driven and sometimes they swapped mid shift. Nicole enjoyed driving the sedans more than the trucks. So if they were on a truck together, Leila would often drive. Nicole was an awesome driver and Leila was good on the radio and cool under pressure. This was very important, especially in a pursuit.

Nicole wanted to ease Caroline in so the back seat was the best place for her. Even though Caroline was no longer a student Police Officer, City Central's usual policy was to have a 3 person crew for the first couple of weeks. Suburban commands tended not to do this as much but sometimes busy commands took a new officer by surprise.

There was so much that Caroline could learn about the area that she was policing so the commander preferred to ease their new officers (experienced police or not) into the area. It was better that Leila handle the radio because she knew through experience exactly where she was. It was very common for officers to come to Central direct from their initial training but it was uncommon for otherwise experienced officers to arrive at Central at Constable or Senior Constable level. In time, people tried to cut their commuting time down once they had some seniority and experience. After all, many more people lived in the suburbs compared to those who lived in City Central's area.

A MOMENT IN TIME by Eric Brook

Initial station and area familiarisation was all a part of officer safety and situational awareness. While Caroline could be trying to work out where she was, it could be possible that she did not see something that could be very important. At City Central, even the most experienced officers needed to remain switched on. Throughout the day and night, there was so much noise, so many lights and so many people around the various parts of the city. While New York had the reputation as the city that never sleeps, Sydney (or Melbourne in Victoria) was not far behind in Australian terms.

Having a car full of female officers was no longer a novelty, either. When women started being cops, they were usually used in cases involving children or what was now known as domestic violence. In those days, women did not investigate the number of crimes they do in the current day. In days gone by, supervisors would pair up a woman with a male officer. It's not uncommon to see a tall female officer with a short male officer. Occasionally though, members of the public wondered where the male officer was when an all-female crew arrived. Leila in particular did not like that and sometimes that annoyed her. She was more than capable of doing the same work as her male workmates.

Today, however, Sabrina decided who went with who. She knew who worked well together and kept those pairs together when she could. Tomorrow, Sabrina would probably put Caroline with another pairing. That way, Caroline got to work with everyone and vice versa. Also, people could see how Caroline was performing in a variety of situations. It could be potentially life threatening if you did not work as a team with your partner and the rest of the team. Some people who were on the job regarded policing as a contact sport much like the various football codes.

But unlike the sportsmen, it was realistic to keep in the back of your mind that you might not come home at the end of the day. So far in history in the state of New South Wales, 249 police officers, their families & colleagues had discovered that chilling fact out the hard way during the state's history of policing. While it was a relatively small number compared to the thousands of crimes detected each year, each officer still needed to be careful. When an officer was badly injured or killed on duty, the mental effect often extended beyond the officer's home station.

Nicole turned the car onto Goulburn Street. Many streets in the city were named after major cities or historical figures. Bathurst Street to the north of the station was a great street if travelling from west to east. It was in part paralleled by the newer Cross City Tunnel. To the City Central crews, the Cross City Tunnel was almost useless to them but it was a good way to avoid the city while travelling east or west.

When leaving the station from the parking bay out front, Goulburn Street would be the first major east-west street that could be used to access the rest of the city. Caroline would soon get very familiar with Goulburn Street as well as George Street, Liverpool Street, Pitt Street, Park Street and many others in the nearby vicinity. In time, Caroline would know every square inch of her command's area. She already had a basic understanding of the major streets but not of the many lanes and alleyways that ran off the major streets.

The time was now 1700. Peak hour traffic should be starting now, Caroline thought. The police radio in the car was broadcasting jobs, mainly for Surry Hills, Kings Cross and Redfern. The radio channel was not dedicated to City Central alone. Often, neighbouring commands would help each other out with attending incidents. Caroline kept listening for her car's call sign, City 36.

Leila heard City 16 receive a job for a shoplifter at Myer. As that car had a prisoner pod, City 15, 16, 17 or 18 usually got the shoplifter jobs allocated to them in preference to the sedans that were 35 & 36. Leila said "Looks like Col & Dave will be busy for a while."

It was not common for a shoplifting job not to end up with a prisoner on board or "Returning with 1 on board" in cop speak. Sometimes, the person would be calm and a sedan could be used. However, no one in authority wanted to risk their officers or the offender so a Caged Truck was used when possible. Most of the time, "Returning with 1 on board" was a trip back to the station but at other times, it might be to the Sydney Hospital, for instance. Due to the time involved with paperwork and interviewing the offender, a simple arrest could mean being back at the station for a good 2 or 3 hours. That period extended for a more complex investigation. Some offences and some offenders could now be dealt with by way of a Penalty Infringement Notice in order to reduce the amount of time that police were spending on paperwork. Often, an officer could spend more time on the paperwork than the item was worth. It was often easier to fill in a penalty notice on site, especially for first time offenders.

Nicole was pointing out to Caroline various trouble spots on George Street including the cinema strip, numerous pubs & clubs. Some venues had remained the same for many years while others often changed management. Some even changed type of business completely. For most places, the incident would be broadcast with the name of the street and the cross-street. Once the police got close to the scene, it often was obvious where the heat was.

Caroline's brain was mentally filing the information away as she knew that soon, she'd be in Leila's seat in another car. While she could not expect to remember every single premises, it would be handy to know where the major trouble spots were. While the driver also would know the spots as well, it was important for each officer to be prepared mentally and to know the area well.

A MOMENT IN TIME by Eric Brook

Suddenly, the radio was calling them. Caroline had been waiting for this moment. "Standing by for any available car in the vicinity of Central railway station.", the radio broadcast. Because of Central station's location, it was an even money bet between City Central and Surry Hills to see who got there first. Also, the radio operator did not know if there were any specialist units in the area who normally did not give their location.

It must have been an urgent job. If it was routine, a particular car was often nominated. Radio (as the operators were often called) obviously wanted a car - any car - to get to Central sooner rather than later. It did not matter who those police were. They could determine the resources needed once the first arriving officers assessed the situation.

Nicole knew that if need be from where she was, she could get there under lights and sirens in 3 minutes, not including the time it took to run to a platform. Nicole looked at Caroline and asked "Ready?" Caroline nodded to Nicole and Nicole nodded to Leila.

Leila knew what she had to do. "Radio, City 36", Leila said into the radio. The radio operator told Leila to report to platform 16 at Central. The next thing Caroline heard was not the details of the job but the sirens, activated by Leila. Leila worked the siren as Nicole weaved through the traffic.

A MOMENT IN TIME by Eric Brook

As City 36 weaved through the traffic and the lights bounced around from the LED light bar, this was real. This was not an Academy drill or a simulation with someone in your class or an actor pretending to be a crook. This was real. Your first big job was one you talked about for years. This job sounded big Caroline, even if it turned out to be a nothing job.

Caroline's life was about to change forever.

Chapter 3 – Wake Up, Train!

12 noon, Thursday 01 April 2010

It was days like today that Judy Sanders was glad that she had moved closer to the depot. She used to live in the suburbs 30 minutes drive away but she got sick of driving so she moved closer to work. It was a bright sunny day, too good for working, she thought. Judy had been a train driver for 10 years. Some women used operational roles to get a free ride into an office job. They would put up with it for a while and either get sick of the shift work or she would fall pregnant and never come back to her old job. Judy on the other hand enjoyed driving trains, it was what she wanted to do since she was a little girl. Of course, back in her day as a young girl, there were no female train drivers, only men. Most of those men also seemed to be really old.

Female train drivers were now a lot more common than they used to be on the modern electric trains in Sydney. On freight trains in days gone by, it was very uncommon to see a female crew member. Crewing a steam train was hard, physical work and diesel locomotives were noisy, rattly and dirty. The electric trains Judy was driving was a different world to the steam and diesel locomotives she remembered as a little girl but she was happy to drive the sparks, as some of the older enginemen called the newer electric trains.

A MOMENT IN TIME by Eric Brook

It no longer mattered if you were physically strong or not but mental toughness was needed on the ever increasing workloads that Judy and other drivers had. She made it look easy but her brain was continually working overtime, even if she looked like she was on auto pilot. And no, Dave, there was no auto pilot.

There was a lot of repetitive arm movements because of how the trains were driven. On most trains, a lever operated with the left hand worked the brakes. The right hand controlled the power and also activated the so-called deadman handle. If Judy relaxed her downward pressure on the handle, the brakes would rapidly apply. In an emergency, letting go of the handle was the easiest way to stop the train by the driver.

The constant downwards pressure required on the deadman handle and the regular repetitive movements with both handles led to over-use injuries. Judy had been lucky. While she might be a bit sore after a long stretch of driving, she had not suffered any problems that several of her workmates had. The worst case scenario was that some drivers had needed shoulder reconstructions. Judy was not looking forward to that possibility but it was in the back of her mind.

A MOMENT IN TIME by Eric Brook

Also in the back of her mind was the chance that someone could jump in front of her train to kill themselves. She had been warned about it as a trainee driver and remembered the words of the instructor at the time: "Most drivers can expect to hit at least one person in their career."

Most people chose railway station platforms as their venue of choice. A smaller number chose random locations in between stations. It was something that lived in the back of Judy's mind. She was realistic enough to know that it could happen to her. Most times, she thought about the usual things that people who are not train drivers think about including her upcoming weekend off, her upcoming holiday, doing the shopping. Sometimes, though, she visualised about death by train whether she liked it or not. Maybe this was her brain's way to prepare her. Judy had previously had some close calls but had not hit anyone yet.

Shaking off another death vision, Judy tried to concentrate on her current task. Driving her old but faithful car up the hill, a bridge carried her car over two railway lines. The top of the bridge was a bottleneck as there was a sharp curve to the left then the bridge went steeply down hill down a narrower road. The bridge was an afterthought because of a new train line so it had to be shoehorned into a smaller than optimal space due to the surroundings.

A MOMENT IN TIME by Eric Brook

Often, a car had to wait at the top of the bridge for a truck coming the other way to climb up the bridge from the depot side. Trucks often visited the depot to deliver parts and take away the rubbish collected on the trains among other things.

Luckily for Judy though, this was not the case now and she could zoom down the other side to a short straight section before a staff car park to the left and a security checkpoint straight ahead. Judy stopped at the security checkpoint because the boom gate was down. She reached into a compartment in the car and found her green parking permit. She was in full uniform complete with orange safety vest so the security guard did not have to come over to the car and give directions or a site induction. Judy clearly knew where she was going and she belonged there.

She held up the green parking permit in her left hand and waved to the security guard. The boom gate then opened and Judy drove through. She threw her permit onto the dashboard and drove across a small bridge before following a narrow road which snaked around a building before reaching another car park. She parked as near to a set of stairs as she could. It was a strange time of day at the depot as some people were at the middle of their day while Judy was at the start of hers. Some drivers were at the end of their work day. So to finish work at this time of day, a driver would have needed to start work around 5am. That is what time Judy loved to go to bed.

A MOMENT IN TIME by Eric Brook

She looked at the clock on her dashboard and saw that it was 12:02. She had exactly 6 minutes before she was due to sign on duty at 12:08. Train crew rosters were strange like that, they had lots of weird starting times. Indeed, every minute of the day was a potential start time. Every minute of Judy's upcoming day was mapped out to the second on what she called a diagram.

She knew that she had 16 minutes in which to sign on and check her diagram, read any special information required. She then knew that she had 5 minutes to find her train and then 5 minutes to walk to the train. On today's diagram, she had the next 80 minutes to get her train ready for service.

Ten minutes after that, she was due to leave the depot on her first run. Then she had the train timetables dictating to her until she changed trains. Then she had to have at least 30 minutes for her meal break, 10 of this being walking time. Some days, she would drive two trains on longer trips. On other days, she might drive five or six trains for shorter distances. Depending on the trip, Judy loved the longer trips as she loved driving trains.

Judy reached into the back seat of her car and got her massive orange work bag. It contained a lot of paper and instruction manuals that Judy hardly ever needed but would get in trouble for if she did not have it with her. For years, people on the job were trying to reduce the amount of things a driver had to carry. In the electronic age, Judy had a lot of paper in her bag that could have been placed onto a smart phone or an electronic organiser but was not.

Walking down the stairs, Judy saw the occasional worker wearing an orange shirt. She did not know what half the people in the orange shirts actually did because they could be doing a range of jobs including cleaning the train, replacing windows and doors, fixing the brakes and a lot more. Occasionally, she would see people in overalls who she knew as painters.

She knew that she was the only person she could see on her short walk to the sign on room that was dressed like a school girl. Her work uniform reminded her of her school uniform. The uniform was very uncomfortable. At the end of the day, Judy could not wait to get her heavy work boots off her feet and to change into something a little more comfortable.

Entering the small sign on area, Judy was a minute or two early. She enjoyed being 5 minutes drive away from the depot and the managers had noticed a nice change in her personality since she moved closer to the depot. Judy enjoyed the work at the depot and found working occasional depot based shifts to be a nice change rather than driving endlessly for hours.

A MOMENT IN TIME by Eric Brook

She squeezed her way through a sea of bodies hovering around the roster cabinet looking at the new rosters for the next fortnight that was posted yesterday. She thought that some people seemed to live in front of the roster cabinet trying to find people to swap shifts with.

Judy preferred afternoon and late afternoon shifts. She knew that she was due to do a fortnight of very early morning shifts from Sunday so she had a note pinned to a cork board looking for a swap. She had a couple of swap buddies but one of them was on holidays and the other was already on mornings. Most times, she managed to get a swap but at other times she could not. A fortnight on mornings was not great for Judy as it turned her world upside down. Super Duper Early Mornings (as she called them) started somewhere between 1.30am and 6am in her eyes. The later she started, the better.

Once she got to the sign on window, she saw Grant sitting there, a new addition to the depot. Judy often did not have a lot of time to talk to the people who signed her on duty but she was always nice to them.

"Hi, Grant. I'm here, mate. Don't worry about my sheet" Judy said. Judy had a theory that she would only fill in her time sheet at the end of the week. It did not matter either way because the weekly time sheets were sent into the timekeeper at the end of each week.

A MOMENT IN TIME by Eric Brook

Without looking up from his list of trains in front of him, Grant said "No worries, Judy. Your train is on 20 Top, sets M1 and M35." Grant was telling Judy where her train was. Each track (in railway speak also called a road) had a number and because the tracks were long at the depot, 3 trains could fit on the same track.

A train closest to the concrete walkway from the sign on room was called on top. If it was in the middle, it would have been called 20 middle. If it was furthest away from Judy's current location and the concrete walkway, it would have been called 20 back. It was a lot longer walk to 20 back than 20 top and Judy was happy about that - 20 top was far enough away as it was. Because her train was on 20 top, Judy did not have to worry about trains in front of her having problems and not being able to move and delaying her. Judy made a mental note of the road and train numbers and said goodbye to Grant.

Judy quickly made sure that her swap note was still on the cork board. It was useless trying to check the rosters for possible swaps at this moment because the area in front of the roster was filled with people writing their rostered shifts down for the next two weeks. When it came to the rosters at the depot, there were two types of people. If you were new to the depot, you were a relief driver.

A MOMENT IN TIME by Eric Brook

A relief driver was nicknamed a swinger as they could swing from line to line on the roster. Your role was to cover for other drivers when they were on holidays, long term sick leave, special projects, people not driving for various reasons. If you were not filling in for other drivers or on holidays yourself, you would be on standby.

Standby shifts were a nice break from driving but they were very important for the running of the network. Sometimes you would not drive at all during a shift. At other times, it was possible that a driver might drive more than someone on an actual diagram. The reasons for being needed on standby could include driver illness or injury, toilet breaks, a near hit or fatality and late running trains. Rather than holding the train for the late running driver, the standby driver would take the train instead, usually until the next scheduled driver took over.

Unless you managed to get a straight answer from the roster clerk, the only advanced notice of the rosters was when the roster came out on Wednesday to start on Sunday if you were a swinger. This usually only changed when you were filling in for someone for a long time, during their holidays for instance.

Several swingers were in front of the rosters looking at what they were rostered for. Finding a swinger when the roster came out was often a good way to find a swap at the last minute. The other type of drivers were like Judy who had enough seniority not to be a swinger. When a roster came out, they knew where on the roster they were and it was possible to plan ahead and work out what you were doing in the future. Sometimes the roster clerk could throw a curve ball with things like training. Usually though, it was easier not to be a swinger.

Judy thought of her roster clerk as a God because more than anyone else in her life, the roster clerk controlled Judy's life. In the case of the swingers, it could be worse as the roster clerk could change what you were doing on a daily basis. Some people were swingers for a short amount of time but the depot average was between 12 and 18 months.

Judy had a look at the diagram in her hand. She had a book in her bag called a Diagram Book. This book had every single diagram for the depot inside. Each separate job had a different diagram number and some diagrams were good and others not so good.

Judy's diagram for the day was average, only two Bankstown Circles, she thought. Later, she had to drive to Liverpool via Granville and back to Lidcombe before ending her shift. Some people judged their entire day based on their diagrams.

Unlike bus drivers who stayed on the same bus all day, train drivers were relieved by another driver for their meal break. Judy saw on her diagram that her meal break would be at Central just after 5pm which suited her. Central was a great place to buy food with a variety of eateries a short walk away. On a short meal break, there was no time to spend 10 minutes walking to an eatery, buying the food, walking back then eating. Sometimes if she was on standby at Central, Judy would walk further than she normally did. Central was close to Chinatown and Judy did enjoy the whole Chinatown experience. The location of the meal break and the time of the day could be the difference between a good & a bad meal break.

Train crew often brought food from the shop at their meal break location because they did not want to carry their food around with them. Carrying around the food was more trouble than it was worth in the opinion of many people. They did not have a fridge or freezer to store their food on the train and often their starting location was not the same as their meal break location. Besides, some people left food in fridges and other people would steal it, no matter how well it was labelled.

With her bag still on her back, Judy walked over to 20 road. Occasionally, she would have to stop to let a train pass by. Unlike a modern depot, there were different places in the depot for different tasks. There were special roads for working on the brakes of the train and replacing the brake pads. There was another special area for working on the roof equipment where the overhead wiring could be easily turned off. There were special areas to replace the train's air conditioning units, train wheels, graffiti removal and monthly detailed inspections. This meant that trains would have to be moved around from one place to other if a train needed multiple tasks completed during a day or night.

It was the job of the Shed Driver (that Judy called Mr Shed) to move the trains around. Most of the time, there were four Shed Drivers on duty at any time. Often, the Shed Drivers would be in the meal room waiting for a task to be completed. Then the train would need to be moved from (for instance) the brake road so another train could be checked.

There was a modern depot under construction which was needed to maintain the new trains under construction. These new trains would replace many of the older trains in the depot that Judy could see in front of her. In this new depot, many things could be done to the train without having to move it from one place to another. Judy was in two minds about the new depot. It would be a great place to work because it is new and there are new trains there. It would not have the atmosphere of her current depot, though.

The new trains (called a Waratah train, named after the state floral emblem) would be a revision of the current Millennium Train. In a way, Judy was about to get a sneak preview of the new trains that she would soon be driving in the next year or so. She would miss the older trains but comparing a Millennium or a Waratah train to a train as old as she was - it was like comparing the Model T Ford to a modern car.

A MOMENT IN TIME by Eric Brook

She could see that a couple of the roads were closed because the tracks were getting concrete sleepers installed to replace the old wooden ones. Judy hated wooden sleepers after she dropped one on her big toe several years ago while doing some gardening at home. Her big toe was broken and bleeding badly but she managed to get herself to hospital. Sometimes it would give her pain, especially in winter. Wearing the big heavy work boots that she was now wearing would have been great at that time but sometimes today the boots would aggravate her toe.

However, Judy had been passed as medically fit to drive a train when she became a driver and at regular intervals since. The medicals increased in frequency as a driver got older. Some people had found out that they had conditions that they had no idea that they had simply due to their regular medicals. Depending on the nature of someone's condition, they were either given time for medication to take affect or they were monitored more closely. In rare cases, they were not allowed to drive trains any more and had to find another job or retire.

Judy could now see the front of her train now that another train had finished passing by. Because there were a lot of people walking and working around the depot, the train speeds around the depot were very low compared to the mainline outside the depot where trains zoomed by at up to 80kph. Some of the people who worked in the depot had no fear of trains and thought nothing about walking in front of them at will, often at the last minute. A constant battle that the depot management was having was people working on the trains without the drivers knowing about it.

In one such incident, a tradesman was working between two carriages while Judy was preparing her train for service one day. Only by chance, Judy found the man who was working on the train without giving an indication by means of a red flag on the front of the train saying that he was there. Especially in that situation, it was important that Judy not be driving or testing the train as the man could have been killed had the train moved. But instead of being happy that Judy was looking out for him, the man was abusive.

If she had of written the details down, she would have been able to double check to make sure that she was at the correct road (20) and that she had the right train (M1/M35). Each road had a yellow circle and the road number painted in black in the yellow circle but some people still got their roads mixed up, especially the newer train crew or those crew members that were not locals. Sometimes though, the train had been moved or parked in the wrong spot so while the road number was correct, it was the wrong train.

Each train had a set number to identify it. In this case, there were two set numbers because there were two 4 car sets to make an 8 car train. Judy knew from her diagram book that the run number (train number in railway speak) was 711G. Because it was not 711A, Judy knew that the train had been in service for the morning peak hour and was taking a break in the depot. Often, the same train would be in service all day.

Happy that both her and the train was in the correct place, Judy looked at the train. She noticed that the train was very wet but it was bright and sunny outside. After coming out of service, the train had been driven through the train wash. The train wash was a building which was longer than the train and a driver drove the train slowly through. Like a car wash, the train wash had acid, brushes and high pressure water jets to rinse the train.

Sometimes it was Judy's job to drive the train through the train wash but her train was driven through by the day shift wash drivers. It would remind Judy to be extra careful getting into the train because the handles and the steps to get in the train were still wet. Often, the trains would be washed at the end of the day as soon as they arrived at the depot. After arriving in the depot, the train would be cleaned and any faults fixed.

The train that Judy was about to get ready for service was called a Millennium Train. It was the most modern train that Judy was able to drive. It was not the newest train on the system, though. The newest train was called an OSCAR train but it was not named after the Sesame Street character. OSCAR was one of hundreds of railway acronyms that had made it into a train crew member's common language. In this case, OSCAR stood for Outer Suburban CARriage. An OSCAR train was similar to a Millennium Train but there were subtle differences. OSCAR trains did not operate on Judy's sector of operations as they were mainly meant for longer trips that extended to the edges of the metropolitan areas and beyond.

One improvement that Judy loved was the ability to open the driver's door with a key while she was standing on the ground like she was now. The older trains were easy to open if they were on a platform. If there was no platform, some people (men and women alike) had trouble unlocking and opening the door unless they climbed a step or two on the small ladder to reach the floor of the train. Judy placed her key into the lock located near her eye level and turned it.

Like a door from the Spaceship Enterprise, it slid open. Judy placed her bag on the floor of the train and climbed into the train using the ladder and handrails. She was very careful because the handrails were still wet from driving through the train wash earlier. Some people even wore cotton gloves so they did not touch any dirty surfaces.

Looking around the cabin of the train, Judy saw no steering wheel. Of course, she knew that a train did not have a steering wheel but many children (and some adults) did not know this. If she was stopped at a station for a while, some people asked to have a look inside the cabin. If she could, she would open the door and give the person a look. She asked a train driver to have a look inside when she was a small child and he did not allow her to have a look. So if she could she would open the door or window. Many people asked "Where is the steering wheel?". Judy knew that the rails did the steering for her. Sometimes she joked that it was the man in the signal box that did the steering for her so she could go from one track to another.

Judy knew that the train was in a sleep-like state. To non-railway people who asked, she would talk about putting the trains to bed at night and waking them up in the morning. Indeed, as a child, she had asked her own mother where the trains sleep at night. Now, she was about to wake this modern train up. It was eerily quiet because things like the air conditioning and compressors that pumped air throughout the train to work things like the horn, doors and brakes were effectively asleep. Judy was about to change that.

Putting her key into a hole in the dashboard, Judy moved a couple of levers and the train started to wake up. Immediately in front of her seat were two computer screens which enabled Judy to send requests to the train and the train could give a response back to her. She thought it would have been cool if the train could talk to her like in sci-fi movies.

A MOMENT IN TIME by Eric Brook

Most things that Judy had to do with the train could be done via these screens while she was sitting in the driver's seat. In a moment, the train asked Judy to put a code number into the system. This code told the train that Judy was a driver and that she wanted to drive the train from that end. Judy checked a few screens and gradually saw boxes changing from red or yellow to green.

Once she had enough green boxes, she reached over and pressed a button labelled "Pantograph up." Pressing this button would raise an arm like device from the train to the electric wires above the train. The power would go from the wires to the train via the arm (called a pantograph). She could not see the pantographs rising (there were 4 in total) but could see them on the computer screen which showed a diagram on the train complete with raised pantographs. Shortly after this, the air conditioning and the compressors kicked in and the train sounded like a train again.

On the screens in front of her, Judy could see on various pages that the boxes were going from red to green as power went through the train. It was a touch screen based system so it looked like Judy was playing a poker machine. Her arm and finger were moving rapidly up and down on the one spot. Red alarm warnings were flashing on the top of Judy's screen and she had to acknowledge each one to clear it from the queue.

A MOMENT IN TIME by Eric Brook

Often when a train first woke up, there were several alarms as things that were not working because they were shut down were reportedly failed. Clearing these alarms could sometimes take several minutes but was important to do because then new alarms could appear as the train was running.

A couple of times in the past, a smoke alarm had activated on Judy's screen so she had to stop and check the affected carriage. The screen could even tell you by a red flashing light which carriage the problem was in. It was not always reliable though but Judy had to check anyway. Luckily for her, they were both false alarms. She had had a couple of fires on older trains however. People would light small fires, usually using the free newspapers that were handed out to the afternoon commuters.

One thing that Judy could ignore for the moment was the number of passengers on the train according to the screen. On one half of the train, the computer said that she had 120 passengers on board and the other half said that she had 45. She knew this was impossible because she knew that she was in the train in the depot and that she was the only person on the train.

The screen said that it was now 1225 and her diagram said that she was due out at 1400. Over the next 70 minutes or so, Judy did a series of tests from both ends of the train to make sure that everything was working as it should and that the train was fit to enter service. She walked through the train twice, once via the lower deck and once via the upper deck. In older trains, there were less steps going to the lower deck than the upper deck so she would always go downstairs first.

There was an official way of doing things but often the unofficial way was quicker and more efficient. It was usually a lot easier and made a lot more sense doing things the unofficial way. After all, if you wanted to find a quicker way to do things, ask a driver. They will usually find a way. As long as the job got done, many people were quite happy to do things the unofficial way.

The train guard was responsible for opening and closing the doors, making the announcements on the train and also passenger security. Some guards in the future would make the next step up to becoming a driver while others would remain a guard for year. The New South Wales system still had two crew members despite many systems in the world having only a driver or an operator. For many years, the two crew system worked well so remained as it was.

A guard that Judy did not know well joined the train and Judy and the guard did their last couple of checks that Judy could not do alone. The preparation of the train went well and it was 10 minutes before the train was due out. The train should be able to now leave the depot on time. This was not always the case.

A MOMENT IN TIME by Eric Brook

Judy took the chance to go to the toilet that luckily for her was located right next to her train. She knew that she would not get another chance for a while. Management took a dim view of people who left their train sitting at a station for a while to go to the toilet. Sometimes it could not be helped though with a person driving on the same train for up to 4 & a half hours. So now was a good time to go.

The lime green shirt that James was wearing made him stand out. He was the shunter whose job it was to make sure that the trains came in and out of the depot at the right time and that the trains were parked in the right places. Sometimes this meant changing the points (some people might call them switches) so the train would go to the correct track. James was walking over towards Judy's train to tell her that it was time for her to leave the depot. The shunters did a lot of walking and many of them preferred to wear shorts. Judy was not sure if this was meant to show off their legs or if it was just more comfortable. Some of the shunters wore shorts year around and you knew it was cold when certain shunters wore long pants.

Judy left the toilet and could see James standing next to her train. "Hi Dave!", Judy said. Judy knew that Dave's name was actually James but with several of the shunters in the depot called Dave, she preferred to call them all Dave. James had a sense of humour and Judy knew that. If James did not like being called Dave, she would not have done it.

A MOMENT IN TIME by Eric Brook

"Hi, Judy, you peanut", said Dave/James, jokingly. "Are you ready to go? Have you finished powdering your nose yet?"

Judy climbed into the train without answering that question just yet. "The Peanut Express is now ready to depart now, Dave", Judy said. Dave told Judy that she was authorised to depart and he walked away laughing. Unlike many drivers in the depot, you could have a joke with Judy and she would have a joke back if the time and place was right.

She told the guard on the internal communications system that they were ok to depart. It was Judy's job to make an announcement to say that the train was leaving just in case any cleaners had snuck on board, looking for a place to hide away from actually doing work. The cleaners were supposed to report to Judy or the guard before they worked on the train.

It was the guard's job to make announcements but on this rare occasion, it was actually Judy's job. While she was in a playful mood, she made a different announcement to normal. "Good afternoon, ladies and gentlemen. The Peanut Express from Blue Depot to the City via Bankstown is due to depart. Cabin crew, arm doors and cross check. Prepare for take off."

A MOMENT IN TIME by Eric Brook

She knew that no one would probably hear it because they should not have been on the train. The cleaners and other workers carried a sheet of paper with all the arrivals and departures on it so they knew when Judy was due out. If they were on the train, it was not Judy's problem.

If the trains were arriving or departing from the depot near the times that people working there signed on or off, some people would catch the train directly to or from the depot. In years gone by, many trains passing the depot made an unofficial special stop there to drop someone off. This practice was replaced with a dedicated bus service from nearby Lidcombe due to delays and safety concerns. 20 minutes was allowed to travel from the depot to Lidcombe as a part of a train crew member's diagram.

While Judy had worked her way up the ladder from working on stations to train guard to driver having joined the railways as soon as she could after leaving school. She had worked mainly on the City Circle line stations and so she was used to busy stations. She loved working on the platforms, making the announcements herself or with an early version of recorded announcements. There were no computers which showed her where the trains were like there was now. She thought that the station staff today were princesses, especially now that a lot of the City Circle's station cleaning was contracted out. She knew what it was like to work hard and sweat.

Chapter 4 – On The Road Again

2pm Thursday 1 April 2010

A couple of horn blasts later, Judy inched her way out of the depot right on time at 1400. Once she was fully on the main line and heading in the right direction a few minutes later, Judy moved the combined power and brake handle towards her and the train went faster. Older trains had two handles and many drivers had a hard time adjusting. The newer train that she was now driving had one handle used by the left hand. This left the right hand with not a lot to do in comparison. All the right hand had to do was to use the horn, press the vigilance button and to press the touch screens.

During her initial training as a driver, she was taught to look out for various landmarks to either shut off power, increase power or to start braking. Some of the landmarks changed or disappeared during Judy's 10 years of driving the trains but mostly, she got it right. She was driving an all stations train which meant that she was stopping and starting every couple of minutes. The landscape varied widely during the next three hours, not that Judy really noticed.

The vast majority of the time, Judy was looking out of the front window. She could glance out the side windows from time to time, especially when she was stopping her train at station platforms. From her seat she could not see the exact end of the train so needed to line her body up with a sign or marker which told her the train was in the correct place.

She was watching for the traffic light-like devices that railway people called signals. The signals tell Judy if the track ahead was clear or not. Sometimes they would tell her how fast she could go or if she was changing tracks. Various coloured lights meant different things but once you understood how they worked, they were relatively simple. A driver would go past many signals on a trip.

Judy really enjoyed seeing two green lights which meant that she did not have to worry about trains in front of her. She would have to obey the speed limits which varied a lot. Many times she would not even reach the speed limit because she had to stop at a station. She had to know the speed limits though because sometimes, she would not be driving an all stations service. Judy enjoyed the express services.

During the afternoon, Judy passed many trains going in the opposite direction. She was not sure how this particular tradition started but every time two trains passed, the two drivers would wave to each other if they could. It would not matter who the driver was. Judy presumed that it was a respect thing to say "Hey mate, how are you doing." Most people waved but it was not really a reportable offence if a driver refused to wave.

A MOMENT IN TIME by Eric Brook

During a training course once, Judy waved to a computerised track worker while she was driving in the simulator. At the time, the people laughed at her and wondered why she did that. She told them that she would do it in the real world so she would do that in the simulator. She did it for her own amusement. She often did things for her own amusement.

Judy was proud of her driving record. She had been driving for 10 years, most of them at her current depot. During that time, she had not passed any stop signals illegally (yes, you can pass them with permission under some circumstances and this does not count as a breach) or had she hit anyone. On the rare occasions that she was socialising with people she did not know and the subject of her work came up, most people asked:

"Have you hit anyone?" (no)

"Where's the steering wheel?" (there is none)

"Why is my train late?" (there are various reasons)

"Can you fix the air conditioning?" (she could turn it on or off, that was about it)

"Do you like your job?" (usually)

A MOMENT IN TIME by Eric Brook

It was Judy's job to know the various speed limits on the tracks. Just like when driving a car, there were regular signs around the network when the speed limit changed. The slowest speed limit was 4kph when a train was being driven through the wash plant and the highest for Judy's train was 115kph. These speeds were often possible in the other suburbs where the stations were further apart.

During her training, Judy learnt to drive the train like a roller coaster. Unlike a car, it was not essential to be powering around the network the entire time. On an express run at higher speeds, Judy could roll through a few suburbs without needing to power. The built up speed and the topography would do the work for her. Judy enjoyed it when she got those sections right. It was her job to know how to drive the train well. One scenario that was often quoted during training was "imagine a grandmother walking through the train and you brake hard and she falls down the stairs."

Another important task that Judy had was to be able to identify and fix faults on the train. With the newer train that she was on, it was a lot easier to diagnose and fix a fault, often without leaving the driver's seat. While some of the older drivers did not like this type of train, Judy loved it. It was unrealistic to expect someone who had been driving a type of train for 20 years and did not know how to use a computer to cope with a touch screen based system. Over time they adjusted but from time to time, another driver would ask Judy about a certain type of fault.

On older trains, however, sometimes a driver had to leave their seat to fix a fault. Depending on the fault and the location of the fault, it was possible for Judy to fix it herself but sometimes to save time, she asked the guard to do this for her. Faults had to be reported to be fixed either while the train was in service or when at the depot.

Sometimes, a fault was serious enough for the train to be taken out of service straight away. Judy prided herself on her knowledge but sometimes even she could not fix a fault herself. There was a group of people called train technicians who were placed around the network to attend to faults while the trains were in service. Sometimes, an extra pair of hands were handy so Judy could keep driving the train. Most of the technicians were former drivers themselves so they understood what it was like and understood how the trains behaved. Judy hated calling the techs for every single little thing and she could fix a lot of problems herself. She liked it when the train tech said "I can't fix it" because that usually meant that the problem was serious. There was only so much that a driver or a technician could do outside the depot.

To her, there was nothing worse than the fault being repaired by the tech because of something simple that Judy had forgotten to do.

Another constant problem was vandalism. Vandalism came in many forms including graffiti, etching, breaking things, throwing objects at the train. Often this meant that a carriage had to be locked up for the safety of the passengers. Gone were the days where passengers could be trusted not to stick their head out of where a window should be. People often sat down without looking and sometimes sat in wet graffiti.

Shattered glass was an obvious problem. The Tangara train (introduced in the late 1980's/early 1990's) had a lot of glass including for windows and others for decoration. The black glass between the two decks of the train was like a magnet for rock throwers. It was a single layer of glass that broke into really fine pieces when smashed. Until the rest of the glass could be removed, a heavy speed restriction would be in place while the train was passing a platform or passing trackworkers.

On one weekend trip, this happened to Judy's train. Without the help of station staff and not near a depot, the train had to continue with speed restrictions for 90 percent of Judy's trip from the outer suburbs. No one came to fix the problem so when Judy changed over with the next driver, the speed restriction remained for the entire trip on the north shore.

While she was driving her train, she had a small speaker on the dashboard with a blue iPod attached. Sometimes she liked to listen to music podcasts and sometimes she listened to her own type of music. Unlike management's opinion, she found that listening to the iPod relaxed her and helped her concentrate. She thought that she would go mad without listening to something as she was driving.

A MOMENT IN TIME by Eric Brook

In years gone by, many people brought small radios with them, especially some of the senior drivers during football season or when the horse races were on over a weekend. Over time, Judy got sick of the radio and had discovered podcasts instead. She listened to a range of shows depending on her mood. Today she was in a music mood so she was listening to music shows.

She had enough podcasts of a given category to listen to the same type of podcast for the whole shift. Time seemed to go faster when listening to these shows, especially comedy podcasts. Sometimes people must have wondered who was doing the laughing inside the cabin when Judy played those sort of shows.

Sometimes, it was fun to hear the one sided conversations in the passenger area immediately behind Judy. Most of the time, they would start with a raised voice saying "Hi! I'm on a train!". The one sided domestic disputes that were very public on the train were sometimes funny, sometimes sad. Judy hated the screaming children. School kids mucking around on the train and trying to hold open the doors and delaying the trains annoyed Judy too.

But most of all, people who pretended to jump in front of the train (or pretend to push other people in front of the train) was the thing that Judy hated above else. She failed to see the humour the first time and also the 50th time and the 150th time. No one higher up the food chain treated these issues seriously. She did however find the penguin promotion funny where the passengers were shown as penguins trying to get on the train.

Overall, the train was performing well, Judy was driving well and she was on time. Sometimes, it did not feel like she was on the same train for 3 hours. She knew some people who complained about catching the train to and from work for 15 minutes each way. Judy loved to tell them "try being on the same train for 3 hours at a time staying in the same seat and see how you go."

She liked running on time, especially if she had a short meal break. Unlike office workers that often had morning tea, lunch and afternoon tea, it was common for Judy to get only one break a day. She did not consider changing from one end of the train to another at a terminal station a real break unless it was over 10 minutes. By the time that she arrived at the right spot on the platform, cut the controls out at one end, walked to the other end of the train, spoke to the guard and cut the controls in at the departure end of the train, 5 to 10 minutes could easily fly by. 5 minutes was the quickest time it could be done in.

Sometimes, the passengers would ask Judy questions as she was walking down the platform. Because of the route she was on, Judy had not changed ends of the train since leaving the depot. She was looking forward to going to the toilet again (lucky she left before she left the depot!) and having something to eat at Central.

http://www.amomentintimenovel.com

A MOMENT IN TIME by Eric Brook

Judy's train was now arriving at Erskineville station. Several people got off the train as it was quicker to get off the train there and walk to nearby Newtown. If someone wanted to get the train to Newtown from Erko (as the station was called by the locals), they would have to go one station to Redfern, change platform, wait for another train and go two stops. Often when leaving the city, the trains to Newtown might be running late so people would catch the on time train to Erskineville and walk the short distance to Newtown.

It was Judy's last chance to go relatively fast for the line she was on after leaving Erskineville. She blew the horn, released the brakes and powered up until the train reached the next signal. She shut off the power while the train was going about 40kph and the train rolled a distance.

The newer trains did not have a major problem in this section but the older trains did. There was a device attached to the overhead wiring called an airgap which separated two electrical sections of wiring. It enabled one section to be alive and another to be dead if need be. If a driver powered under the airgap, they could kill the power to the train. So the best thing to do was to power to just before the airgap and then shut off the power and coast. There were many airgaps in the network, This one was very important for some reason and every trainee driver was told about this particular airgap.

A MOMENT IN TIME by Eric Brook

This is what Judy did even though the newer train she was on was smart enough to be ok. Driving the train the same way for every type of train was the best thing to do. The more a driver did things the same way, the more that it was an automatic thing to do.

On either side of her, there were yards to park trains. The depot on the right was where her train was maintained. Once Judy's train had passed the next signal, she powered up to near the track speed of 65kph and shut off the power again. The train would continue to roll at that speed until it was time to put the brakes on for the stop at Redfern.

The train braked for Redfern station. It was the station before Central. Some people used it as a convenient interchange. Other people found Central to be better for changing trains as it was their view that Central was safer and easier. Central had lifts and Redfern did not. Central also did not usually have riots and major disturbances at the front entrance to the station, unlike Redfern. The name of the station was a lot nicer than the reality. The timetable usually had a couple of minutes of inbuilt slack at Redfern so it was easier to be on time at Central. If you were a little late at Redfern, a short stop could mean being back on time at Central.

A MOMENT IN TIME by Eric Brook

Central was important to the bean counters driving a desk somewhere in railway headquarters because On Time Running was measured from there. On this occasion, Judy was on time at Redfern so she had time to wait.

She used the time to put her iPod in her pocket and her speaker in her bag. She made sure her bag was shut with everything in it and the bag was closed. There was nothing worse than to leave something important on the train and rely on the incoming driver's honesty. A few phone calls would usually have to be made to retrieve the item. This had not happened to Judy but she had left a few half finished drinks on the train, to her annoyance. She saw that she was on time at Redfern at 1700 with arrival at Central due at 1703.

The doors closed and just like at all the other stations previously, the guard gave Judy a single short bell. This was Judy's sign to leave the station. Checking to make sure the signal in front of her was not at stop, Judy blew the horn and released the brakes again. She powered to 45kph and shut the power off again. She hoped that, for once, she had green lights all the way to Central. At this time of the afternoon, there were a lot of trains in the area starting their peak hour trips from the city to the suburbs.

She coasted over a sandstone series of viaducts which enabled the train to switch to different platforms at Central. These sandstone viaducts were very old but was an important piece of infrastructure on the approach to Central. The trains that were about to arrive at Central were high off the ground while the trains that were leaving the city were at ground level. This way, trains could switch from one track to the other without affecting trains heading in the opposite direction.

Train drivers relied on their knowledge of the track that they were driving over. Sometimes the signals would give Judy an indication about which way she was going. As she got closer to Central, the signals changed from green over green to green over yellow to yellow over yellow.

While there were always exceptions to every rule, the signal before the turnout told Judy which way she was to go. The top light on the signal was very important. If the top light was red, Judy was not going anywhere. A yellow top light meant that Judy was going to switch over to platform 17 and had to slow down. The green top light meant that she was going straight ahead to platform 20 and 21.

On this occasion, she had a top yellow light to change from the line called the Up Illawarra Local to the Up Local so she was on platform 17 as the timetable required for the train's next trip. Judy did not normally care where the train was going after it left Central if she was getting off the train. Unlike some drivers, she did not read the driver's version of the timetable which told them exactly where the train was due to change tracks. She knew that things could change at a moment's notice and as long as she got to where she was going and stopped at the stations she needed to, she was happy.

She hoped that her relief driver was standing at the Town Hall end of Central where they should be and not in the meal room. If the train did not need to change from one track to the other, it would have been sailing at the track speed of 50kph. Instead, the train needed to change tracks and the speed limit was 25kph instead.

Judy approached Central. It was a grand old railway station, especially if she looked towards the main terminal. Because she had to drive slower to switch tracks, she did not need to brake as early compared to if she was driving at track speed. She was looking towards the end of the platform and subconsciously scanning the people on the platform. The clocks on the platform said the time was 17:03:25. Above everything else, she was looking for the incoming driver.

Judy's arrival onto the platform would change her life forever.

Chapter 5 – Katrina's Cabin Fever

12 noon, Thursday 1 April 2010

The City of Sydney Fire Station was a mixture of old and new. The station needed to keep up with the times on the inside but the mostly sandstone front ensured the station maintained a historic look which was very important considering that the station was built in 1887. Over time, the station had been upgraded on several occasions with the last renovations and additions being in 2003. It was not, however, the first fire station in Sydney. It was commonly called Station 1, Number 1 or Headquarters.

Inside the station, there was a line of trucks waiting for their next call with their cabin doors open. The trucks were lifeless at this point but could be called into action at any point. Like the majority of fire engines in Australia, each truck was painted red. To the general public, the colour was known as Fire Engine Red. Firefighters sometimes joked that red made the trucks go faster. They also said that a fire engine was not a real fire engine unless it was red.

In days gone by, a fire engine was a modified version of a standard truck. In more recent times, fire engines are custom designed and built for the task, often with input from those people who used them. Each vehicle was designed to have the same equipment in the same location regardless of the station where it was based.

A MOMENT IN TIME by Eric Brook

Near each truck was a set of protective gear for each person. Known as turnout gear in Sydney, it was designed to protect the user from the elements, usually fire. Fire is not the sole enemy of the firefighter in a modern fire and rescue service. Various forms of rescue bring different hazards and being outdoors also present a wide range of hazards. By design, the gear was strong and tough but this also made it heavy. As a result, most people only wore their turnout gear when needed.

When not in their turnout gear, everyone wore service supplied navy blue shirts and long pants. Some people call this station wear. In the event of a call, the turnout gear simply went over the top of the station wear. Some smaller suburban stations might be able to remain in the station the entire time but not City of Sydney. Station 1 was extremely busy and a different world compared to a single truck station.

The large whiteboard at the main entrance to the station showed who was allocated to each truck. Everyone on shift knew this already but the whiteboard was a tradition. Next to the whiteboard was an older blackboard which was no longer used but was used in the past for the same reason.

The same group of firefighters remained together as a group called a Platoon. Each station had 4 groups or Platoons labelled A, B, C & D. Across the state, each platoon of the same letter would be working (or not working) at the same time. For instance, the current shift at City of Sydney was A Platoon. This meant that every person on A Platoon was currently working regardless of their location across the state. Each person was given a pocket calendar pre-marked with their platoon details so they could work out a year in advance if they were working on a particular day.

Most permanently staffed stations worked what was known as a 10-14 roster made up of 10 hour day shifts and 14 hour night shifts. On average, it worked out that people worked 2 day shifts followed by 2 night shifts followed by 4 days off. Unlike many shift working jobs, there was no such thing as a permanent day shift or a permanent afternoon shift.

A Platoon at City of Sydney were on shift and about to eat lunch. Because the station had several trucks, a riding list was needed for each shift. There was a copy on the whiteboard, a copy on the Station Officer's computer as a part of their daily report as well as a copy in each truck.

A MOMENT IN TIME by Eric Brook

The current day's list consisted of:

Senior Station Officer – Wagner

Station Officer - Morris

Flyer – Morris (SO), Sigler, Hutchins, Lafferty, Evans.

Pumper - Wagner (SSO), Crawford, Chambliss, Wallace, Davis

Rescue - Gibson, Miller

Bronto - Thorpe, Thorpe

Most crews at City of Sydney preferred to remain on the same vehicle day after day. The Flyer and Pumper crews were able to rotate between the two trucks as they were basically doing the same job. The Rescue and Bronto were specialist positions with extra skills and training required. While everyone was expected to know how those trucks were to be used, it was up to those crews to be the experts on that vehicle.

The central focus point of most fire stations was the meal room and kitchen area. The room was large as all of the rooms needed to be at City of Sydney. The eating area was a long table with room for one person at the head of the table at each end. The head of the table was usually reserved for the Senior Station Officer. If there were any guests, they would take the head of the table positions.

A MOMENT IN TIME by Eric Brook

Sometimes, a firefighter or senior officer from another station of fire service might visit. Being the main fire station in Sydney, everyone at Station 1 were used to unexpected visitors. As always though, if the alarm bells went off, the crews had to go. Being a multi-appliance station though, it was possible that someone would be still at the station, even if it was the Bronto crew.

Off to the side of the eating area was a large square shaped kitchen. It was fully equipped to cook a wide variety of food but it was commonly only used on special occasions, at least by A Platoon. It was often easier to send a couple of people out for food. Most of the local eateries around the station knew A Platoon well and would often allow them to phone order. Some places even delivered to the station. There was a large variety of things to eat nearby and each person usually had a personal favourite.

The meal room was full because everyone on shift was in the station and no one was at a call. If all the trucks were not in, each truck's crew would stick together as a team. Each truck could be called out together or separately. The platoon stayed together year round except for when people were on various forms of leave. As a result of this and the long shifts, the people in the room knew each other well. It was 12 noon and midway through the shift.

A MOMENT IN TIME by Eric Brook

Unless out on a call, it was traditional for the entire platoon to have lunch together. Like most stations, the crews all put in some money and a couple of people would take a radio and walk to a nearby store.

Today was pizza day thanks to the Bronto crew of Bill and Bob Thorpe. Bill and Bob were brothers and usually operated the Ladder Truck together as they were specialists on that truck. Whoever was on the Bronto usually got the food because the Bronto was called out the least. The Station Officers preferred that the crews not spilt up whenever possible.

The Bronto was called a Ladder Platform officially these days but everyone who had been at City of Sydney for a while called the truck Bronto. Bronto usually only went to calls that involved high rise fires. LP1, as the radio would call Bronto, was great in that situation but was not much use on a regular call. Like the namesake dinosaur, Bronto found it difficult to run in traffic.

When it was fully set up, the Bronto was an imposing sight. There were limited numbers of Bronto type trucks in service. They were handy for aerial rescues and fighting large structure fires from above. As they were a rare resource, sometimes they drove longer distances to larger fires to support other vehicles. A large working fire with a Bronto was often newsworthy. Bill and Bob had found themselves at many large fires in the densely populated inner city suburbs.

A MOMENT IN TIME by Eric Brook

Back from their important mission, Bill and Bob laid the pizza boxes on the table. There was 3 separate boxes because no one could agree on what sort of pizza they wanted. With a large crew present, the pizzas were always large. If there was a call right at that second, the pizza could be reheated later although some people took the slice they were eating with them to eat on the way to the call.

Sitting at the head of the table was a cute, petite blonde woman. Far from being a special guest, Renee was the Senior Station Officer. In a strong but still feminine voice, Renee announced "Lunch is served!" She was the leader of all of the firefighters on shift on A Platoon. Each Platoon had their own Station Officer who worked exactly the same hours that the crews worked. Because the station had two pumpers that could be used together or separately, each vehicle had a Station Officer.

Station Officer Craig "The Sarge" Morris had only just transferred into City of Sydney on a temporary basis which gave Renee the Senior Station Officer job on A Platoon pretty much by default. He was very confident in his ability and made friends easily with the crews. As a relief Station Officer, it was important for Craig to be quickly settle in to a routine and know the people that he was working with. Like Renee, he had been stationed at several stations on different platoons in the inner city areas.

A MOMENT IN TIME by Eric Brook

With 15 years in the service, Renee still enjoyed her job without being too set in her ways. There were people who had been in the fire service a lot longer than Renee but they were often happy not to climb the ladder, so to speak. They were quite happy to keep a hose in their hands. They enjoyed being one of the crew and did not enjoy the thought of becoming a manager like Renee was. Renee had worked hard to become one of the few female Station Officers in the state and was respected by most of the station as soon as she walked through the door. It was common to find that the title of Station Officer demanded automatic respect. Some of the crew needed convincing about Renee, though.

She had spent her early years at Bondi which was a busy station, partly due to the number of tourists in the area. Tourist areas were often busy as the owners of accommodation often tried to maximise their income and not spend a lot of money on maintenance and safety. Renee enjoyed educating the owners and also the tourists about fire safety but found that it was mostly the Station Officer doing the educating.

After several years at Bondi as a firefighter, Renee applied for a relief Station Officer position. This meant that she was filling in for other Station Officers at various stations. After working in several stations during her first 12 months, Renee was based permanently to Station 1. She preferred to be at the one station and get to know her crew and her area. She had now been a Station Officer of City of Sydney's A Platoon for 12 months.

A MOMENT IN TIME by Eric Brook

That might not sound like a lot but in terms of the workload, 1 year at Station 1 or one of the other Sydney CBD stations was like 5 years at a suburban station. Through her performance over time, she earned the respect of her Platoon. She knew when to have fun but when it was time to be serious, she was serious. In Renee's case, it was usually easy to tell the difference.

"Hey Chicago!" Renee called across the table to Richard, the Pumper driver. "Have you finished with that pizza box?". Renee called Richard "Chicago" because he was really good at getting through the traffic, just like a Chicagoian taxi driver.

Richard "Chicago" Crawford nodded and said "You take it, Reno", a play on Renee's name and also the city of Reno, Nevada. Reno (nicknamed "The Biggest Little City In The World") was often regarded as the little cousin to Vegas (also in Nevada). Vegas also happened to be the nickname of another Station Officer on another platoon because he liked to gamble on anything that moved. One thing that firefighters were good at was giving their workmates nicknames, especially if they were the result of a screw-up.

Richard was A Platoon's Pumper driver and the longest serving man on the platoon. He had driven several different vehicles during his time at the station. If Richard said something, everyone listened. He could have been promoted to Station Officer several times but chose to remain where he was. Richard's opinion of the Station Officer was sometimes the difference between a happy ship and the Station Officer moving to another station. He was also the main dispenser of nicknames and the station comic.

Reno (as Renee was quickly nicknamed by Richard soon after her arrival to Station 1) grabbed the pizza and started eating. She looked over at the other female on shift, Katrina. "You going to eat, Kat?" Renee asked. Katrina shrugged, looking at the various boxes. Katrina could not decide what to eat. After a minute or so, she grabbed the closest piece of pizza and started to eat.

Katrina Miller was the newest member of the platoon. Despite 7 years in the fire service, she was new to Rescue and new to City of Sydney and a multi appliance station. She previously had been at Lidcombe fire station in the inner west of Sydney. Most fire stations in Sydney only had one appliance. Katrina was looking for a new challenge and she certainly had that in front of her at Station 1.

Katrina had model looks but was attracted to the fire service at an early age. She grew up on a farm and she saw herself as a tomboy. She had many adventures and loved things fast and powerful. Her favourite activity outside work was rock climbing. Now that she was in rescue, there was the possibility of doing some high-rise abseiling with the bonus of getting paid to do it.

A MOMENT IN TIME by Eric Brook

Renee looked around her team and thought about how much they were eating. If people ate too much at lunchtime, they might not feel like working in the afternoon. She knew, however, that if the station alarms went off, the crew would always spring into action.

"How you doin' over there, O?" she asked Shawn (also known as Shawno), one of the Pumper crew. Mouth full of pizza, O nodded. Renee knew that pizza was Shawno's favourite food to eat at work. He was a quiet man who also played guitar in a band which he fit in around work.

"How 'bout you, T?"

"I'm good, Boss!"

Troy enjoyed riding with Shawn on the Pumper as it was busier than the Rescue Truck and the Bronto. Most people had some sort of nickname, even if it was the first or last letter of their name. Like many firies, O and T had met on the job but had become firm friends on and off the job. Troy was the platoon's computer genius. If Renee had problems with the station's computer, she would ask T for help first. Often it was a problem that was easily fixed, saving Renee a call to the IT help desk. She thought that T would be great on a computer help desk but he had actually became a fireman initially simply to meet women. He had never told her the real reason that he signed up.

A MOMENT IN TIME by Eric Brook

As the pizza supply died down, the conversations started between several people. Some of the crew were talking about the start of the football season. Depending on where someone was sitting, they may have been able to take part in two conversations at once. Katrina and Renee did not care about football which was the current topic of discussion. It was near the start of the football season. In the station, there was a football tipping competition across all of the platoons. There was a cash prize for the top tippers overall and in the platoon at the end of the season.

Renee and Katrina moved away from the main table as they wanted to talk to each other about the news of the day. The news of the day consisted of late night violence towards public safety workers. While it mainly affected the police and ambulance services more than the fire service, it was still possible for firefighters to be attacked on the job. It was something to keep in mind.

Often, the problems of the day were discussed over the table during and immediately after meals. It was often a great way to let off some steam, especially if the platoon had not been on many calls lately. This could have been a problem at busy stations when jobs dried up suddenly. The long table approach was handy if the platoon wanted to talk as a platoon to sort out a problem informally. It was amazing to listen to many of the world's problems were solved around the long table at Station 1.

A MOMENT IN TIME by Eric Brook

Looking across the room, Renee thought about starting a conversation with Robert and Mike but thought better of it as she was more concerned with Katrina's mental welfare as she was showing signs of cabin fever. She knew that every day, Robert & Mike were like twins. Together on the Flyer, they looked and sounded similar. When Renee first arrived at Station 1, she got them confused unless they spoke.

Robert liked to speak in the third person around the station after seeing it happen on an older TV drama called Fire. The character was called Grievous so Robert gave himself that nickname. The series had a single female in a platoon set in Queensland. Like TV's Grievous, Robert spent much energy trying to bed Renee. He had more chance of getting a job on a breakfast radio show than sleeping with Renee.

As far as the crew of A Platoon knew, only one woman slept with Renee and that was Renee. Even if she wanted to, she found Grievous to be very strange. She might not have minded as much if she was not the platoon's Station Officer. She needed to keep her romantic and personal distance between herself and the blokes. This could be hard considering the close quarters in which they lived.

Flyer crew member Mike earned the nickname Chaos because he was the person that everything seemed to happen to. If something was going to happen, Mike was involved somehow as the joker or the subject of the joke.

A MOMENT IN TIME by Eric Brook

Some people even wondered how Chaos had not managed to blow himself up or lose several body parts. Somehow, Grievous and Chaos worked well together so most people allowed them to work together. As Chicago said once "They are a problem but they are our problem."

Renee had to keep a close eye on Mike at a fire. Robert usually did his best to keep Mike in check. If there was a metaphorical big red button to press, Mike would want to press it and Robert would be egging Mike on to do it. It was Renee's job to make sure it was not pressed.

The Flyer was the bigger of the two similar looking red fire trucks in the station. It had more water and a bigger pump and in a normal station would be called a Super Pumper. But Station 1 was special in so many ways. To avoid confusion, call signs were changed for some multi appliance stations such as City of Sydney. Rather than have "Pumper 1" and "Super Pumper 1" over the radio, Super Pumper 1 was called Flyer 1 instead.

In days gone by, Flyer 1 went to every call in the city. As the city got bigger, Flyer 1 could not keep up with the calls. The easiest way for the layman to tell the Flyer apart was the yellow line around the body of the truck. It was also a throwback to tradition as the crew of the Flyer always used to go to every job they could in the city.

A MOMENT IN TIME by Eric Brook

With lunch over, Katrina went over to her Rescue truck. She did not believe in just sitting around the station doing nothing. The Rescue truck needed special qualifications and Katrina was new to Rescue. She took the time to look through the various compartments and lockers of the truck. She had only recently completed the Rescue course after spending a few years on a Pumper at Lidcombe, Station 30.

One of her bigger jobs was when the railway station across the road was on fire one night. That incident late on a Saturday night saw several Pumpers and a Bronto attend the fire. Luckily, the fire occurred late on a Saturday night when there was not as many people around. That fire totally destroyed a shop and several offices on the station's over bridge. At one stage, the concrete bridge was in real danger of collapsing. She even managed to get onto TV because at the time, a camera crew were riding along with Station 15 (Burwood) as a part of a show called "Fire 000."

Good teamwork and a lot of water contributed to that result. There were many stations present from the surrounding areas and each station usually worked in a sector of the fire. An Incident Commander had to work with the various Station Officers to keep track of the fire and work out various strategies to protect firstly life and then property.

http://www.amomentintimenovel.com

A MOMENT IN TIME by Eric Brook

That night was a long night for Katrina as there were several hotspots and smaller fires in the one structure. The fire could have easily spread across the road to the nearby shopping precinct. If the fire had of spread to the shops across the road, the fire could of spread quickly because many of those older buildings were connected.

Renee came over to see Katrina. "What are you doing, Kat?" Renee asked. It was fairly obvious to Renee what Katrina was doing but the Station Officer was slightly worried about her new Rescue Operator. Cabin fever soon after doing an intensive course could be a bad thing. The Rescue truck did not go on every call which did not help Katrina's state of mind. She had seen the Pumper and Flyer leave the station under lights and sirens many times and she wanted some of that action. She could not go onto the Pumper or the Flyer, though. That would leave her Rescue partner Scott as the only Rescue Operator at the station which was unacceptable. Scott and Katrina had to work together and that could not happen if Katrina was on another truck.

Katrina closed a locker and said "Just making sure everything is here, Renee." Katrina said. "I want everything to be here when we get a call. I want to make sure that everything is how it should be."

Renee looked at her new Rescue operator and smiled. "You checked this morning, right?". Renee knew that Katrina had checked the truck already. Katrina nodded.

A MOMENT IN TIME by Eric Brook

"And you haven't been anywhere in the truck." Katrina did not disagree. "So everything is still where it was when you checked it this morning."

Unless the truck was out at the start of the shift, the first thing to do after roll call was to check the truck. After each call for a Pumper, the wet hoses were removed and other consumables were restocked. Katrina was used to handling wet hoses and scrubbing them before hanging them up to dry. But on the Rescue truck, there were no hoses to worry about and everything was supposed to be returned to the truck on scene.

As the Rescue truck had not been anywhere while Katrina was on shift, she knew everything was there as it was supposed to be. Regardless, Renee was happy that Katrina was looking over the equipment. It showed Renee that Katrina was keen and eager.

Like most larger cities in the world, Sydney had many shops and multi-storey skyscrapers. There were a lot more people in the city during the day compared to overnight. Many people worked but did not live in the centre of Sydney. There was always a high fire risk regardless of the time of day. There were many buildings that had lifts installed and rescuing people out of lifts was an important function that was high on the call statistics.

A MOMENT IN TIME by Eric Brook

City of Sydney had a relatively small area of responsibility in terms of land area but often were assisted by (and assisted) their surrounding stations. Much like the Police, there was a station at The Rocks (station 3) to the north, Redfern (station 10) to the south. To the east a hop away from Kings Cross was station 4, Darlinghurst. It was common for trucks to cross the imaginary lines on the maps into another station's area.

Number 1's day at been reasonably slow by their own standards. The Rescue had not been out yet. The Flyer and Pumper had been out to a couple of separate calls for fire alarms that turned out to be false alarms due to a fault in the system. There was a very rare day that there were no calls at all for City of Sydney.

Renee knew that Katrina was feeling a bit on edge. Katrina had only spent a couple of shifts at the station and had not been on a rescue call yet. Rescue operators stayed with their truck and did not switch to the Flyer or Pumper under normal circumstances. All of the team were expected to be able to assist in a rescue but Katrina now was a specialist as a Rescue Operator. She was still expected to remain current with a hose, though. "You miss the Pumper, Kat?" Renee asked. Katrina nodded as she looked towards Pumper 1.

A MOMENT IN TIME by Eric Brook

Katrina knew that rescue is what she wanted to do and had worked hard to get through the 2 week course. The equipment was not light and required a lot of skill to use correctly. During the course, Katrina had played the parts of rescuer and victim during several different types of rescue. The rescuers had to work in pairs as a team much as they would in the real world. A lot of time was spent practising on crashed cars using the Jaws of Life. Used by an expert, a sedan or station wagon could easily be converted into a convertible.

Some stations now had a combined truck that had rescue gear and firefighting gear on the same truck. These trucks not surprisingly were called a Rescue Pumper. While City of Sydney might receive a new Rescue Pumper in the future, Rescue 1 was still a dedicated Rescue vehicle for now. It contained all the tools for various forms of rescue including Urban Search and Rescue (USAR), Road Accident Rescue (RAR), general Search and Rescue (SAR) and more. In the event of a large scale rescue such as a natural disaster, there were a couple of dedicated semi trailers that would be driven to the scene filled with extra rescue equipment.

As important as Rescue 1 was, it could not be filled with every piece of rescue equipment known to man. It carried enough equipment for the type of incidents that it would regularly deal with. In addition, every pumper also carried basic rescue equipment.

Rescue 1 also contained basic hazardous materials (HAZMAT) protective equipment like all fire engines. Like Rescue, HAZMAT was a specialised area within the fire service with specialised personnel and vehicles. At larger events, Rescue & HAZMAT would work closely together. There was a dedicated HAZMAT section with specialised vehicles scattered around the state for larger incidents.

HAZMAT was a very technical area because there were so many chemicals that were in common usage. Not only would you need to know what these chemicals were and how to stop them, you also needed to know what happened if the chemicals were mixed with water, foam, fire and other chemicals.

Renee had an idea. "Let's go for a drive, Kat. You need to know the city. Comms can get us on the radio if they need us. Go warm the truck up. I'll go and talk with Scott." The Rescue truck could only seat a driver and a passenger which was one reason that there were only two rescue operators at the station. The rest of the crew had more basic rescue skills that could be useful to assist the operators if needed.

Rescue itself was in a state of change in the greater Sydney area. Mostly, each emergency service had a core function. For instance, Police were responsible for law enforcement and did not put out fires. The fire service put out fires. Rescue was an interesting situation, though.

A MOMENT IN TIME by Eric Brook

Each service decided that they needed a rescue function. This led to turf wars between the services as they fought to get their rescuers to as many calls as possible. There was also a lot of duplication of personnel and equipment. Eventually, the Ambulance Service lost most of their rescue function with the fire service taking over. Now, the City of Sydney area was the only major area that had two rescue services. Both the Police and Fire services had rescue functions. This was a possible reason that Rescue 1 had not been on a call today.

Katrina disconnected the power cord from the truck which keeps the various electronics charged. She put on her turnout pants on over her blue drill pants and grabbed her turnout jacket and put it over her seat back. Renee went and saw Katrina's partner Scott and Chicago, the Pumper driver. Scott and Chicago were senior firefighters that Renee could rely on. "Guys, I am going to take Kat out on the Rescue. She is getting cabin fever." Renee said. "Scotty, ride in my seat. If you get a call, I'll meet you there." Both men agreed to the idea. "We'll be back soon."

Renee walked over to the Rescue truck. She did a quick lap of the truck and saw that the doors and lockers were closed and the power cord was disconnected. Happy, Renee grabbed her turnout gear just in case of a call and climbed into the truck that was running. "Let's go, Kat."

A MOMENT IN TIME by Eric Brook

Renee pushed a button and the door in front of Rescue 1 opened. Katrina turned the fire truck's heavyish steering wheel to the right and drove the truck down Castlereagh Street. Renee grabbed the radio handset and pressed the button.

"Sydney Comms, Rescue 1, yellow." Renee said. This told the radio operator that the message was not urgent or fire related. After the operator answered, Renee continued. "Rescue 1 in local area for familiarisation. SO1 on board the Rescue. Send me to any call for Station 1. I'm available via RT."

While it was 2010, the fire service stuck with some terms from the past. While Renee would have preferred to use the word radio, RT (short for Radio-Telephone) was still used. Renee was telling Comms that she was the SO, another term from the past. Surprisingly, Station Officer (SO) had not been replaced by a title developed by a bunch of suits in a brainstorming session armed with some markers and butcher's paper.

"Message received, Rescue 1. 1437"

Katrina and Renee did not need to look at their watches. For safety reasons, they did not wear watches. The last thing one needed was a melted watch in the extreme heat of fire. They were used to hearing the radio tell them what the time was.

http://www.amomentintimenovel.com

A MOMENT IN TIME by Eric Brook

Waiting to turn right onto Hay Street, both woman saw a tram turn right to climb a hill to Central station. "See that tram?" Renee asked. Katrina nodded while waiting for the light to turn green. "We get a few tram versus pedestrian calls, especially down near the Hay/George Street intersection. There's not a lot of room under that tram bumper. So even for a skinny person, you'll need an airbag. Let's go down there and have a look. The easiest way to drive down there is to follow the tracks. The trams don't go fast down there but people don't watch where they are going. The tram normally wins. The street section we are on is slow but at the end of this street, it's like a normal train."

The lights turned green and Katrina turned right into Hay Street. Following Renee's advice, Katrina moved the big truck onto the tram tracks. The Big Red Truck (BRT - sometimes a term of affection for a fire engine) was similar in bulk to the tram but not as long. It was a lot easier to drive down the tram tracks as cars were not allowed to do the same. In this situation, there was nothing to gain by doing so but in an emergency, every second counted.

"Don't forget about the bus lanes either, Kat", Renee explained. "Use every little trick you can. Here in the city, don't go down the wrong side of the road if you don't have to. Multiply the traffic that you've experienced around Lidcombe by 50."

A MOMENT IN TIME by Eric Brook

"Are they as stupid around here as they are outside my old station?" Katrina wondered out loud. "I used to hate coming out of the station during the peak hours because you'd need to be a mind reader to figure out where the drivers were going around there!"

Katrina continued to steer the truck west towards Darling Harbour. On one side was the local markets that came to life on the weekends. On the other side was the Sydney Entertainment Centre and the Monorail. The monorail was regarded as a tourist ride by many locals but the city's Emergency Services needed to know how to deal with any form of situation here just as much as the other types of transport. Renee saw a monorail train above her head. She changed the tone of her voice. "Mono means one and rail means rail. Here ends your extensive course so you can be a monothingy guy."

Katrina recognised the line as being from an early episode of The Simpsons. She never pictured Station Officer Renee Wagner to be a Simpsons fan nor to have a sense of humour. Being new to the station, Katrina did not know Renee very well yet. Katrina laughed and started to sing the end of the Monorail song from the same episode. Renee joined in. The song ended with both women singing "MONO – D'oh!"

"Speaking of D'oh, did you hear about the monorail crash the other week, Kat? That was here." Renee pointed to the monorail track above the ground. "We had to send everything we had to that, even the Bronto. We even called for Darlo's LP. Some of the carriages were on the platform but the LPs were very handy for the rest. You can't walk people through the monorail carriages like you can on the tram or trains. And they don't have emergency slides like large commercial planes."

Talking of trains reminded Renee of something else that she needed to tell her new rescue operator. "We've have to get you down into the train tunnels and the train rescue course. There's a big difference between the train tracks in the suburbs compared to the trains under our feet here in the city. Remind me about it when we get back. You'll get a railway job sooner or later, usually people jumping in front of a train. Let's turn around and head back towards George Street."

Katrina found a corner to do a complete u-turn rather than a 3 point turn. She preferred to a complete u-turn in the large truck. Renee looked out the window and said "It's a lovely day, isn't it? Too bad we are working all weekend, though."

Katrina partly disagreed. "I think it rains many times in Easter. My old station had the closest pump to the Easter Show. I can remember heaps of times going out there in the rain. But if it stays like this, it will be awesome. But Easter itself doesn't worry me that much. A few bad crashes on Parramatta Road, though. I saw the guys on

15's Rescue and that's when I knew I wanted to cut people out of cars. So I applied for the Rescue course. I was very surprised to have got onto the course so quickly!"

Continuing the trip back towards the station, the radio attracted Renee's attention. She was used to being able to filter out in her mind the many messages that did not apply to her station. Every Station Officer had to learn this important skill, especially when they were out of the fire station.

Chapter 6 – Katrina Gets A Job

3.12pm Thursday 01 April 2010

"Sydney Comms calling Rescue 1, message" said the speaker. Katrina thought "That's us!". Renee picked up the handset and answered. The operator asked for Renee's location. By this time, they were near the corner of George and Hay Streets, just around the corner from their station. "Rescue 1, attend Myer on George Street with your pump, person stuck in a lift."

Katrina accelerated down the tram tracks for the short distance to George Street just as Renee suggested minutes earlier.

"Rescue 1, code 1", said Renee in an urgent tone. Despite having a joke with Katrina a few minutes ago, Renee knew that this was serious business.

Katrina switched on the lights and sirens as Comms announced the time as 1512. Code 1 meant that the driver was using lights and sirens and possibly using authority to break some road rules, usually red lights and speed limits. While they were exempt from most rules of the road in this mode, they still have a duty of care to themselves, the crew and the motorists and people around them.

Renee knew that lights and sirens were nice but did not make the truck resistant to crashing. The truck was not like a dodgem car nor was it wrapped in bubble wrap. Besides, you would need a lot of bubble wrap to cover Rescue 1.

"Left! Left!", Renee yelled to make herself heard over the siren. Katrina slowed for the corner then punched the steering wheel. This changed the tone of the siren. Renee called "Clear left" and then "Clear right" as the truck arrived at the traffic light. Good luck rather than technology ensured the light was green. Katrina wrestled the steering wheel to the left. George Street was the main street of Sydney and was busy most of the day and night with frequent intersections.

The city pedestrians reminded Renee of crash test dummies. As Renee knew and Katrina would soon discover, a Volvo nerd in a lab coat could not repair these sorts of dummies. Sirens blaring, Renee reminded Katrina to use the bus lane when she could. The bus lane was mostly clear and a couple of buses pulled into traffic to give Rescue 1 a clear run. Some cars moved, others did not despite Renee's twiddling of the siren knob. It was her experience in the city that a simple siren was not always enough to make yourself heard.

Being careful with the various intersections, Renee kept an ear on the radio. The truck approached the Queen Victoria Building and Renee reminded Katrina that the building they needed was a block ahead. "Where do I park?", Katrina asked, looking around. Renee pointed to the bus lane on the other side of the road outside the store. While it was on the wrong side of the road, the truck needed to be as close to the front entrance as possible.

In Renee's eyes, going around the block or carrying tools across George Street were not options. Katrina slowed the truck down, Renee blipped the sirens a couple of times. Despite being a large truck with red and blue flashing lights and a siren, sometimes twiddling the dial to change the sound of the siren would attract attention.

As Rescue 1 moved slowly through the George/Market intersection, both women could see Pumper 1 arriving at the same time on Market Street. The store had entrances fronting both George and Pitt Streets and the George Street side at the corner of Market Street was the agreed meeting point in the Pre Incident Plan for the building. George Street was easier because it was two way.

Pitt Street on the other hand was one way and had a mall in the middle. The mall was a bigger obstacle for Station 3 than City of Sydney for this call. Pumper 3 could come down George Street from the station in The Rocks a lot better than Pitt Street. The Rocks was the secondary station for this call if Station 1 were at other calls. Major locations had primary and secondary stations in the Pre Incident Plans however Comms could change that if needed. The plan was simply a guide to what the crews could expect. It was not a substitute for the first arriving Station Officer to size up the situation and ask for the resources required, even if they needed more resources than the plan stated.

For this type of call, it was sometimes overkill for a Pumper to attend with the Rescue but it was hard to predict why people were stuck in a lift and where the lift was in relation to a level. In outer suburbs, a Pumper would attend a similar job solo as each firefighter did have basic rescue skills and equipment. If they needed help then, they could call their nearest Rescue station via the Comms Centre.

Renee turned the sirens off but left the lights on. She knew she was not parked in an ideal situation. All of the city's emergency workers had to do the best they can with no spaces allocated to them so if that meant parking in a traffic lane on the wrong side of the road, that was what had to be done. The Rescue would not fit on the footpath like the Police's paddy wagon from City Central was, lights also flashing.

"Where are the Ambos?", Renee thought to herself. It was normal to send paramedics to these calls for high risk patients. Unlike America, Renee's crew (and indeed her service) were not paramedics. It was not uncommon for the Ambulance to be on scene first.

A MOMENT IN TIME by Eric Brook

She grabbed the radio handset. "Sydney Comms, Rescue 1, Blue".

The blue colour code meant that it was an incident related message. After being acknowledged and allowed to keep talking, Renee continued with her message.

"Rescue 1 and Pumper 1, code 3, Myer on George Street. Police on site, no Ambos. Further message to follow." She was telling Comms that both her and Chicago on Pumper 1 were on scene.

"1517."

Grabbing her Incident Controller vest, both women left the truck. Renee told Katrina to bring the Lift Rescue Kit. It contained all the main items Katrina would need if a set of keys did not work. "Nice driving, Kat. Bit slow, Chicago!", Renee said to her two drivers. She said that on most calls to Richard even if he had done well.

Richard laughed. "It must have because Reno was not in Nevada", Nevada being Richard's personal name for Pumper 1 when Renee was in it. Pumper 1 or Flyer 1 were Renee's normal ride. Normally, she would not be riding in the Rescue.

A MOMENT IN TIME by Eric Brook

Katrina's rescue partner Scott climbed out of Pumper 1. As driver and pump operator of Pumper 1, Richard remained with the trucks. Even though Renee was the Station Officer, she was not a rescue operator. Scott was Katrina's rescue partner so Scott, Katrina & Renee entered the building. Renee told the rest of Pumper 1's crew to stay in the truck. Often the Pumper crew were not needed but could be handy if the person was in a bad way and needed to be lifted out into an Ambulance.

A Police Officer met the trio at the door. It must have been his wagon on the footpath. "This way", he said. "There's an elderly couple stuck in the lift. They are stuck near the second floor."

Renee led the growing number of emergency workers towards the lift. Renee said to Scott "Try your key first, Scotty. This might save you a walk, Katrina. Better to try this rather than rip the lift apart as Plan A."

The Police Officer showed the fire crew which lift was the problem child. "Your partner is upstairs?" Katrina asked the cop. He nodded. Scotty inserted his special key into the lock. It was designed for the fire service as a universal key that could over-ride the way the lift worked. That was the theory, anyway.

Thankfully, Scott and Katrina could see the numbers on the display changing from 2 to 1 then to G. The doors opened and a happy elderly couple emerged from the open door, somewhat bewildered to see a policeman and three firemen waiting. Renee told Scott and Katrina to check the couple in the absence of the yet-to-arrive paramedics and the cop to go and find his partner.

As Scott and Katrina checked the patients, Renee called Comms on her radio. "Sydney Comms, Pumper 1, green."

Strangely to the untrained ear, green meant stop and meant that the crew would be available. The incident was over. Normally, green meant go and red meant stop. In the fire service, it was the opposite. It was good for things to be green (incident over) compared to being red (life threatening emergency).

"From Myer on George Street, 2 elderly people freed from lift by Brigade, assisted by Police. Nil damage, nil injuries, Ambos not on site and are not required. Both crews returning shortly."

"1532. Channel clear."

Scott and Katrina finished up with their patients. "Go back to the truck, I need to speak to the store manager." said Renee. Renee caught a different lift to the second floor. The last thing that Renee wanted to do was to get stuck in the same lift that she had just helped rescue the elderly couple from. That would have been an embarrassing call for help!

For many years, the store's lifts had a lift operator inside whose job it was to drive the lift and announce what was on each floor. Several years ago, the store was modernised and modern lifts without a lift operator was installed. Instead of the lift operator's voice, a recorded voice told Renee that she was on the second floor.

The doors opened and Renee saw a couple of Police Officers and the Store Manager. Renee spoke to the Manager and she was convinced that the lift was not going to be used again until the lift company had a chance to look at it. The last thing that Renee wanted was a return visit for the same problem with the same lift.

With all the required information written down briefly, Renee got back into the lift and headed to the ground floor. She would head back to the station and type the details of the call on the computer system for the fire report. Comms would have most of the information but there would be some details that Renee would add that would not be suitable for transmission over the radio.

A MOMENT IN TIME by Eric Brook

The crews of Rescue 1 and Pumper 1 were waiting for Renee to come back to the trucks. Scott and Katrina were waiting on the footpath. Scott thought that Renee might like to ride back to the station with Katrina. Renee headed towards Pumper 1 so Scott and Katrina headed back to the Rescue truck.

Renee called Comms on the radio again. "Pumper 1 and Rescue 1 are code 4 to station."

"Station 1, code 4 at 1552."

Code 4 meant that the crews were returning back to their station and were available for another call. If they were heading somewhere else (like another station), they gave that location. Most crews effectively were partly repeating themselves, much like people used the term ATM Machine. Why people were effectively were saying Automated Teller Machine Machine was stunning to Renee. But like most Station Officers, Renee would say that she was going code 4 to station. Normally at a scene, each truck would talk for themselves but considering that they were from the same station and travelling together, Renee thought she would save time and speak for both trucks.

It was relatively simple for Chicago on Pumper 1 to drive back to the station. All Richard had to do was to go straight ahead for a couple of blocks, turn left into Sussex

Street, then left into Bathurst Street and then right into Castlereagh Street. Katrina had a more difficult job, however. She was in the bus lane on the wrong side of the road. With Scott acting as her guide and temporary traffic controller, Katrina reversed the big red truck into the intersection with warning lights flashing. When she could turn left into Market Street, Scott climbed into the truck and Katrina turned into Market Street.

Once on the correct side of the road again, Scott turned the lights off. They could see Pumper 1 in the distance but Scott knew which way Chicago would drive back to the station. Not that it mattered, of course. Renee was now in her rightful position in the passenger's seat of Pumper 1 and Scott was in the same seat on Rescue 1. If need be, they could be diverted to another job at any time.

When Rescue 1 got to the corner of Bathurst and Castlereagh Streets, Scott reminded Katrina about the special fire lane between the intersection and the station. The station was midway down on the right hand side of Castlereagh Street. It was a one way street heading south towards Central railway station. This was the direction that they were currently going. In a rare design for the city, there was a dedicated fire lane between the fire station and the intersection that the trucks could use in both directions, thus negating the one way Castlereagh Street for a short distance. That was handy for calls to the north of the station as they could then go east on Bathurst Street then north via Elizabeth Street to head further north. There were warning lights but Scott reminded Katrina to take care when leaving the station. It was certainly a lot easier to leave the station under lights and sirens than if the station was located on George or Pitt Streets.

Even with the growing afternoon traffic, it was a short trip back to the station. Chicago stopped Pumper 1 in the fire lane and Renee climbed out of the truck. Luckily the street was quiet and there was really no need for Renee to be standing in the middle of the road blocking traffic. She knew, however, that the traffic could change instantly. Once Renee was out of the truck, the lights of the truck were turned on and Richard swung the truck in an arc and ended up in line with the door. Renee stood in the middle of the road like a traffic cop would on point duty. Richard pushed a button on the dashboard on the truck and the garage style door opened. Lights flashing, Richard reversed the truck into the station like he had on many occasions before. Once the truck was in the building, the door closed and Renee moved off the road.

Knowing that Rescue 1 was not far behind, Renee stood on the footpath to save Scott from doing the same thing with his truck. Soon enough, Rescue 1 rounded the corner and the lights on the truck came on. Renee and Katrina repeated the procedure and both trucks were now back at the station ready for the next call. It was now 1603.

A MOMENT IN TIME by Eric Brook

Renee hooked both trucks up to the power points again. During this call, there was no equipment to replace so the crews went upstairs to a recreation room. The large room had a large screen TV and lounges in one corner and a snooker table in another. Leading away from the recreation room was a large gym. There was a lot of down time while on shift so the powers that be encouraged the crews to stay active. One way to keep fit and still be ready at the station to go at a moment's notice was to use the gym. On many occasions, there would be a couple of people working out with a couple more people helping them.

While the gym was large, it was not really large enough for the whole platoon to work out together at the same time. Sometimes on weekend day shifts, the whole platoon would leave their station in their trucks and go for a run in the nearby Hyde Park. On more than one occasion, the run was interrupted by a call. Comms knew where the trucks were and the Station Officers would be sure to keep their portable radios on, listening for a call.

Listening for a call at the station was easy. There would be a series of tones over the speakers in the station. There were separate tones for each truck as not every truck went out on each call. The robotic female voice would also announce the name of the trucks needed. Whoever was closest to the teleprinter would grab a computer print out of the job and give it to the Station Officer.

Each truck also had a Mobile Data Terminal (MDT) which gave the details of the job. While the MDT had different buttons for leaving the station, arriving on scene, leaving the scene and back at the station, the fire service preferred the use of voice comms with codes. Most of the time, the radio operator would not give the details of the calls over the radio.

Some Station Officers were looking forward to the day that the various buttons on the MDT were allowed to be use. After all, they thought, the Ambulance Service was already doing it. Renee, however, preferred to use her voice and talk over the radio. She knew that there would be a day though where she would not have a choice.

The crews from Rescue 1 and Pumper 1 were taking advantage of the down time they now had. They knew that there was under two hours remaining in the shift. They did not want to be out on another call when 6pm rolled around and the next Platoon came on shift. Sometimes though, this was unavoidable.

Renee completed her paperwork from the previous call while she had the chance. Sitting in her shared office that she shared with the other Station Officers, she was typing on her computer when Katrina came into the room. Luckily for Renee, she could talk and type at the same time. Renee invited Katrina to sit down. Katrina sat down.

A MOMENT IN TIME by Eric Brook

"Thanks for the tour, Renee. I really did need to get outside. The tram tracks and the bus lane thing really did work well. And Scotty told me about the lane to Bathurst Street, too." Renee concentrated on her report but continued talking to Katrina.

"Kat, if you think you need to get out and about for a while, let me know. Grab Scotty and he'll look after you. I can see that you are eager to learn. And trust me, there's a lot to this city that you'll learn about."

Renee was about to dismiss Katrina when she remembered their earlier conversation. "Oh, while you are here, I'll do the paperwork for the train rescue course. Hopefully you'll get on the next course. They do a hands-on exercise and show you around the train one day and then another day they'll take you into the tunnels. That will probably be when the tracks are closed on a weekend."

The printer whirred and one piece of paper came out. Renee grabbed the paper off the printer and put it on the desk in front of Katrina. "Sign this form and I'll put it in for you. You'll need to do the course sooner rather than later." Katrina looked at the form quickly and signed it.

"Go relax, Kat. There's not long to go now before home time." Katrina handed the form to Renee who also signed it. She then placed it in her out tray.

A MOMENT IN TIME by Eric Brook

"Thanks, Renee."

There were a group of people around the TV. At this time of the afternoon, there was not much use in watching a DVD or a movie because it was close to home time. Being near the afternoon peak hour, there was a lot of people eagerly leaving the city and they all wanted to get out at the same time. The older men preferred to watch the news on the TV, regardless of the channel. Now that there was a 4.30pm bulletin on Channel 7, the TV usually found itself on that channel. The news was just starting. At the station, the TV would often be on as background noise even if no one was watching it.

Assuming there were no interruptions from calls at the end of the 30 minute bulletin, someone changed the channel at 5pm to Channel 10. The shift changeover happened at 6pm as the Channel 10 news ended. Most times, the TV would remain on Channel 10. The Simpsons would often play to an empty room as the Platoons changed over and the incoming Platoon checked the trucks. That might explain Renee's love of The Simpsons that she demonstrated in front of Katrina earlier in the Rescue.

If something big was happening in the news, Sky News was the station of choice as they covered stories in detail that the other stations could not. Many stations now had Pay TV and the crews put money in to keep the service, usually with a social club arrangement. The crews often relaxed in front of the TV. They saw the news of the day, including traffic reports. There could be a lot of down time for a modern day firefighter as fire safety and suppression had improved dramatically over the last few years.

On today's news, they could see a lot of people heading out of town for the Easter long weekend. Often, the traffic helicopters would show car accidents and the team would see other stations on scene from a great distance. The traffic would usually be back for miles. Often, you could not tell the normal traffic apart from traffic that would be normally occurring on a normal day. Channel 10 were infamous for this. They would show heavy traffic and someone would scream at the TV "That's because it is peak hour! There's nothing special going on!"

The Channel 7 news was just finishing. This meant that the platoon only had 60 minutes to go before it was home time. Most times, the incoming shift would arrive 10 minutes or so early. 12 hours later, the night shift would be hanging out for the day shift to arrive. 12 hour days suited the station a lot better than the traditional 10 hours of day shift and 14 hours of night shift. Outer stations did this, not City of Sydney. People were moving around the station.

Some people were in the gym, some intently watching the TV, others lounging around. A couple of people were cleaning the kitchen to make sure that it was clean for the incoming shift. Renee was starting her end of shift report. Someone turned the TV across to Channel 10 and the first commercial break was just ending. The blonde female newsreader welcomed viewers back from the commercial break saying "News just in........"

"WHOOP WHOOP WHOOP WHOOP WHOOP. Pumper. Rescue. Pumper. Rescue" the robotic voice said, interrupting the newsreader.

Suddenly people came running from everywhere. Chicago headed for the Pumper. He was going for another drive under lights and sirens. Scott and Katrina headed to the Rescue. Renee ran to the teleprinter and gave a copy to Scott. "Central railway, Scotty. Look after Katrina." Renee said.

Katrina disconnected the electrical cable from the Rescue as Richard was doing the same to the Pumper. It was normally the driver that did this because it was their duty to be responsible for anything that could damage the truck. It was usually the very last thing they did before climbing into the truck. To most drivers, it was a habit that they got themselves into.

The two crews climbed fast into the trucks and the doors of the station opened automatically. Richard was slightly quicker than Katrina into the seat and was first out of the station.

A MOMENT IN TIME by Eric Brook

"Right!" Scott yelled to Katrina as he turned on the siren of the Rescue. Renee did the same on the Pumper.

"Sydney Comms, Pumper 1, Blue" Renee said using a loud voice over the radio, trying to be heard over the siren. After being answered, Renee said "Pumper and Rescue Code 1". Again, she was speaking for both trucks. Scott did not get a word in while on the Rescue if Renee was on the call in the Pumper.

"Pumper 1, Rescue 1, code 1 at 1708."

Katrina drove the truck hard down Castlereagh Street. Scott told Katrina to head to Central station. The easiest way for them to drive there was to again follow the tram tracks, this time up the hill to Central. Katrina and Chicago gunned the engines of their respective trucks as the traffic parted for them. Renee was sure to have her siren on a different tone to Scott's. That way, people might be able to tell that there were two trucks coming rather than one.

Just before the right hand curve of the tram track to arrive at Central, Scott told Katrina the nature of the incident and said "When we get there, head to Platform 16. All we'll need is a first aid kit for the moment. If we need anything else, we can come back for it when we assess the situation. You'll need your turnout gear."

Katrina's life was about to change forever.

Chapter 7 - Run, Natalie, Run!

12 noon, Thursday April 1 2010

The engine of the late model BMW motorcycle roared into life. The floor of the garage was slick and a sudden application of power from a standing start caused a squeal from the rear tyre. The rear end of the bike squiggled slightly under load.

Being careful not to be car-food right after leaving the garage, the helmeted rider was on a mission. Wearing a full faced red and white helmet and tight blue racing leathers with some hi-visibility stripes, the rider looked like she was racing in the Australian MotoGP. This was not the Phillip Island racetrack but the busy streets of down town Sydney.

Unless you knew what to look for, you would not have known there was a woman riding the high powered BMW motorcycle. She was not in the same spot for long enough to look closely at her. Compared to the traffic around, she looked like a streak of light. On a bike, nothing stopped her. Stopped traffic? No worries. She would go between the cars. Red traffic lights? Sure, she would slow down but she would go right through them. What about the main concourse of Central railway station? That was no obstacle either.

A MOMENT IN TIME by Eric Brook

Weaving around a sea of travellers waiting to travel, the bike slowed to a crawl over the tiles that were never intended for motorcycle use. Heading towards the male toilets, the bike stopped and the rider leapt off the bike.

Taking a short moment to take off her helmet, she shook her head and her long brown hair was free of the prison that was the red and white helmet. Putting her helmet on the handlebars, the woman grabbed a bag of supplies from the carrier on the bike and raced into the male toilets, passing a female Police Officer and a railway security guard guarding the entrance.

Paramedic Natalie Murphy was one of the new breed of paramedics. Until recently, some paramedics were known as Ambulance Officers. The Ambulance Service recently decided to change to a more functional uniform and at the same time re-branded their Ambulance Officers so everyone was a paramedic. Natalie loved calling herself a paramedic but she also enjoyed treating patients. She was not merely happy to "scoop and run" but where possible, work on the patient to stabilise them if possible prior to transport.

Central Station was the largest railway station in Sydney and millions of passengers and other people not travelling passed through the station complex every year. It unusually had a dedicated First Aid Officer on site around the clock. In modern times, no other station had this. Sure, other railway stations had staff who had first aid training but those staff members also had other station duties to do. The dedicated First Aid Officer was able to treat many minor injuries and illnesses and make a decision about further medical treatment. Sometimes, some bandaging and a reassuring word was all the person needed. This freed up Ambulances for more urgent jobs.

On this occasion though, the First Aid Officer could only do so much. A staff member was preparing to clean the toilets and found a man passed out in a cubicle. The staff member called the First Aid Officer who attended right away. The First Aid Officer saw that the man needed CPR. The Officer remembered his First Aid training. He remembered that when he did CPR training with the training aid Resus Annie, he either had the "patient" on a table or on the classroom floor where he had plenty of room. In that cubicle at Central, though, it was dirty, smelly and cramped. He was doing a good job under difficult circumstances.

The First Aid Officer was glad to see Natalie. He knew that he needed some professional assistance. Without the bulk of a medium truck sized Ambulance, Natalie was able to whiz through the traffic. As designed for by the Ambulance Service, Natalie beat her colleagues to the scene. Until her initial assessment, the Ambulance was also en-route. She could start treatment and decide if the Ambulance was required. Obviously she could not transport the patient herself on the back of her motorcycle.

A MOMENT IN TIME by Eric Brook

Natalie saw the open cubicle door with the shaken staff member outside the door. Seeing he was upset, Natalie said "I'm here, mate. Go wait outside. Make sure no one flogs my bike, please."

The man was relieved to leave the area. Next, Natalie spoke to the First Aid Officer. "Hey mate, I'm Natalie from the Ambos. I'll take over." Allowing the man to take a breather, she went into her patient assessment routine.

"Ambos here, mate! Can you hear me?" No response. Natalie knelt beside the man to feel for a pulse. If it was there at all, it was really weak.

To make sure, Natalie reached for her bag and retrieved her heart monitor. As quick as she could, she hooked up the 12 lead ECG. Happy the leads were in the right place, Natalie turned on the machine. It did a short self test and it confirmed her fears. There was a perfectly flat line. Natalie knew there was nothing she could do. Unlike the world of TV where they routinely shocked flat line patients and brought them back to life, she remembered her instructor's voice from several years ago saying "You can't shock a flat line, Nat."

A MOMENT IN TIME by Eric Brook

She watched the screen for a minute before turning the machine off. "He's gone." She looked to the First Aid Officer. "You did your best, mate. He's gone." She patted the man on the back. "C'mon, mate. Let's go. Do you want me to tell your colleague or can you do it?"

"I'll tell him. What an awful way to go. Out of all the places, I'd hate to go here.", the First Aid Officer said to Natalie.

On the way out, she called her base. "Sydney, Bike 1. Code 4, Central Station. Police on site." Code 4 was the discreet way of telling the base that the patient was dead. The base called off the responding Ambulance. Natalie told the Policewoman guarding the toilet that the man was dead. The Police Officer used her radio to call her base. Until proven otherwise, the toilet was now a crime scene. It was very important to make sure that no one who was not supposed to be there entered the area.

There appeared to be no suspicious circumstances that Natalie saw. She went back into the cubicle with a Police Officer for a more detailed examination. Natalie disconnected the heart monitor and put it in her bag. She left the sticky pads on the man. Checking the man, she did not see anything such as a needle or track marks which was a tell-tale sign of drug abuse. The man could have died naturally, he might have been assaulted or he might have fallen.

A MOMENT IN TIME by Eric Brook

There was nothing else Natalie could do. She would be debriefed today about what she did on site. If she was extremely lucky, she might find out what happened to the man after the autopsy. If she was curious, she could look at the Coroner's website if it was newsworthy enough. There was one sure way she would find out what happened - if there was an allegation that she did the wrong thing. She would find out very quickly if that was the case.

Natalie left the toilet again with the Police Officer. She obtained all the details of the railway staff and the Police. Natalie did not want (or need) to wait around for the Government Contractors whose job it was to collect the body and take it to the State Coroner's office for an autopsy. Nor did she want to wait for Sydney's version of CSI. She wanted to get back on her bike and back in service. While death did affect her, she knew that she could do nothing for the man. She wondered how the First Aid Officer and the station staff member who found the man would cope. It was quite possible that the man was already dead when found by the station staff member.

The arrival of Natalie's Supervisor was a welcome distraction. It was customary for a Supervisor to attend on a difficult call and there was no more difficult call than one involving a death of a patient. This allowed the Supervisor a chance to see if the Paramedic was holding up ok straight after the incident. Any Supervisor worth their salt would not wait to be called to the scene by the

A MOMENT IN TIME by Eric Brook

Communications Centre after hearing one of their paramedics call code 4 over the radio. In this case, there was nothing that Natalie could have done. However on other occasions, the paramedics could have been working on the patient for some time. This situation was often hard for a paramedic to deal with.

Natalie looked and acted fine but one never knew. The Supervisor would be the paramedic's representative on the scene until the man's body was taken away. In any case, it was planned that the Supervisor was going to see Natalie in any case in between calls today. The Ambulance Service was taking part in an internet (and hopefully later, TV) reality series called "The Chronicles of EMS" (http://chroniclesofems.com).

The show started when a firefighter/paramedic working in San Francisco met up with a paramedic from the UK to compare various paramedical services. After the first episode in Justin's home town of San Francisco and Mark returning the hospitality in his English city of Newcastle, they were visiting various cities including the city of Sydney. It was a long trip for both men but it was part work and part holiday. They had been working hard on getting the concept working in addition to their paid work of being paramedics. Chronicles was like a second job, albeit one that does not pay the bills at least in the short term.

A MOMENT IN TIME by Eric Brook

Natalie knew that she was going to be one of the subjects of the visit. She had previously agreed to being filmed and she was wearing a small camera in addition to a helmet camera. Both Justin and Mark were interested in Natalie's motorcycle role. Justin had shown before that there was nothing like the motorcycles back home it but it would be very handy. In many ways, San Francisco was very similar to Sydney.

Over in England, Mark at least had the use of a chase car for rapid response which also would have been handy. As a supervisor himself, it was often Mark's job to drive the chase car. While the Sydney suburbs had chase cars (as Mark called them), the centre of Sydney had motorcycles and people like Natalie riding them. Out of the two men, Mark thought of himself as more likely to be a motorcycling paramedic rather than Justin.

The Chronicles crew knew they would not be able to get permission to film the victim to ask if he was OK because he had died. In that case, they may decide to use the footage anyway but blur the face. The death of a patient was a difficult dilemma for the project. Death was distressing for some people to see on TV. However, death was a realistic option when it came to para-medicine.

Death did happen and the paramedics had to be prepared for that fact. It was often hard for them but some time out, counselling and support was always available.

http://www.amomentintimenovel.com

A MOMENT IN TIME by Eric Brook

Supervisor Keith and the crew briefly spoke to Natalie before setting up to film Natalie talking about the scene for the program. "The guy over there found the victim passed out in the cubicle. He called the station's First Aid Officer who was doing CPR when I arrived. I found no sign of life and confirmed that via ECG. There was nothing I could do and nothing obvious which would tell me why he died."

"OK, thanks, Nat. You alright?"

"Uh-huh."

"Anything else you need to tell me?".

"Nothing really stands out. I didn't see any obvious reason for him to code.

"Let's grab a coffee and have a chat to the imports."

Natalie made sure her bike was fully loaded up and said goodbye to the Police. She could do no more here. She walked her bike out of the concourse area and directed the gathering to a nearby coffee shop where she could park the bike and make a quick getaway to the next job if - no, when - she would get called on the next call. Keith went back to the toilet to get started on the paperwork.

A MOMENT IN TIME by Eric Brook

Mark and Justin grabbed the coffees and Natalie welcomed the caffeine hit. After drinking the coffees and a bit of social chit-chat, Justin and Mark started their interview. Justin started off with "So how exactly do you transport a patient on THAT?" as the cameraman focused briefly on Natalie's bike. She laughed a much needed laugh after that call. The camera then moved to a shot where all three paramedics could be seen on camera.

Natalie explained the system to the overseas paramedics. She recalled the story of how she was told about her current job. "I was working in a station in the suburbs. My Station Officer knew that I loved to ride bikes and suggested that I put in for the position as they are hard to get. First of all, I did not know about the motorcycle rapid response group so I thought that there was a new type of Paramedic - one that could be confused with a bicycle courier." Mark had a laugh at that one in his jolly English accent. A different Ambulance service to Mark's used bicycles to respond around the terminals at the very busy Heathrow Airport.

"But then he told me that it was motorcycles. I love riding my bike here at work. My work bike is better than my own bike that I ride off duty. So I get paid to ride fast which I love. I love trying to beat the Ambulance to the scene. And I do love treating the patients. I do miss driving the ambulance and treating the patient in the back, too. I don't miss babysitting patients in the Emergency Department, though. I love being out on the road."

A MOMENT IN TIME by Eric Brook

Justin asked Natalie for a tour of the motorcycle. That was a bit of a misnomer as he could see the bike in front of him. He wanted to see what gear Natalie carried. Justin was surprised to see how much gear she could carry.

"Wow, you've got a lot in your kit!", Mark exclaimed. "How much of that stuff do you need on a daily basis?"

"Most of it are the nice-to-have category. But you never know what you'll need from call to call, though. I want to make an assessment and if I can, start treatment.", Natalie said.

"So what's the advantages of you and the bike on the call you just had?", Justin wondered out loud to the camera.

"Well, I beat the Ambulance. I was able to do an assessment and I saw that the male had died so I cancelled the vehicle that was coming. They are now on another call as we speak. But if I needed the extra pairs of hands or the transport, I can handover to them when they get there or give them a hand." Natalie said.

"So you mentioned that the last patient didn't make it. How does that make you feel when that happens, Natalie? Are you seeing more death now that you'll be highly likely to be first on site?", Mark enquired.

A MOMENT IN TIME by Eric Brook

"I've had some counselling before but I've never been asked the question in that accent before!", Natalie smiled.

"Sure, I get sad. I feel for the person who died and the family they leave behind. I'm sure you guys feel the same. We deal with the call and move to the next one. But to answer the last part of your question, Mark, I haven't really thought about it. Interesting question, though!"

"So, have you been a paramedic all your life, Natalie?", Justin asked. She looked into the camera. She paused before thinking some more and finally started to speak.

"Well, I've done some office work before but I'd rather drive an ambulance rather than a desk. I ended up getting a dispatch job here and did that for a while. It was a good job but when they advertised for Ambos, I applied. I got knocked back the first time, though. They thought I wasn't up to the job even though I was sending people on lots of calls every day."

After the interview, the crew grabbed photos and video of Natalie, Justin & Mark on the bike, both separately and together. It was the highlight of Natalie's day so far. She had a nice break and called her base saying that she was now available after the previous call and her meal break. It was one of Natalie's more interesting breaks.

A MOMENT IN TIME by Eric Brook

The film crew asked Natalie to do a dummy run up the shared roadway leading from Hay Street to the station. It was easier to grab as much footage as they could because they would not be back any time soon. After a couple of runs up and down the ramp, the crew were happy with the shots.

During some more on camera discussions, Natalie received a call. This pleased the crew as well as Mark and Justin. There was nothing worse than doing a reality series about paramedical work and having no calls. The call was close by. A bus and a car collided on Broadway at the corner of City Road. This would be a multi unit response.

Natalie sped off on her bike with the Chronicles of EMS crew and Keith in hot pursuit in the supervisor's vehicle. Natalie's helmet camera was recording things from her point of view because it was difficult to have a cameraman on the back of her motorcycle. In the front passenger's seat of the supervisor's vehicle was the cameraman and in the back seat were the director and the two overseas paramedics.

As viewers would see in coming weeks on the internet, Natalie gunned the motor of the motorcycle. The siren wailed and various LED lights on the bike flashed. Because a bus was involved, Natalie knew Ambulances would be coming from everywhere. She knew that at least two fire trucks would arrive for fire protection.

Natalie also knew that there was a high chance of someone being trapped, most likely in the car. Unless the caller to the emergency services was really specific, these calls were often described as "possible persons trapped". In that instance, separate rescue trucks (either from the Fire Brigade Rescue or Police Rescue) would probably attend as well as a couple of Police cars for traffic control. If the first responders found that no person was trapped, the Rescue trucks would be often stood down to be made available for other calls.

Depending on the circumstances, the Police Crash Investigation Unit might need to attend too. Hopefully the non injured would be off the bus, Natalie thought. That would make her triage a lot easier. She was hoping that it was not a school bus. The city was popular for excursions and 2pm (the time of the accident) was a good time to leave the city to be back in time close to the normal end of the school day.

Inside her helmet, the noise of her base on the radio was competing with the various sirens approaching the scene as well as the surrounding traffic. Luckily for Natalie, her base did not talk as much as the Police or the Fire Brigade.

The intersection of Broadway and City Road was busy at the best of times. Heading west, it was a popular turnoff for the inner west and the southern suburbs. Heading east towards the city, it was a final chance to bypass the city. There was a lot of pedestrian traffic as well as there was a university, a large park, a large shopping centre and other shops nearby. As Natalie and the other emergency vehicles got closer to the accident, the traffic got heavier. Natalie was able to slide between the lanes of traffic. The larger fire trucks and ambulances had no hope of doing that.

The Supervisor's car weaved in and out of the traffic joined by three Ambulances. The procession tried to stay on the correct side of the road when they could but it was not always possible. Like a train, the line of emergency vehicles ran through the traffic like a snake if a snake was 50 metres long and had various colours of reflective tape, red and blue flashing lights and a voice of sirens.

Like a precision motorcycle rider in the Police Force, Natalie was the head of the snake by a long way. She arrived on site a good few minutes ahead of the rest of the vehicles.

Traffic was at a standstill around the site, despite the traffic lights going through their normal cycles. By chance, a Police motorcycle and the Public Order & Riot Squad were passing by soon after the incident and had set up their vehicles to try and establish a hot zone for the crews. Being a car full of heavily armed Police who were not always designed to be seen, the squad had to remember to put their high visibility vests on. Some of the officers were checking the bus and clearing the uninjured passengers.

A MOMENT IN TIME by Eric Brook

The Team Leader of the Police team saw Natalie arrive and climb off her bike. "One dead in the car, one trapped. The bus driver is trapped, my blokes are clearing the uninjured off the bus now." Natalie thanked the cop and assured him the troops were coming. "I'll be the judge of the dead and the injured. We need to clear this traffic. Can we do something about those lights?" Natalie asked.

Looking over at the blue and white commuter bus, most of the damage was on the driver's side. Luckily, the driver was fit enough to open the two undamaged side doors even though he was pinned by his feet. This action meant the emergency exit windows were not needed on this occasion.

"Sydney, Bike 1." Natalie called her base. On site with Police. Police assessment as follows. One possible code 4 and one trapped in car. One person trapped in the bus. Further triage to follow."

Based on the damage, Natalie was most concerned about the occupants of the car. She saw the driver was not wearing a seatbelt. He had massive head trauma and was clearly deceased. Nothing could be done for him. Natalie went to the passenger. She saw that the lady was trapped by the legs. Natalie could not access the lady via the door as it was severely dented. The window was up, too.

A MOMENT IN TIME by Eric Brook

Seeing this, Natalie went back to her bike and grabbed a blanket and some oxygen. She returned to the car and went to the driver's side and opened the door. She covered the dead driver with the blanket and reached across the body to access the patient. "Sorry mate" Natalie whispered to the dead man. She placed an oxygen mask on the female passenger.

Natalie spoke on the radio again. "Sydney, Bike 1. One code 4, one female trapped in car 1 by the legs. Confirm Rescue."

By this time, the snake of emergency workers arrived. Natalie confirmed the status of the car. The troops were here to look after the bus. The traffic lights changed to flashing yellow and a policewoman started traffic duty. Two fire brigade pumpers from the nearby Glebe and Redfern stations arrived along with two Police Rescue trucks.

The Chronicles of EMS crew headed to the bus while the two cameras went to work between the two vehicles. While Mark and Justin were paramedics in their own services and were wearing their normal uniforms, they could not treat patients here. There was nothing wrong with Mark or Justin talking to the patients as it was an official visit. And technically, if a person was not injured, they were not a patient. Besides, they thought, they were still First Aid qualified. With the assistance of Mark, Justin, the Police and other Ambulance crews, most of the people on the bus were found to be uninjured and were taken off the bus. They would need to take another bus to complete their journey.

Natalie spoke to Keith. "Do you want me to clear and head back into service? I'm quite happy to stay here and work on car 1 if you need me to."

"Keep going, Nat." Keith sent Natalie back to the car with another paramedic. Natalie climbed over the deceased man again and the other paramedic climbed into the back seat. Now that she had started treatment, Keith wanted Natalie to keep working on the patient.

The paramedic at the rear put a c-collar on the patient and Natalie placed a cannula into the patient's arm. With the cannula in place, Natalie could give the woman drugs and fluids intravenously. First though, Natalie wanted to put a heart monitor onto the woman.

"Hi, I'm Natalie. I'm a paramedic. What's your name?". Introducing herself to the patient was normal for Natalie but some of the old school Ambos did not believe in such niceties.

"Michelle."

A MOMENT IN TIME by Eric Brook

"Ok, Michelle. We are going to get you out of here as soon as we can. My buddy Frank is behind you. We'll get you out as quick as we can. Do you know what day it is?"

"Thursday"

"And do you know where you are?", Frank asked from the back seat. Frank did not need to talk but it was important that he did. Patient Michelle could not turn her neck to look at Frank but Frank did not want his voice to be a mystery to her in case he needed to talk later.

"Car crash." It might seem like a stupid question for the paramedics to ask but they were standard questions to determine how the patient's neurological system was working. It could help diagnose a head injury.

"Have you passed out at all?", Natalie asked while she was taking Michelle's blood pressure. "Did you hit your head?"

"Don't think so", Michelle groaned.

Natalie grabbed the heart monitor that was in her bag that she placed on the roof. Applying the pads to the woman's chest, Natalie soon saw on the monitor that unlike her last two patients, this patient had a heartbeat.

A MOMENT IN TIME by Eric Brook

In case things changed during the rescue, Natalie had her defibrillator at the ready. The woman was screaming in pain. Natalie asked "on the scale of 1 to 10, 10 being the worst you have ever had, how's the pain?"

Through the oxygen mask, the woman rated herself an 9/10.

Natalie keyed up her radio to give a progress report. As far as Natalie could tell, Michelle had no head injuries and had not lost conciousness. Her blood pressure was good and her heartbeat was strong. She was in extreme pain, possibly due to the entrapment as well as a possible broken leg at the least.

Right, Natalie thought, this woman needed pain relief. Natalie got onto her radio and asked Keith on an incident channel to bring some morphine over. Natalie did not carry drugs for security and logistics reasons. Keith came over and handed Natalie the drug. "You'll be feeling a pin prick that probably feels like nothing. Can you feel your toes? The woman nodded. Natalie injected the woman via the cannula. Natalie knew the woman would not have felt the pin prick. She injected the drug into Michelle using the cannula rather than piercing the skin again.

A MOMENT IN TIME by Eric Brook

Shortly after, the morphine started to work and the woman reported her pain levels decreasing. Finally, a white overalled man opened the driver's door to talk to Natalie.

"Finally!", Natalie said. "Get stuck in traffic, Joe?" Joe the Police Rescue Operator knew Natalie well and laughed.

"We all don't have cool bikes with lots of flashing lights, you know!". It was Natalie's time for a brief laugh.

"What you got, Nat? Are we ok to start cutting?". As far as she could tell, Joe's face barely registered that Natalie was sitting next to a covered deceased male. However, she knew that Joe had seen his fair share of blanket covered bodies. Often, it was Joe's job to recover the body from a difficult or dangerous location before it was taken away.

Joe knew that Crash Investigation would want the male in the driver's seat to remain in situ and that's why Natalie rightly left him there, albeit covered for public decency and respect for the dead. Natalie looked at the heartbeats on the monitor that was improving slightly now that Vitamin M (a street name for morphine) had kicked in. Natalie knew that the woman would be better in the back of the Ambulance rather than trapped by her legs.

A MOMENT IN TIME by Eric Brook

The paramedic knew that she had to watch the patient extra carefully while on the morphine. Natalie herself had been a patient herself, most notably when she broke her leg badly while motocrossing in a remote area. Great way to experience what the patients experience, become one themselves. Natalie became more flirty and giggly while on the morph but other patients had trippy experiences to the point that people forgot they were injured.

In addition, Natalie knew she had to be concerned with Compartment Compression Syndrome, otherwise known as toxic crush. While this case did not appear to be at the high end of the scale, the release of the compression (in this case, the mangled front of the car) could see toxins built up in the body be released and end up killing the patient. So Natalie had to take precautions, which is what she was doing with IV fluids, pain relief, oxygen, a heart monitor and hopefully a steady release by Joe.

"Joe, she's stable. Not super urgent but not next week, either. Pinned in by the lower legs."

Natalie had to stay where she was to treat the patient and the other paramedic keeping the woman's neck still. Joe went and found goggles and hearing protection for the two paramedics and the patient. He then put a couple of plastic shields up to protect them as well. Once that was done, Joe said "Ok, Nat. We're ready to cut. How she doin'?".

A MOMENT IN TIME by Eric Brook

Speaking to partly to Joe and partly to Michelle, Natalie responded. "We are doing OK, aren't we, Michelle?"

Joe continued talking, barely waiting for Natalie's answer. "Let me know if you need a rapid extraction or we need to stop." A thumbs up from both paramedics saw Joe's team start cutting.

With a fire team on standby for fire protection, Joe and his team worked slowly and carefully. One team worked on the B Pillar. The B Pillar was the metal column between the front and back seats. That enabled the rescuers to fit a spine board into the car, lie the patient on it and then lift them out flat. That way, it could help prevent a spinal injury caused by the rescuers. The signs were good so far based on Natalie's monitoring.

Another rescue team were working near the woman's feet. There would be no use cutting the B Pillar if the rescue team could not move the woman due to entrapment. It was likely that the cutting would have been a smaller amount compared to the other team. They only needed enough room for the legs not to be trapped.

After a few minutes, the team at the front had finished cutting. A pair of paramedics were waiting with a stretcher so Michelle could placed on the stretcher, secured to it and then loaded into the Ambulance. One of the paramedics went to the front seat of the car to speak to Natalie. The second cutting team had finished. Natalie gave a quick progress report to the other paramedic. The paramedic went to the other side of the car to assist in the removal of the woman.

Joe had a spine board at the ready. Natalie told Joe that she was ok to go. The team worked together to load the woman onto the spine board. Once on the spine board, Natalie asked for a moment to observe the woman's heart rate. Happy that she was going to ok for the moment, Natalie disconnected the heart monitor but left the pads in place. The crew that would load the woman into the Ambulance would shortly hook their monitor up.

"OK, Joe. We are right to go. Everyone right?", Natalie asked. Joe nodded. Various people murmured in agreement. "On my count, everyone. On 3."

"1. 2. 3."

In a rehearsed move, the combined team of paramedics, firefighters and Police Rescue officers lifted the woman as Natalie had instructed. She was quickly loaded onto the stretcher and loaded into the Ambulance. The paramedics climbed into the Ambulance and left the scene slowly in the direction of Royal Prince Alfred Hospital. The care of the woman was now up to the new crew and the medical staff at RPA.

A MOMENT IN TIME by Eric Brook

With the release of the woman, Natalie thanked Frank the rear seat paramedic for his help. Luckily, Frank did not have a lot to do. After climbing over the dead male driver for the last time, she whispered to the man "Mate, we got her out. You aren't in pain. See you on the other side."

The Chronicles of EMS crew had returned from the bus. Mark had spent most of his time watching Natalie in action. Justin kept an eye on the rescue of the bus driver. Both men, however. were waiting for Natalie as she left the vehicle for the final time. It was a warm day and the car was small and hot. For the fittest paramedic, that would have been more than enough to raise a sweat. However, Natalie the motorcycle paramedic was wearing Ambulance Service issued motorcycle leathers. So Mark's comment should not have come as a surprise but with his English accent, Natalie was a little surprised.

"Nat, you look hot."

She wasn't sure if Mark meant that she was uber attractive (she was) or that she was really sweaty under those leathers (she was).

"Good job" said the American and English accents together. Both men gave her a high-five and Mark earned a sly wink from Natalie for his previous comment. "How's

A MOMENT IN TIME by Eric Brook

the bus driver? Need me for anything else?" asked Natalie, unzipping her top half slightly.

Keith the supervisor said that the bus driver was ok (considering) after being cut out of his bus. A handful of passengers were walking wounded but did not need an ambulance ride to the hospital. A new bus picked up the remaining passengers.

In the meantime, the Police were busy traffic coning the area off and were able to control traffic better. Peak hour was fast approaching but the accident required the Crash Investigation Unit to attend because it was a fatal smash. Also, the Government Contractors were having a busy day too. They could wait though until called by the CIU.

With the Ambulances off the scene except for Natalie, Keith, Justin, Mark and the Chronicles crew, Police Rescue packed up and left the scene. The Police on site told the tow truck drivers that they would not be needed for a good couple of hours at least until CIU attended. One fire truck left the scene but one crew remained for fire protection and clean up. The Glebe Station Officer volunteered his platoon stay behind as Redfern was a busier station.

Nearly 4 hours after the call to Central, Keith told the troops to return to the station. He needed to debrief Natalie (again) and to let her cool down a bit. Leaving a motorcycle paramedic on site for that long was unusual but Keith determined that she was doing a good job and she should continue.

Climbing on the back of the motorcycle, Natalie headed back to the station driving without lights or sirens. There was a lot for the Police and Fire Brigade to do on scene but it was no longer a place for the Ambulance Service. Natalie was still available for calls but a chance to get to the station and get out of the motorcycle leathers for a while would be great. Hopefully she would even get the chance to grab something to eat but more importantly, re-hydrate. She had been in the leathers now for at least 4 hours and two calls, the second one a very long call. She had just under 3 hours to go, finishing work at 7pm.

It could be a very long and exhausting day going from call to call under lights and sirens. Riding a motorcycle was very physical indeed but trying to avoid the traffic and get to the call as quick as possible was mentally draining as well. Then adding to that mental drain was working on the patients. As much as Natalie loved the lights and sirens calls, she was enjoying the chance to take her time under no pressure.

In the Supervisor's car behind Natalie, Mark and Justin were taking the chance to talk about the call they had just seen. They saw that the rescue teams from the Police Rescue group worked very well with the paramedics. There were two difficult rescues and everyone was happy with the result with the obvious exception of the dead car driver. The further the two Chronicles stars travelled from home, the more that they saw things being similar to home. They knew they could not save everyone but so far the scoreboard since they were with Natalie read 2 deceased, 2 major traumas and a handful of walking wounded out of two calls after lunch.

They talked about how they expected Natalie to arrive at that call, do an initial triage and then go to the next call. Sometimes it is a case of "all hands on deck" and this case was a good case in point. While the damage to the car would be fairly obvious when the call was given as a car versus bus accident, who knows how many people were on the bus and how many of them were injured?

Arriving back at the station, Natalie parked her cycle in the garage. She left her helmet on the bike and walked inside to the kitchen area where she had some energy drink in the fridge. The cold energy drink felt great on Natalie's lips and down her throat. It was a lot better than tap water. If it was good enough for elite athletes, it was good enough for her, she thought. Drink bottle still in hand, she went to the female locker room.

Mostly the station was empty as the Ambulance Service encouraged their officers to be out on the streets a lot, especially in the city. Natalie went to her locker and opened it. Inside was a spare shirt which she grabbed along with a towel. Taking the chance while she had it, she took off her motorcycle leathers. She was hoping that there would be a day where standard overalls would be enough instead of the leathers. While she felt and looked great in the leathers and felt safer, it was also very hot.

Today was one such occasion. She also took off her shirt and work pants. Her body was covered in sweat. With 3 hours to go in the shift, having a shower would probably not be a good move. She would have a shower at the end of the shift anyway and technically, she was still available for calls.

The last thing Natalie wanted to be was naked in the shower and receive a call. Murphy's Law of Emergency Services dictated that saying certain words could be enough to get a call as well as having a shower, having something to eat or having a nap in the Ambulance.

Before wiping the sweat off with the towel, Natalie admired herself in the mirror. She knew she was fit and it was days like today where being fit was a bonus. She towelled herself down with one end of the towel being wet and the other end being dry. After the cool water hit her skin, she felt a lot better. Her pants were not as damp as her shirt was so she put a clean shirt on and put her newly cooled lower half of her body back into the blue work pants. Back in a dressed state, Natalie threw the towel and the damp shirt into her washing bag at the bottom of her locker, sprayed some deodorant and took her drink toward the supervisor's office.

Natalie knocked on Keith's door. Keith usually had an open door policy and was well liked as a Supervisor. Some people like to think they can make the step up from Paramedic to Supervisor but not everyone could. Keith could. Unlike supervisors in some other industries, he had put in the hard yards as on the road and could still be asked to assist on calls today if need be. Like the paramedics under him, he was expected to keep up to date with current practices and procedures.

"Oh wow, Natalie. What an afternoon you've had. 2 people dead, one trapped - great job by the way - and I think the Englishman wants to take you out for an old fashioned debrief over dinner. I think he likes you."

Natalie blushed but smiled at the first time. Romantic relationships between paramedics were discouraged but many stations had at least one couple who had met solely because of work. "How are you feeling? You've had two code 4 calls this afternoon. Do you need some time off the bike? Do you need to talk to someone?"

Natalie said that she was fine. Realistically, she was probably still running with adrenaline and wanted to be on the bike speeding to another call right now. She had enjoyed the chance to have a drink and get out of the leathers, though. "Don't forget that you do have the option of the Employee Assistance Scheme if you need it later down the track. If you have some paperwork to do, now would be a good time to go and do it. Otherwise, take the time to relax before your next call. I think the Yank and the Pom want to have a bit of a chat to you about those calls, too. Go find them, they are in the rec room."

In the rec room, Justin and Mark were having one of their UK versus US versus Australia talking sessions on camera when Natalie arrived. They took the chance to ask her about the two calls they had seen her on and asked for her opinions on what she knew about their systems. It is not too often that someone gets invited to two different countries in the same afternoon.

"Maybe the San Fran PD would let you borrow one of their police cycles so you feel at home", Justin said. "You'll love the hills and you'll love going down the crookedest street in the world."

Natalie raised an eyebrow. Justin went and got a laptop out of his bag and showed Natalie the video that they shot on Lombard Street, San Francisco. It was a street that literally zig-zagged down a hill. The road is lined with hedges and hundreds of people a day drive down the hill while hundreds more people watch the people driving down the hill. People's houses adjoined the street and seeing the footage, Natalie wondered how they would ever leave their homes.

A MOMENT IN TIME by Eric Brook

"I dare say that those houses are the safest and most carefully watched houses in the city based on the people watching", Mark laughed. "When Justin and the crew took me down there, I could not believe the number of people watching us driving down the hill. It was surreal. Nothing like that would ever happen in Newcastle."

"So what do you think of our system, guys?" Natalie asked the two visitors. "I've really enjoyed watching your series and I hope you've both like what you've seen here."

"Oh yeah!", Mark and Justin said in unison.

"It's a little bit hot in here!", Mark said. For most of his life, April meant the end of winter. He was not used to being in the southern hemisphere and being in this heat.

"It would be a lovely day down at the Bay", Justin sighed as he thought of home. It was a long way from the Golden Gate Bridge.

"Let's just relax before the next call.", Natalie suggested. Shame we can't take the bike down to the Quay down by the harbour. It gets manic down there over summer."

A MOMENT IN TIME by Eric Brook

Relaxing before the next call sounded like a good idea to everyone. It was not a typical day for any of them and Natalie needed some down time, even if she would not admit it. She turned on the TV and there was some American soap that Natalie and Justin were very familiar with. "Normally I don't get to see this show", Natalie said. "Normally I'm on the bike at this time of day."

Mark thought that he did not see the point on having shows like this on TV. At least with this type of show, he did not yell at the TV when they did something that was totally unrealistic. Like many people, he did not like watching shows about his own profession. That was one thing that he did not want Chronicles of EMS to be. He wanted it to be real.

Sometimes, there was down time like now that was greatly needed. There needed to be a way to blow off some steam. Watching the upcoming news bulletin was not usually one of them but being in a strange country, the news was sometimes interesting to them.

The news started and no one in the room thought that the accident they all were at earlier would be on the news. They all had been involved in treating the patients with all sorts of accidents that going to watch it on the news was so different. They did not notice many media on the scene.

A MOMENT IN TIME by Eric Brook

Before you knew it, there was a wide screen version on the news showing the accident scene with the bus and the car. It was lucky that Natalie covered the dead car driver with a blanket because while she was so busy treating the female passenger, the TV cameraman filmed right through the window of the car for the world to see.

For Natalie, it was a real out of body experience watching herself on TV treat the patient. As far as she knew, it was the first time she had been on TV. Realistically though, it was probably not the first time that a member of the media caught her in action but it was the first time she had seen it.

"Drinks at the bar on Natalie tonight!" Mark laughed.

"What are you on about?" Natalie threw him a quizzical look.

"We have this tradition", Mark explained. "If you get on TV while at work, you buy the drinks that night." The footage changed and on the bus, you quite easily could see a firefighter/paramedic from America and a paramedic from the UK wearing a green jumpsuit talking to the people on the bus.

A MOMENT IN TIME by Eric Brook

"Looks like Justin and Mark are getting the second and third shouts then!", Natalie laughed back at them good naturedly. It was time for the foreigners to look puzzled.

"What?"

"If I have to buy the first round because I'm on TV, you blokes were on there too! So that's the second and third rounds sorted! Oh, and there's Keith buying the fourth!" That gave Mark and Justin an idea to approach the TV station to see if they could get the footage. While they had their own footage from their own cameras, it was interesting to hear the local newsreaders describing the scene.

Right on cue as if he was watching the same news bulletin in his office, Keith walked out of his office and entered the recreation room, a paramedic's home away from home.

"Natalie, you ....." Keith said importantly as she cleared her throat, almost as if the schoolgirl had her hand in the cookie jar and got caught by the school teacher. "Have a job. Central Railway. Get dressed and get on your bike. Maybe we'll see you on the 6 o'clock news and you'll be getting the fifth round. On ya bike!"

It was 5.10pm. Natalie's life was going to change forever.

http://www.amomentintimenovel.com

Chapter 8 – Another Day, Another Drama

Thursday 01 April 2010, 12 noon

It felt like the 100th time that the elderly male appeared in the cubicle. He smelt really bad. It smelt like he had been drinking heavily, again. Once again, he had drunk too much and fallen over. This time, he had badly cut his head, again. Sitting down on a bed in the cubicle, the man looked like he was going to fall over, again. He looked around the room but even if there was a good looking woman in the cubicle with him, he could not focus on her. Not that he realised it, there was a very attractive woman trying to look after Ol' Trev.

Lisa was tall and slim and somehow managed to look attractive in a pair of green surgical scrubs. That was no mean feat according to some of the experts on the subject, Lisa's fellow male doctors. Little that Ol' Trev knew or cared, Lisa was one of the best doctors in the very busy Emergency Department of Royal Prince Alfred Hospital (RPA).

If RPA was not the busiest Emergency Department in the Sydney Metro area, it would have been in the Grand Final playing against St Vincent's. RPA was a major go-to hospital for patients in the southern half of the centre of Sydney as well as many of the inner western suburbs.

A MOMENT IN TIME by Eric Brook

Lisa was busy and that is the way she liked it. She had decided early on that she wanted to be a doctor and that the best place to work was in a hospital's Emergency Department. She had thought of being a nurse when she left school and went to university to start to learn all she needed to be a nurse. After a few months, she was enjoying learning about how the human body worked so much and how to fix it. Because she was still early in her course, she made enquiries about how to convert her current learning and leave university as a doctor.

During her course, Lisa was rotated through various specialities in the hospital setting as well as in general practice in a surgery. She did not enjoy the general practice as much as she thought she might have. She thought that she was being treated as a machine in the surgery, being encouraged to get through as many people in an hour as she could. She found that in the hospital environment, she enjoyed the Emergency Department the best. She loved how the doctors and nurses worked together. She also enjoyed being able to call in the specialist doctors if needed and learn from them.

Often, Lisa had to play the role of medical detective. A patient would often have no idea what was going on. They knew that they were in pain in a certain area of the body but not specifically why. Lisa would ask a series of questions and make some physical observations to try and work out what was wrong with the patient. That was a challenge that she enjoyed.

A MOMENT IN TIME by Eric Brook

Despite it being a hard road with many long hours, Lisa enjoyed the various challenges that patients came through the door. There was more to being an ED doctor than traffic accidents and people with foreign objects placed where they were not supposed to go but that is what most people thought of when they found out where she worked.

Her current patient was better known as Ol' Trev. He was what the hospital staff and paramedics would call a "frequent flier", a regular to the hospital. Even if Lisa could understand him, she knew why he was there. She knew that he was homeless but did not know why, that story changed with every visit. Somehow, Ol' Trev would get drunk. Sometimes, he would safely find somewhere to sleep. But on some occasions like today, he would fall over and hurt himself. He could not get himself to a doctor. Most doctors would not treat homeless people. If he could, he would go to a homeless shelter. Today, someone had called an Ambulance who assessed him and brought him to RPA.

If the Emergency Department was extremely busy, Ol' Trev found himself sliding down the waiting list. In some ways, this could be seen as a win/win situation for him, surprisingly. The triage nurse would make sure that he was not still bleeding. Pending being stitched up and x-rayed, Ol' Trev could wait in the warm waiting room.

A MOMENT IN TIME by Eric Brook

Trev liked this hospital because unlike sheltering where he could, it was warm there. If someone else had exactly the same symptoms as Ol' Trev, the other person would probably be seen first. Trev most of the time would have had no concept of time.

Lisa carefully looked at his bloody head. Unlike most patients, he was not capable of telling her how he felt because he was very drunk. The more alcohol he had, the worse it got. So she had to do her best with what she had. Looking at what she could see, the best Lisa could do right now was to clean the wound and see how big the cut was. She knew that stitching or stapling his head was not the best thing to do in his current state. He was unstable when sitting up and lying down was not ideal.

Getting to work, Lisa cleaned the wound. She wanted to tightly bandage the wound first and hopefully that would be enough. She would let Ol' Trev go back to the waiting room for a while and have the triage nurse keep an eye on him. She needed to keep the queue moving otherwise the hospital would go "code red". This meant that the hospital would only treat major trauma patients.

"There you go, Trev. All done, mate.", Lisa said in a sympathetic voice. She led the man down the hall to the waiting room and said to him that he should sit down. Lisa talking and her body language was enough for him to understand. She was used to dealing with people who could not speak a lot of English so having a range of non verbal ways to communicate was an important tool for her.

A MOMENT IN TIME by Eric Brook

After washing her hands again, Lisa was ready for her next patient. She was happy that unlike Ol' Trev, her next patient could fully understand her. Eric was a train driver who had a history of kidney stones. He usually needed strong pain relief and a day or two to pass the stone. "I've got your tests back and they confirm what we thought. I am going to put you on a drip to replace your fluids. The nurse will be here soon to do that for you." He nodded.

"We'll see how you go when that bag's gone. You'll be better off with some more fluids. The scan shows that the stone has a little way to go before it comes out." Eric lay back on his bed. The morphine had kicked in and he knew that in a matter of time, the stone would come out. He usually did not need the drip but over the last 12 hours or so, things were coming out very quickly of his top and back entrances but not his front, he coyly explained.

Lisa went to the next cubicle and saw Peter. He was doing a self defence course when his knee dislocated during a scenario. Lisa had some obvious news for him too. "We know you've dislocated your knee. Luckily for you, the kneecap went back in by itself. There's no bone fracture which sometimes happens. That means no plaster for you. Over the next few days, you'll be sore. You might get some soreness because you've stretched the ligaments and tendons. Keep the brace on for a few days until you get to see your doctor. Keep it elevated and keep off it as much as you can. Keep up the pain relief. You can go home now."

Peter was pleased as he hated hospitals. He would make the best of a bad situation and spend all day watching TV, something he rarely did. Peter hobbled out of the cubicle with one leg straight as could be because of the brace.

In cubicle 3 was Sam. She was being treated for a partially severed finger. She was cooking lunch and the knife slipped. She was in a lot of pain and was waiting for a surgical consult. Lisa stuck her head in. "How you doing, Sam?" The painful look said it all. "The Surgeon will be down soon, I hope. Doctor Saunders is magic when it comes to this sort of things. You are in good hands with Rob." Almost as soon as she made that last comment, she knew that Sam could have taken that the wrong way. "I'll organise some more pain relief for you. Try to keep that hand still as you can. Back soon."

Cubicle 4 saw a little baby by the name of Justin. He had been in a car accident with his parents Jason and Sarah. Justin had some cuts from broken grass. Lisa found babies challenging to work with. Jason was in cubicle 5 with internal injuries from the crash which happened near Sydney's version of Little Italy, Norton Street. Sarah was concerned about her husband but her baby needed her help more, as did the doctors. It was always better to have a parent present with babies and small children.

A trauma team were looking after Jason the best that they could next door. He was in a lot of pain. At least baby

A MOMENT IN TIME by Eric Brook

Justin did not know what was going on and in time to come, he would not remember it. Jason, however, could remember every second. He was frustrated that nothing he could have done would have prevented the accident which occurred after another car ran a red traffic light and t-boned Jason's car. Jason's door received most of the impact.

Luckily, he was able to get out of the car himself by sliding out of the passenger's door. Once he did, he collapsed onto the side of the road. The paramedics who found him thought that it would be better to "scoop and run" rather than try to stabilise him on site. They knew that they could only do so much for him on the side of the road and in the back of the Ambulance and that the best place for Jason was right where he was now, in one of the best trauma centres in the country. Sometimes, though, not even the best trauma teams could save every patient.

Cubicle 6 was being cleaned after Rod had a massive vomiting attack and not all of it landed in the bucket provided. He was unsure exactly who he was or how he got there. Perhaps he was a younger and not homeless version of Ol' Trev. At that stage, all Lisa wanted to do was stop the vomiting. A big, long, sharp needle would fix that, she hoped. She had to wait until he stop vomiting for a couple of minutes. Hopefully that would do the trick. Finally, he stopped vomiting much to the delight of Lisa, the lady cleaning the vomit and - of course - Rod himself. Lisa left nurse Jen to inject Rod.

A MOMENT IN TIME by Eric Brook

Lisa went back to check on train driver Eric but he was not in his cubicle. Hopefully that meant that the rehydrating drip was working and Eric was using the toilet. Maybe it was a false alarm. One of the symptoms of kidney stones was the urge to urinate but being unable to. Often, people suffering would go to the toilet more out of hope than anything else. Maybe he was going to vomit? Eric was an experienced sufferer so apart from the very first time that it happened, he knew what to expect. Lisa looked at the chart and saw that the drip had not been started yet so it was more than likely a false alarm. She would check on him again soon.

Suddenly, the sound that many people hated was echoing around the department. Baby Justin was crying a lot. Lisa checked the cubicle and his little body was not happy with having the little particles of broken glass removed. Using tweezers, fellow doctor Heath was trying his best to grab only the glass but that was easier said than done. Sometimes Heath would grab skin, too. Either way, some pain was to be expected in the circumstances. Heath said that he did not need Lisa's help. He was quite capable and was being assisted by nurse Leanne. It was going to take some time to get all the glass. They started with the obvious pieces they could see but later there would be the problem of smaller pieces they could not see.

A few minutes later, Rod was feeling a lot better in cubicle 6. The cubicle was minty fresh and hopefully now it was going to stay that way. The medication that nurse Jen had injected into Rod was designed to work very quickly. If the vomiting stopped soon, they could get to the bottom of why Rod was in the hospital in the first place. Both Jen and Lisa wanted to figure out if there was a reason that he was vomiting. Was it food poisoning? Alcohol? Drugs? Illness?

Now that he did not have his head inside a bucket, Lisa could get a complete history and update his observations. She saw that his blood pressure was elevated but that could have been because of the effort involved in vomiting. Of course, she would note it now and then check it in half an hour to compare the two readings. Hopefully there would be no more vomiting before the next set of observations. Nurse Jen also took some blood out of Rodney's arm to test it. Based on what he just told her, Jen might be able to rule out drugs and alcohol but would wait until the blood test.

Rod would not be the first patient in medical history to lie (or not be entirely truthful) about the reasons he was there. If he was on drugs, he might be so high that he thinks he is a talking towel and might not even realise where he was or what was happening to him. The blood test and a little more time would be more helpful than Rod was being at the moment.

Eric arrived back his cubicle. A nurse had not inserted his drip yet so as both Eric & Lisa knew that his trip to the toilet was a false alarm. Lisa was about to talk to Eric when she heard "Code Blue, Cubicle 5. Code Blue, Cubicle 5." She knew that she had to rush to cubicle 5.

"Back when I can", Lisa whispered to Eric. She raced over to cubicle 5 where the trauma team was working hard on car crash victim Jason. He was losing a lot of blood internally and externally. As soon as the team would pump fresh blood into Jason, his body would lose it from elsewhere. There were so many potential places where it could be coming from.

Entering the cubicle, Lisa saw fellow doctor Ashley prepare to shock Jason's heart to get it onto a better rhythm. "Clear!" Ashley half yelled. The other doctors and nurses stepped back. Pressing a button, Ashley gave Jason a massive shock. "What you got, Ash?", Lisa asked with concern in her voice. Both Ashley and Lisa looked at the screen.

"Not good, Lis", Ashley said. "We keep giving him blood but it keeps coming back out. He needs surgery but he's not stable enough." The shock brought them some time but not a lot.

"If only we knew where that blood was - shocking again - CLEAR!" The medical team was running out of time. A nurse was already breathing for him. Blood was being pumped into him. The defibrillator was helping his heart beat stay in some sort of rhythm. His heartbeat was really low. "We don't have much time." Ashley sighed. She knew she was fighting a losing battle.

The heart monitor's tone was broadcasting a slow "beep beep beep" tone. While the tone was a slow "beep beep beep" or faster, Jason was still alive. It was better for him if the tone got faster, indicating a stronger heart beat. Lisa and Ashley studied the monitor. One dice Ashley had not rolled yet was adrenaline. Ashley posed the question to Lisa. "We have to try", Lisa gasped.

Ashley ordered the drug which tries to simulate the natural "flight or fight" response. Another shock to Jason's chest would push it around the body. Apart from a short spike that was the machine, the heart monitor beeped slowly. Both doctors knew they had to give the drug a short time to work.

This was the moment that would determine if Jason would live or die. He was still losing too much blood. The nurses could try their best to patch the external holes but the internal holes needed to be fixed too. Just like there was only so much the paramedics could do when they arrived on scene, there was only so much they could do in the Emergency Department.

The heart monitor continued to beep beep beep. Lisa wished that she could pause time and send Jason to surgery. She wanted to be able to fast forward 5 years and watch a healthy Jason take his son Justin (who was still in the next cubicle) to school. Lisa held her breath.

A MOMENT IN TIME by Eric Brook

Beep. Beep. Beep. Beep. "C'mon dude. You can make it. You can make it", Lisa whispered into his ear. Faith, prayer and whispering into his ear was about all Lisa had left. "You've fought hard. Do you have anything left?". Lisa squeezed his hand. He did not squeeze back.

Beep. Beep. Beep. Beep.

His eyes were closed like they had been since just after the accident. Should they get Jason's wife to say goodbye? Did she need to see the man she loved battered and broken? Pluses and minuses entered Lisa's mind. She squeezed his hand again.

Beeeeeeeeeeeeeeeeeeeeeeeeeep

A flat monotone replaced the previous beep beep beep. Jason was gone. Lisa knew it. Ashley knew it. The entire team knew it. "Call it, Ash. He's gone. You did your best.", Lisa said.

Looking up at the clock, a nurse had already turned off the heart monitor. Ashley whispered, knowing Jason's wife was in the next cubicle. "Time of death, 1527. Thanks, everyone."

A MOMENT IN TIME by Eric Brook

A nurse pulled a sheet up to Jason's chest. Now he looked like he was sleeping. Ashley and Lisa went to the next cubicle to give the bad news to Jason's wife Sarah. Under normal circumstances, they would take her to a quiet room. Sarah was obviously concerned with baby Justin's condition and did not think that Jason would die. Lisa told nurse Leanne and doctor Heath to take a short break from removing broken glass from Justin's baby skin.

Once they had Sarah's full attention, Ashley took a deep breath. Death was just as a big a part of life in the Emergency Department as life was. Never made it any easier, though.

"There's no easy way to tell you this, Sarah", Ashley explained. "We worked really hard but Jason lost too much blood from inside. As fast as we pumped it in, it was coming out. We couldn't stop it. I'm sorry to say that Jason is no longer with us. If it is an consolation, he isn't in pain any more."

"Oh no! Oh no!", Sarah started to sob. "That can't be right. No no no no no!". Needless to say, Sarah was in shock. Lisa nodded. Sarah cried loudly. Lisa hugged Sarah. Sarah's sobs were cushioned by Lisa's shoulder. This was one of many normal reactions with a death message. After a short time, Sarah asked to see Jason. Lisa took Sarah in with Ashley hanging behind.

A MOMENT IN TIME by Eric Brook

To someone who did not know any better, you would think that Jason was asleep or in a coma. Lisa and Ashley were used to death but this was Sarah's first time. After seeing that she was not going to fall over or rip the cubicle apart, Lisa and Ashley took a step or two back and left Sarah to say goodbye.

Sarah bent over and placed her face next to Jason's. "Oh man! Why did you have to leave me! There's so much that we haven't done yet! Justin needs you. I need you. I want you. Come back!" As soon as she said that, she knew he was not coming back. The tears flowed.

It was so unfair, Lisa thought. An average small family out driving and through no fault of their own, now little Justin has no dad and Sarah has no husband. There was no doubt Sarah could make it through. After all, single parent families were very common in the modern age.

Who knows, Sarah might even find a new life partner. That was down the track, not this second. Sarah had a couple of busy months ahead of her. Ashley went to see the Nursing Unit Manager to put Sarah in contact with a Patient Relations Officer who could guide her through the next steps. There was a lot to be done with a lot of paperwork that needed to be filled in and arrangements that needed to be made.

http://www.amomentintimenovel.com

A MOMENT IN TIME by Eric Brook

There was nothing more Lisa could do for Sarah. Sudden death was always frustrating but Eric's kidney stones and Rod's vomiting conditions were waiting for her. They seemed insignificant now to her compared to Jason's death but they were not expected to know (or care) about what just happened in cubicle 5.

Lisa went to the scrubs room to clean herself up. She had become quite bloody from dealing with Jason. The last thing her next patient needed to see was their doctor covered in blood. The last thing Lisa wanted to be was covered in blood. She had to be as clean as possible and did not want to pass anything onto another patient.

Lisa entered Eric's cubicle and saw that he now had a drip in his arm. Eric must have spotted a change in Lisa because the patient asked the doctor how she was. Needless to say, this was not normal and Lisa was stunned. "Um.....", she stammered. "Rough time. Not good. Not easy being a doctor, sometimes. Can I ask you a question?"

"Sure.", Eric said.

Lisa knew Eric was a train driver. Most of the time, they presented with the same illnesses that other people had. Sometimes, they had trips and falls. Medical centres would deal with things like RSI through overuse of certain muscle groups. But there was something in particular Lisa was curious about one thing in particular.

A MOMENT IN TIME by Eric Brook

She lowered her voice and the tone of her voice changed. "I know this isn't usual but I need to know." Lisa asked.

"What is it like facing the fact that every day, you know that you might kill someone by doing your job?" Eric knew Lisa was asking about death by train. It was a common question. Sometimes, people even thought that it was a great topic for a dinner party conversation or on a first meeting. He told Lisa what he tells everyone, that he expects it but he can't let it worry him.

"It's an awful feeling, isn't it?" Lisa asked. "It doesn't matter how much they tell you about it in training, does it? We have to expect it, you have to expect it. And when it happens, you don't know how it will affect you. And if it happens once, twice, five times, ten times, every time is different. They expect you to be able to just keep going. I have to keep going. When will it stop? You'd think it would get easier after each one. It doesn't. Sometimes it is very hard, especially if you don't expect it. Sometimes I wonder what it would be like just to sit back and just work a normal 9 to 5 job." Lisa lamented.

"I know what you mean", Eric empathised. "It would be nice to cruise through each day and the biggest thing that you have to worry about is when to leave your desk to have a coffee."

A MOMENT IN TIME by Eric Brook

"Speaking of coffee....", Lisa interrupted. "I know this is unusual for someone in my position ......" as she was searching for the right words. "When you get better, I want to take you out for coffee. So let's get you better." Switching back to doctor Lisa mode, she asked "Has that drip worked yet?". Looking at the bag, he still had a long way to go.

"Not yet but you've given me a great incentive to get better", Eric smiled. "I will take you up on that coffee."

"I've got to get to my other patients now but I'll check you out .... um ..... check on you ...... again soon." Lisa winked and left the cubicle. She felt a connection with Eric that she did not have with many people outside her profession. Sure, she cared about people but Eric was different. She did not know why. It was not her normal style.

Heading to the next cubicle, Rod was feeling a lot better. The needle that nurse Jen had given him worked a treat. The blood test results had not come back yet but he was well enough to wait in the waiting room. He had not vomited since the injection. It was still a mystery what was happening with Rod. He had been asleep much of the time since the injection. Lisa showed him to the waiting room. The needle would wear off in a few hours but that gave the test results time to come back. It would also give Rod a break from the physical effort of vomiting.

A MOMENT IN TIME by Eric Brook

Lisa was thinking of grabbing something to eat quickly but she was passing the Ambulance entry doors when paramedics Mike and Sharon entered, wheeling in a patient. There was no such thing of a set meal break in the Emergency Department. A sandwich there, a quick coffee there, various energy drinks......

"Hi ya'll!" Mike said to Lisa. "Michelle here was the front seat car passenger in a bus versus car accident. Trapped on arrival, morph and 100 percent O2 on board, released by rescue and immobilised. Query broken tib/fib left leg and query broken both feet. No visible cuts or other trauma. Vitals in normal range. Her partner was driving and was deceased on site. No known allergies, we couldn't really talk to her enroute."

"Query ......" meant that the paramedics were not 100 percent sure that the body part in question was damaged or broken. If they were totally sure, they would say so. This was especially important in Michelle's case because the paramedic who did the initial assessment was not giving the patient's handover.

"You'll probably get the bus driver as well", Sharon said. It wasn't pretty. All we did was the transport. That bike ambo and Rescue did all the hard work." The two paramedics at times would carry on like the married couple that they were. They wheeled Michelle into the first Trauma Room and placed her on the hospital's bed.

A MOMENT IN TIME by Eric Brook

"Hi, Michelle. I'm Lisa. I'm a doctor here at RPA. Do you know that you are in the hospital?" Michelle groaned.

"Let's take a look at you." Another groan from Michelle. The first thing that Lisa wanted to do was to see if the backboard and cervical collar were still needed.

"Michelle, I am going to touch your feet. I want to know if you can feel my hand touching your feet. Wave your hand if you can feel it, ok!", Lisa said. Lisa touched both feet and Michelle screamed in pain. That's a fair indication to say that she felt that, Lisa thought to herself. Lisa repeated the procedure with Michelle's hands and found that Michelle could feel that, too. That was a good sign. Before she sent Michelle for scans just to make sure,

Lisa checked Michelle for other injuries and could not find any more that the paramedics had not told her about. A full body scan would be done just in case. It is very rare to be cut of a car and not have any injuries at all. If Michelle only had the injuries that the paramedics described, she was very lucky. An orderly came to take Michelle for her scans. More than likely, these scans would be the first of many that she would have to have during her recovery.

Next door, the bus driver from the same accident had just arrived. According to the paramedics who treated him, he was in shock. He also had a broken left forearm and a couple of finger dislocations. He also was tender in the chest and ribs after hitting the large steering wheel in his bus. He felt responsible for the death of the car driver. As it turned out, the driver of the car who died had turned in front of the bus. The car did not have right of way but thought that he could get around before the bus reached the intersection.

Michelle was lucky she was wearing a seat belt. Maybe if her partner had of done the same thing, he could have been sitting in the next cubicle rather than be still at the site of the accident waiting to go to the State Coroner's office. This of course did not stop the bus driver from feeling bad. In reality, he had done an excellent job of saving his passengers. He tried to slow down as much as he could when he thought that the crash was unavoidable. He knew that a sudden turn of the steering wheel could have produced an out-of-control swerve and that he might of caused the bus to roll or hit another car. How only the two cars were involved was a mystery.

"Hi, Tom. I'm Lisa, one of the doctors here. How are you?". Unlike Michelle, he could talk. He was in shock and in a large amount of pain but he could still talk. His bus took a lot of the impact and protected him more than Michelle's car protected her.

Tom told her what pains he was suffering from. During his 30 year career in driving buses around Sydney, he had a couple of minor accidents in the past but considering the traffic levels in Sydney and the amount Tom drove in a year, he had a great driving record. His passengers liked him as did his workmates and his supervisors.

Lisa took the same systematic approach with Tom that she did with Michelle. In this case, it was a lot easier. Tom could talk and he did not need to be immobilised at the scene. A scan would still be very handy those especially with his chest and ribs as potential trouble spots. As much as he wanted to talk to Lisa, he found it hard to breath and talk. Tom was soon sent off for scans.

Because of her condition, it was easier to use a portable x-ray machine on Michelle. The staff in radiology did not want to lift her from her bed to the x-ray table and then back again if they could avoid it, especially considering that she still had the collar and backboard on. Still in a lot of pain, Michelle could not do much more than look at the roof. She had two areas of major concern, her feet and legs. All Michelle really had to do was to lie still. She did not have a lot of choice in the matter. The radiologist tried to talk to Michelle and soon realised that Michelle was not really able to talk at the moment. Reading Lisa's x-ray request, the x-ray machine caught various angles of Michelle's legs and feet.

Just to be sure, Lisa had also requested a head scan as well as the abdomen. There were various clicks from the machine. In between shots, the operator would adjust the machine. With computers, it was a lot easier to tell straight away what Michelle's issues were. Soon enough, the radiologist left the room to get the orderly as well as to show Lisa the scans.

After finding Lisa, it was time to find out what the treatment plan for Michelle was. It was clear to Lisa and the radiologist that Michelle's condition was pretty much like the paramedics had described. She had two broken feet as well as a tibia/fibula break as well. Most times if one bone broke the other one would be broken as well so most medical professionals called it a tib/fib fracture. Due to the extent of her injuries and her current pain level, Michelle would be a perfect candidate for surgery.

She did not need surgery this second but she would need to be pain managed and stabilised in the meantime. Lisa also needed to be able to talk to Michelle. Michelle was not making much sense at the moment, a common side effect from the pain relief. Lisa knew now that Michelle could go back to the cubicle and get the backboard and collar removed. The orderly pushed Michelle back to the cubicle. Once back there, Lisa and nurse Jen got to work removing the backboard and collar.
For the first time in the hospital, Michelle spoke. "Oh man, I'm glad to be out of that collar!". Jen moved the bed so Michelle could sit up and not be perfectly flat any more. "I'm so sore!"

In case Michelle forgot, Lisa re-introduced herself to Michelle. "Hi, Michelle. I'm Lisa, one of the doctors here at RPA. It's good to be able to talk to you. So far, we know that you have two broken feet and two bones in your left leg. I'll give you some more pain relief. We need to get you admitted and watch you for a while on the ward and see what else we can find, if anything. Once you are a bit more stable, we need to operate on your leg and feet. I'll get a Patient Relation officer to get the paperwork started for you. Nurse Jen here will take your vital signs, history and give you some pain relief. We'll have you in a ward soon."

"Wayne. Where's Wayne? Is he OK?", Michelle asked.

Lisa did not know for sure if Michelle knew that her partner was now dead as a result of the accident. Lisa assumed that Michelle did not know, hence the question. It was going to be Lisa's second death message of the afternoon. Lisa took a second deep breath.

"Michelle, Wayne didn't make it. He passed on at the scene. From what the paramedic who treated you said, he would have gone pretty much on impact. He isn't in pain any more. You are lucky you made it." Michelle started to cry.

Lisa was not sure what Michelle was going to do. Lisa did not know the state of the relationship that Michelle and Wayne had. For all that Lisa knew, Wayne could have been the worst man of the world. It was not Lisa's place to judge or counsel. Lisa held Michelle's hand and squeezed it.

A MOMENT IN TIME by Eric Brook

"Wayne's being looked after. We need to get you well again. If you need anything, use the buzzer." Lisa squeezed Michelle's hand again and left the cubicle.

With the second death message of the afternoon delivered, Lisa went in to check on train driver Eric just like she had when telling Sarah that Jason had died earlier. While she knew that she would not be able to run to him every day, she was going to take advantage of that while she could. "How's my favourite train driver going?", Lisa asked. She looked at his drip. It was mainly empty.

Lisa could tell that he was getting better. She should be able to discharge him soon and then they would not have the doctor/patient relationship any more. Before he could really answer, he leapt out of bed and waddled quickly in the direction of the toilet. Hopefully this meant that the kidney stone was going to leave his body now.

Eric was not used to having to drag the drip around that was attached to his arm on one end and a stand on wheels at the other end. Finding the toilet vacant, Eric opened the door. He lifted up his gown and before he had time to control the hose, someone turned the tap on. Hard. It was like a backyard hose being coiled on the ground and the tap was turned on hard right away. In that case, the hose would sway from side to side spraying water like a fast moving snake.

A MOMENT IN TIME by Eric Brook

This was a relief for Eric. He had not urinated for a couple of days and now that he was getting more hydrated more and more by the minute, nature called and off he went. When he was at work, he usually went to the toilet 3 or 4 times during an 8 hour shift. Sometimes, though, that did not happen.

"Oooooooooh man that's good!" he yelled to no one in particular.

His voice echoed around the toilet cubicle wall. He grabbed a sample and placed it in a specimen jar. Being really careful to wash his hands, he returned to the cubicle with the hot jar in his hand. He passed Lisa on the way and smiled. "I did it", he said. "That felt so good." He lowered his voice to a whisper so only Lisa could hear him. "I am so looking forward to that coffee."

She smiled and winked. "We'll get another bag of fluid into you but I'll put some coffee into it." She looks down at his jar. "We'll get that off to the lab to get checked but I think you are ok to go." She walked him back to the cubicle and took the jar from Eric.

Filling in her paperwork, she found a piece of paper and gave him her phone number. "If you are free on Saturday night, you can take me to dinner. If you are feeling ok, that is. You'll need to find a new doctor. Let me do my paperwork and then I'll see you Saturday."

Had Lisa crossed the line? Had her life changed forever?

http://www.amomentintimenovel.com

Chapter 9 – Judy's Afternoon Turns Bad

5.04pm Thursday 01 April 2010

Judy's stomach rumbled. She had been on duty for about 5 hours at this point. If she took food with her like she did from time to time, she could munch on some finger food while she was driving. This was one of the longer diagrams between starting work and a meal break. It was bordering the award conditions which dictated that the meal break could start anywhere between the second and fifth hours of the shift.

The meal break for Judy was waiting for her when she arrived at Central. She was hoping that her relief driver was waiting for her. In about 200 metres, it was eating time, she thought.

Her train was crossing over from one track to another to the west of Central. A rookie driver mistake would be to accelerate once the front of the train was through the turnout. For safety and comfort reasons, the whole train had to pass through the turnout at or under the speed limit of 25kph. Because of the short distance between the turnout and the platform, there was no point in Judy accelerating to the platform. Once the whole train had passed through the turnout, the track speed increased to 50kph.

A MOMENT IN TIME by Eric Brook

Looking ahead, Judy saw many people on the platform. When the station was busy like it was now, it was common for people to be near the yellow safety line. Some people in off peak periods stood near the yellow line and some people stood over it. However, peak periods worried Judy less about people fooling around on the platform as there was less room because of more people on the platform.

Judy's train was arriving on the platform. Under normal circumstances, Judy aimed to arrive onto the platform doing 45-50 kph and gradually slow down until she stopped at the end of the platform at the right spot. Due to going through the crossover and not dramatically speeding up, she would have been around 30kph at the arrival end of the platform.

Out of the corner of her eye, Judy saw a person running toward the yellow line. He crossed the yellow line and he fell onto the tracks. Before she could react properly, the train ran over the man. Dropping the power handle that was in her left hand, Judy's heart raced. Moving her left hand up to the train radio, she pressed the red Emergency button on the train radio and held it down for 5 seconds. The button enabled Judy's radio call to take priority over any others that were going on at the same time.

A MOMENT IN TIME by Eric Brook

By releasing the power handle, the brakes rapidly applied. It might be the difference between the man being alive and dead. Under normal circumstances, drivers were told to brake smoothly. Under this circumstance, all bets were off. In newer trains with better rated braking systems, there was not a lot of difference between emergency and regular braking. In older trains, though, there was a big difference.

Once the train stopped, Judy put the handle into the Emergency position and applied the parking brake by pressing a button. This would prevent the train from moving. In reality, the train stopped quickly, helped in part by the initially low speed of the train. Of course, it seemed like the train was taking hours to brake when it was actually a small number of seconds.

While Judy waited for the signal box to answer, she pressed the intercom button to tell the guard what was happening. The guard did not have a train radio of their own nor could the guard hear what the Signal Box and the driver were saying. A ringing sound filled the cabin. Judy was starting to shake.

The screen on the radio said EMERGENCY. The other trains in the same area should have showed EMERGENCY IN PROGRESS which was an indication and a warning for other trains to slow down. In what seemed forever, the message on the screen changed to EMERGENCY - SPEAK TO SIGNALER.

A MOMENT IN TIME by Eric Brook

"Sydney Box, driver of 711 run, emergency message. I have struck a man who fell on the tracks at platform 17, Central. Send all the Emergency Services."

This radio call would spark a series of phone calls. The signaller would call the train controller. While the signaller operated the signals, it was the train controller who made all of the important decisions. Nothing could happen without the train controller knowing about it. The train controller was a very powerful and respected position on the railway. Sometimes, they were referred to by other workers by the nickname of "God" or "the man on the wall".

The train controller made a call to the security desk inside the Rail Management Centre where they were both located. It was Security's job to call the Emergency Services. This phone call also signalled the need for the security section to obtain CCTV footage for the Police as well as to live monitor the situation. With nearly 10,000 cameras in the whole network, it would have been extremely lucky for someone to have been live monitoring the situation as it was happening.

The train controller then called stations on the City Circle line. Each platform had a control room and a dedicated line to the train controller. The train controller had a touch screen phone and was able to see when each station answered. The station staff were told to urgently pick up the hotline when it rang and not to speak except to acknowledge the message. "711 out of it, fatality on 17 platform. All outer trains via 16." The station staff could expect delays as all of the North Shore trains now had to compete with the City Circle trains using platform 16 at Central. At least this was an option. The train controller then called out the name of each station in order for them to acknowledge that they understood the message.

"Town Hall?"

"Yep"

"Wynyard?"

"Got it"

"Quay?"

"Uh-ah"

"St James?"

"Roger"

A MOMENT IN TIME by Eric Brook

"Museum?"

"Ok"

Meanwhile, the noise of the ringing intercom rang for around 15 seconds then stopped. Finally, the guard answered. Judy told the guard what happened so the passengers could be evacuated from the train. The first two carriages were alongside the platform and the remaining six carriages were hanging out off the platform. It was not a good idea to either move the train or open the doors. Each carriage had emergency exits that could be opened from the outside. Station staff, train crew and some support staff were trained in how to use these emergency exits. Progressively, the emergency services were being trained about those buttons also.

"Hi mate", Judy started to talk. Her voice was wavering which was unusual for her. "We've hit someone. Emergency services are coming. Don't open the doors. Start evacuating." Judy was hoping that the Guard was able to do their job correctly. She would leave the evacuation process for the Guard to worry about. She had enough to deal with, including people on the platform yelling at her to open the doors.

Shortly, the station staff arrived to help out and knocked on Judy's door. Opening the door, she thought that an extra person's help would be very handy. Judy told the male staff member to use the emergency exit buttons but he said that he did not know how to do it. She wanted the

A MOMENT IN TIME by Eric Brook

Customer Service Attendant to open the doors from the outside. Neither Judy or her guard could selectively open doors from their respective workstations on this type of train.

"Oh for crying out loud, it's not that hard! Walk back along the train and if you see a green sticker, open the flap and press the button!", Judy aggressively said, holding back tears. "We don't pay you people to be wannabe radio station DJ's!"

"Um, sorry. I'm new.", the station staff member said. "What do you want me to do?"

Judy's hand mentally touched her head in a face palm action. "Trust me! I get the new guy!", she said to the man who was 19 years old if he was lucky. "Look, you stay here. Don't touch anything. I'll go and open the doors on the platform. If anyone comes to you looking for me, tell them where I am."

Leaving her cabin for the first time, she could see that the platform was very crowded. A couple of carriages away, the unknown man was underneath the train. She could hear the man screaming. Somehow, he was still alive. It was a chilling sound that she could not lock out of her brain or ears.

A MOMENT IN TIME by Eric Brook

Not every door was an emergency door. At the non emergency door, Judy pointed towards the other end of the carriage for the benefit of those people inside. The passengers could not hear her and she hoped that her pointing the way would tell the passengers what they had to do. Only one end of each carriage had emergency exits. Eventually, there would be emergency exits that would be opened from the inside in the future.

Walking along the platform, Judy pressed the emergency exit button when she found them. Opening the emergency exit doors, the passengers were mostly happy to be leaving the train. The guard had been making announcements and walking through the train to tell people what was going on. This was important because some people got scared when their train was stopped for a long time.

One middle aged man abused Judy. "I'm going to Circular Quay and I'm late for a meeting. What are you going to do about it?" Normally abuse flowed off Judy like water off a duck's back. But with a dying man under her train, all bets were off.

"Are you bloody well kidding me? There's a critically injured man under my train and all you care about is a stupid meeting! Go to hell, arsehole!", Judy aggressively screamed. Before the man could answer, Judy walked away. The man and the surrounding passengers were stunned. This was unlike Judy. She was an experienced driver but sometimes in this situation even experienced drivers could lose the plot. There was always a minority of passengers who only cared about themselves. Most people were at the least understanding when the situation was explained to them.

With all of the possible doors opened along the platform, Judy returned in the direction of the driver's cabin. The guard would have to handle the passengers for now. In the front of each crew area, there was a set of emergency stairs which would be handy if the train was stopped in between stations. The stairs could be set up at the front and/or back of the train so people could easily get off the train. In this instance, though, the stairs were not needed and in their stowed away state was actually in the way. The guard had to move two sets of these emergency steps to the side of the cabin. Once this was done, a temporary handrail system would be hung up between the two halves of the train.

Judy returned to the driver's cabin. "Go help the guard.", she said to the man minding the cabin. "The guard is located near the blue light", said Judy, sarcastically. The joke was probably wasted on the young station worker but Judy felt a little better about it.

"Driver of run 711, Sydney Box calling. Are you there, Drive?"

A MOMENT IN TIME by Eric Brook

"Drive" was an unofficial nickname that some people used as a sign of affection or respect to the driver. Having yelled at the passenger and the station staff member calmed Judy down somewhat.

"Sorry, Box. I was helping with the evacuation and the Emergency Door Releases. The guy on the platform is a newbie.", Judy said. "The guy is alive. Any idea where the Ambos are?"

"They aren't far away. Just to let you know, the power has been cut for platform 17 and 18. How you doing?", the Signal Box asked. The Signal Box controlled the signals and points and would be busy diverting trains around the incident but the man on the radio still took the time to ask Judy how she was.

"I've had better but thanks for asking, mate. I hope those Ambos get here soon.", Judy said.

"We are sending an Inspector and a relief driver to you now. Won't be long. Sydney Box out.", the signaller said. Judy thought that the man on the radio was experienced and had been around for a while. A newer signaller would have called an Inspector by their new fancy title of Operations Standards Manager. Judy was disgusted that everyone except the train crew members were getting fancy new titles and a massive pay rise to go with it.

A MOMENT IN TIME by Eric Brook

"Where are these useless Inspectors when you need them?", Judy said to herself under her breath. During the peak hour, there was supposed to be an Inspector on duty supervising how everything was running with regards to the train crew while the train was waiting on the platform. 5 minutes after the incident, the Inspector who was supposed to take over running the incident from Judy still had not come to see her.

Suddenly, there was a tap on the door and a man in a brand new orange safety vest while wearing a tie stood there. Judy opened the door, Frustratingly, she said "About time you got here. The guy's alive under the second car. The power's off to 17 and 18. I've opened the EDRs on the platform myself because the platform staff had no idea. First day, he says. What happened to having trained, experienced staff at Central? Pfffttt."

In a very bossy tone, the manager looked in the general direction of Judy. "I know you are upset, Driver. So I'm going to ignore your little speech. Wait here, your relief will be here shortly. The Police will be here soon to ask you what happened and breath test you. It would be in your interest for me to be here when they arrive. I'm going to check on the man." The man turned on his heels and left Judy alone in her cabin.

In an event such as this, a relief driver was supposed to be sent out straight away to take over the train. Once this was done, all Judy needed to do was to speak to the police and that could be done off the train once a relief driver arrived. She understood that if she was in an outlying area which was not a normal crew changeover point, relief might take some time to arrive. This would be certainly the case if it was peak hour. However, she was at Central. Central was the biggest station on the network and the biggest train crewing depot, so where was her relief?

It was peak hour. Under normal circumstances, there were several people who were standby drivers located on every platform at Central. There should have been someone here by now. What about the driver who was supposed to relieve her? Where was he? Was he in the meal room watching TV?

Judy picked up her mobile phone and started to dial. She was interrupted by a tap on the door. Opening the door, she saw a couple of police officers. Letting them into the cabin, the younger of the two female officers was more interested in looking around the cabin as if she was a small child. Then as if she had remembered that she had a job to do, she asked Judy if they could talk somewhere in private.

"Sorry, here will have to do for the moment", Judy explained. "Someone should be coming here soon to replace me but until then, I have to stay here. There is a manager here but he is checking on the guy. I can't believe he is still alive!"

A MOMENT IN TIME by Eric Brook

Another tap on the door saw the manager and a relief driver waiting to come inside the cabin. Judy was not happy, especially when she saw that the driver had a cup of coffee in his hands. "Hope you brought one of those for me! It's amazing what you have to do to find a standby in this joint!", she said.

"Sorry, I didn't know how you had it. Do you want this one? It's nice and hot!", said the relief driver. He did not offer a reason for what Judy would see as his tardiness. Judy shook her head.

Judy's train key was still inserted into the keyhole on the dashboard of the train. It needed to be inserted to keep the train radio connected to the network. The relief driver handed her his key to replace the one in the lock. Judy needed to hand over to the train to the new driver. Normally this was a quick process as it had to be done in the time that a normal passenger stop took. There was no rush on this occasion except that Judy wanted to get off the train. "It was going alright until this happened."

The relief driver had been briefed by the manager. The relief driver took control of the train and Judy, the manager and the two police officers left the train and headed off to the standby room at the end of the platform. It was often used as a meal room by the drivers, also. The room was full of drivers, which made Judy madder. She did not want to (nor was she required to) be breath tested and questioned in front of a room full of her colleagues. Seeing this room full, they went over to the manager's platform office. It was a lot smaller than the previous room as it was meant as a single person office.

The junior police officer asked Judy for a breath test. The last time Judy had to do this was outside of work, the machine was the type where someone who had to blow into the straw. That night, she had been tested twice on the same highway. Since then, the machines had been updated and all Judy needed to do on most occasions was to count aloud into the machine. As a rail safety worker, Judy's allowable limit was lower than the general road user and was effectively zero alcohol.

Judy counted to seven and the machine beeped. Judy knew she was sober. It was not worth risking her job for. Apart from being able to be tested on the road like a normal motorist, the railway also had their own sections that tested randomly for alcohol and drugs. Then was the post-incident tests such as this.

Judy's test proved she was sober and that factor of driver impairment could be eliminated as a contributing factor. Next, Judy had to explain the incident as a statement of fact for the police.

A MOMENT IN TIME by Eric Brook

Judy made no attempt to translate her commentary into language the police would understand. "I had just driven through a crossover at the flyovers at 25. Soon after I arrived on the platform and the guy jumped in front of me. I couldn't stop the train in time and the train hit him. I used the deadman handle to stop the train but it wasn't good enough. I couldn't stop in time."

That was all she could really say at the time. Tears started to well up. After signing the police officer's notebook, the police left. At a later stage, she would probably have to give a more detailed statement to the police.

The manager and Judy were now alone in the room. Now she could speak her mind. "Bloody shambles, this is! Where did the guy who was supposed to relieve me in the first place? How come the relief guy took so long to get her? And why bother having station staff if they have no frakking idea what they are doing!" She breathed deeply and looked the manager in the eye. "I suppose it is your first day on the job too!"

He looked at her and did not argue. "Typical!", she said. "In the job 5 minutes and you are a manager."

A MOMENT IN TIME by Eric Brook

"I've had enough of your attitude, Driver! Here's your Cabcharge docket. Get out of my sight, freshen up and get into a cab and go home.", he said to her, handing her a taxi voucher. The last thing a train crew member usually wanted to do after a major incident was to get onto another train to go home.

"Gee, thanks for your support. I can see why you are a manager! You haven't heard the last of this!"

Judy wildly left the office, making sure she slammed the door behind her. Going into the meal room, she gave the drivers in the meal room little thought. She stomped into the direction of the toilets like an angry elephant. Some voice called her name but she ignored it. She dropped her shoulder into a large wooden door and then heavily slid the sliding door open leading to the one and only female cubicle in the room. She sat on the lid of the toilet without removing her pants.

With complete privacy for the first time since the accident, the tears flowed. She kept silent, however. She did not want the other drivers to hear her. Some of the tears were for the man under the train but most were because there was absolutely nothing she could do about what had happened. Some of the tears were due to her general frustration with the events of the afternoon.

Chapter 10 – Caroline's First Job

5.07pm, Thursday 01 April 2010

The red and blue LED lights on the top of the police car flashed from side to side. If it was dark, the lights would have had a greater effect. Every little bit helps, though. The siren alternated between a wail and a yelp which was being controlled by Leila in the passenger's seat of the police car, City 36. For the 3 women in the car, they could hear the sirens very clearly. In many cases, they were hearing the sirens better than the other cars they were aiming the noise at. Nicole gunned the engine of her car. The car roared loudly, just like the lion logo on the front of the car. "Caroline, hang on! This chick drives like a madman. She drives rally cars on the weekend, you know!". Leila raised her voice to be heard over the siren, the engine and the radio.

If Leila had a hand free, she would have been grabbing the handle above the door. In her left hand, she held the radio. She only usually did this when they were on an urgent job like this or in a pursuit. She used her right hand to work the siren. Caroline was gripping her own imaginary handle. She had the option of grabbing the handle above her door but chose not to.

A MOMENT IN TIME by Eric Brook

Caroline was totally transfixed, looking out the front window. She had spent some time in various cars during her placements at the academy. This was the first time that she was in a car that was running lights and sirens. Even though the speeds were not extreme, it was a thrill for the first day officer.

A lot faster than normal, Nicole turned the car left. Their bodies shook slightly as the tyres of the car met the tram tracks. Nicole sped up again for one block before she needed to turn right. She slowed down quickly as Leila counted down. "Clear left, clear right", Leila half yelled.

Caroline surprised herself by calling out "Clear right" to Nicole as well. Usually only the person in the front passenger's seat did this. These calls out to the driver enabled Nicole to concentrate on the road. Leila was acting as eyes for Nicole.

This corner was a little more tricky. There was the normal right hand turn from Hay Street into Pitt Street. Then there was the ramp to the main level of the country side of Central. The part of the road the police car prior to the turn was on was usually for trams only. If Nicole got the corner wrong, she still could get to Central but the way she was going would be better.

A MOMENT IN TIME by Eric Brook

Nicole flicked the car to the right and as soon as the car was straight again, Nicole mashed the accelerator pedal. As the ramp was uphill, she needed more power. Suddenly, Caroline could hear another siren. She turned her head and looked behind her. Expecting to see another police car, she saw a large fire engine behind her. For many incidents, the police were racing to the same scene that the Fire Brigade and Paramedics were.

"Fire truck behind us", Leila said. Unlike Caroline, Leila had a mirror to look in. Nicole knew that she had more power than the heavy fire truck even on level ground. Even if this was not the case, there was no room for Nicole to move over or for the fire truck to overtake. Central's famous clock tower was now in sight.

"Platform 16, guys", Leila said. Nicole reached the top of the ramp and parked in a bus zone. Leila turned off the lights and sirens. Sometimes the lights should stay on for safety reasons but sometimes, there was no point. This was one of those times.

"Radio, City 36 off at Central station", Leila spoke into the radio handset. This let the radio operator know that they were now there. In the days before hand held radios, this would mean that the officers would be uncontactable. In the current day, each officer had a hand held radio and most officers also had mobile phones.

A MOMENT IN TIME by Eric Brook

Undoing their seat belts, the trio left the car and started to run through the crowds on the main concourse. It was peak hour but there was several clusters of people waiting for country trains. Many people were rushing to where Nicole, Leila and Caroline were rushing to. Of course, the passengers were rushing for different reasons. A siren to help them get through the crowd would have been very handy at that moment.

The gear on their belts and their heavy boots acted as a quasi-siren. It was about that time that Caroline was thankful she was wearing a sports bra. After all, she did pick out a lacy number to wear today, originally. It was a short run so far but she was already sweating in the small of her back and other places. It was a warm day prior to their run so all three officers easily worked up a sweat.

The upcoming introduction of the utility vest might help somewhat in keeping the female officers' chests under control while running. The last thing that the female officers needed in a situation like this was for it to look like two puppies were having a fight underneath a blanket as they were running towards an incident. The load bearing vests would more evenly distribute the weight of the equipment that all officers currently carried on their belts. The upcoming introduction of Tasers for general duties police would add to that weight. A Taser would come in handy for some violent situations as an alternative to the lethal force of the gun that each officer carried. This situation was not one of them, however.

A MOMENT IN TIME by Eric Brook

To get through the ticket barrier, there was one section that the staff left open for luggage, people with prams, staff etc. Nicole led Leila through the gate but Caroline - possibly full of first day on the job energy - leapt the barrier in a single stride. It was like she was jumping a hurdle on an athletics track. Caroline was, after all, a gifted athlete in her teens. Caroline could have been leading Nicole and Leila but she did not want to show them up too badly on day 1.

At the moment, Caroline felt she was the cameraman on an episode of COPS. It was one of her favourite TV shows. The police in America sure did things differently over there. There was a New Zealand version that she loved called Police 10-7. The cops and most of the crooks were very laid back in comparison. Besides, she loved the accents. She felt like she was not doing a lot and was merely following Nicole and Leila around like the TV cameraman would. As long as it turned out better than an episode of Reno 911.......

Turning left, Nicole and Leila headed down the escalator which was full of commuters who - mostly - were on the left hand side of the moving stairs. Seeing that the two experienced officers were having problems getting through the crowded escalator, Caroline headed down the adjacent stairs that were almost empty. She was able to overtake Nicole, Leila and around 50 people because of the stairs. On the lower level, there were two passageways. The one on the left was crowded with people because it was near another set of ticket barriers.

A MOMENT IN TIME by Eric Brook

The right hand path was a lot less congested. There was a large no entry sign above the passageway. This originally was a crowd control move for the Olympic Games that Sydney had hosted 10 years earlier. This arrangement worked well with lots of staff to enforce it. After the Olympics ended, the staff disappeared and the signs remained. Unlike no entry signs on the roads, many people ignored these signs, Caroline included.

Because of her previous training, Caroline was feeling pretty good. Nicole and Leila were just behind her but were breathing very heavily in comparison. Taking the path to the right, Caroline climbed the stairs to the platform two at a time. Passengers going down the stairs moved out of the way, some stopping to turn around and watched the 3 police officers run up the stairs. Reaching the platform first and without checking with Nicole or Leila, Caroline reached for her radio handset that was attached to her shoulder. She hardly sounded out of breath as she pushed the talk button.

"Radio, City 36 portable"

"City 36 portable"

Caroline paused briefly.

"City 36 portable, on site at Central platform 17."

A MOMENT IN TIME by Eric Brook

Caroline looked around. Near her, she could see a train that was not completely on the platform. There was a female train driver standing near the front of the train. She was looking down at the tracks.

"We've found the train and are about to speak to the driver. No other services on site. Best entrance is via Eddy Avenue."

"Copy, City 36. Advise ASAP."

Leila and Nicole arrived on the platform not long after Caroline. The three officers headed to the train driver. "Hi. What happened?" Nicole asked as she was catching her breath. She did not worry about the formal introductions at this stage. The train driver explained that she was driving into Central as normal and without warning, a man jumped off the platform. He was now under the train. Nicole had to listen hard to the driver as the man was screaming in the background. That was unusual. Normally in this situation, the person died almost instantly.

"We've got Rescue coming. You alright?" Nicole asked the driver, her breath returning. The driver nodded but Nicole was not convinced. Nicole thought the train driver was often an innocent victim in this situation. There was often nothing that the driver could do in this situation.

Sometimes, a driver could be so grief stricken at this moment in time and needed to be treated carefully.

"Have they stopped the trains?"

"So they tell me!"

Nicole asked Leila to find someone in charge from the railway and asked Caroline to stay with the driver. Nicole got back onto the radio to update them from Caroline's initial arrival message.

"Radio, City 36 portable"

"City 36"

"City 36, from Central station. Confirmed train incident here on platform 17. Male still alive under train. Keep Rescue and the Ambos coming. I need you to confirm that the power is off to platform 17 and that trains are stopped, Radio."

"Copy, City 36. Anything else?"

"I'll need 14's attendance here too."

A MOMENT IN TIME by Eric Brook

"Copy, City 36. Standby."

Nicole turned to Caroline. "Stay here with the driver. Find out what you can. When they send a new driver, we need a breath test."

Leila found a railway manager and directed him to Nicole. She then went towards the stairs to await assistance and the arrival of the emergency services. Despite everything that was going on, trains were still running on the other platform which was very crowded with people trying to get home. Some people were asking Leila how to get home. She advised them to watch the screens. There were people trying to watch the action as well which annoyed her.

Leila then went downstairs to wait for the other services. Normally, the railway sent someone to meet the Emergency Services and the location was supposed to be the same each and every time. This way, Leila could brief the other services on the way from the rendezvous point.

It seemed to take forever but shortly afterwards, the Fire Brigade and some paramedics arrived. "We've got a guy under the train. He's screaming pretty hard. We are waiting to know if the power is off." The officers climbed the stairs towards platform 18. Leila thought that was strange but also thought that they know what they are doing so she headed back to platform 16.

http://www.amomentintimenovel.com

A MOMENT IN TIME by Eric Brook

Leila found Nicole crouching on the platform near the second carriage of the train. Nicole was trying to comfort the man and re-assure him that help was coming. "Hey mate", Nicole shouted. "I'm a Police Officer. My name's Nicole. Rescue's on their way, OK!"

Leila bent down and spoke to Nicole. "Hey Nic, the Ambos and Rescue are here. They are going to set up on platform 18." Before Nicole could answer, her mobile phone rang. It was Sabrina, the shift supervisor. She was on her way to the scene to take control. Rather than tying up the radio, they could talk more freely.

"Trains on platform 16 next to you are still running. The railway won't stop that line. There's no need to. They have closed the track the train is on and the power is off. The track next to it is closed too, number 18. The rescue is going to the opposite platform. Better access for them, they say."

On the opposite platform, Nicole saw a group of firefighters. She yelled across two tracks to them. "Alright boys, the power is off. The track next to you is closed too. I'll be over to see you in a second." Nicole said to the group of firefighters, not noticing there was two women in the group.

A MOMENT IN TIME by Eric Brook

The rescue teams got to work. Turning her attention back to Sabrina, Nicole had a list of things she needed. She needed assistance with crowd control, lots of crime scene tape, an alcometer, CCTV footage and if possible, some sort of barrier for the scene. Sabrina was not far away and said that she would work on those things.

Nicole left Leila to talk to the man underneath the train. Nicole needed to talk to the other emergency services to work together on a plan. At this stage, the area was a crime scene until Nicole could prove otherwise. That meant that she had overall control of the the scene. She would not tell the fire brigade or the paramedics how to conduct the rescue, though.

Nicole was surprised to find that the fire brigade officer was female, just like her. "G'day, I'm Nicole from City Central. I'll be the site commander until my supervisor gets here. How are your guys going?"

The two women shook hands. You could be forgiven for thinking they were on a training course. "Hey. I'm Renee from Station 1. We've got a paramedic talking to the guy and she's about to go under the train. We are going to lift the train up a bit and hopefully we'll get him out soon. We're good."

A MOMENT IN TIME by Eric Brook

At the front of the train, Caroline took the driver into the driver's cabin. "Wow", Caroline said. "I've never been in here before. Is it fun? Are there many women drivers?".

The driver looked at her with a blank look on her face. She had just hit someone with her train and the cop in front of her was worried about was finding out how many women were on the job.

"Is there somewhere else we can go? I need to take a statement from you." The driver explained that she had to stay with the train until someone else arrived.

Nicole called on the radio to let them know that the Fire Brigade and the paramedics had arrived. Various people above the food chain above Nicole needed to know what was going on. Often, supervisors like Sabrina listened to the radio to keep an ear on what was going on. Sometimes she would allocate a specific crew to a certain job. Just by listening to the radio, she could tell who was busy, who was taking it easy and who would be at a job for a long time.

In a moment, Sabrina would see how busy Nicole was as the Police Commander of the incident. In a multi-service response, each service would have their own commander, usually the highest ranked officer on the first vehicle from each service. As a Senior Constable, Nicole would be the

A MOMENT IN TIME by Eric Brook

Police Commander until relieved by a higher ranking person on site. In this case, that would be Sabrina.

A few minutes later, Sabrina arrived on the platform and had her hands full of crime scene tape, an alcometer and a camera. She arrived on the platform and Leila gave Sabrina an update on what was going on. When Sabrina arrived, the Fire Brigade and Paramedics were working on getting the man out from under the train. Caroline was talking with the driver and Leila was doing her best with crowd control.

On her way to the scene in her car City 14, Sabrina proactively contacted her counterpart at the Central Commuter Crime Unit who was stationed in another part of Central station. Even though the station was physically located in the middle of her command, the CCU was a specialist resource that she did not directly control. Often, officers from the CCU were the first officers on the scene but on this occasion, Sabrina did not hear any officers calling up on the radio. If they were attending, they should have used their radios to let people know they were attending. Often, the CCU would attend without City Central's help which would enable Sabrina's team to concentrate on other calls.

Once on the platform, Leila saw that Sabrina had crime scene tape and started to tape off the scene. It was a lot easier to convince people to stay behind the tape that people could see. Some people were concerned about going home while others were watching the rescue effect. This was common at many incident scenes but it annoyed Leila no end.

The news media also had arrived by this point. Leila and her fellow officers tried to keep the media back from the incident. The last thing that the rescue workers needed was a TV camera hanging over their shoulder. The media worked quickly. One of the TV channels were currently in the middle of their nightly news with the other two stations starting their bulletins at the top of the hour. Sabrina walked over to the media to give them a briefing and to seek their co-operation. In front of the cameras, Sabrina gave the following statement.

"Emergency services were called to Central Station just after 5pm with reports that a man was struck by a train here on platform 17. Police, Fire Brigade and the Ambulance Service arrived to find the man alive underneath the train. Teams are working now to release the man and assess his condition. As you may appreciate, there is not a lot of room underneath that train. The circumstances of this incident is not yet known and is under investigation. CityRail's advice is that services are disrupted on all metropolitan lines except the Eastern Suburbs and Illawarra lines. If you can delay your journey from the city, this is a great idea. Thank you."

A MOMENT IN TIME by Eric Brook

Sabrina walked across to platform 18 to talk to Nicole. "Sabrina, this is Renee, the Fire Officer in charge. Renee, this is Sabrina, my supervisor." The three women were looking towards the train. "I can't believe the guy's still alive!", Nicole explained.

Renee explained to Sabrina the process that was in progress. By this stage, a paramedic was underneath the train with a rescue officer. Air bags were slowly raising the train to enable the rescuers to get the man out from under the train. This part of the operation was slow. Sabrina officially took charge of the scene from Nicole. Nicole stayed on the scene to keep an eye on proceedings.

Sabrina wanted to find out if a crime was committed so she walked back to platform 16. She was sure that no foul play was involved but wanted to find out for herself. This was often the case. Arriving at the front of the train, Sabrina spoke quietly to Caroline. "How's the driver, Caroline? Do we know what happened?"

"She's ok, considering. She said that the guy simply jumped off the platform", Caroline explained. "There was nothing that she said that she could do."

Meanwhile, the relief train driver had arrived to relieve the shaken driver. Caroline was joined by a railway manager. Once the relief driver arrived, Sabrina directed the railway staff and Caroline off the train. Under the direction of the railway manager, they found a quiet room at the end of the platform to conduct the formalities.

Sabrina handed Caroline the alcometer for the breath test. It was the same sort that would be used on the side of the road for random breath testing. All police cars were supposed to have an alcometer but due to the Highway Patrol operation later that night, the machine that City 36 would have normally was not in the car.

It was a requirement under the Rail Safety Act and internal company procedures that a train driver be breath tested after such an incident. That was a lot quicker than giving a blood or urine test. It was a formality that both Caroline and the driver expected. The driver knew that she could be breath tested by police or company officials at any time during her shift. Even though the breath test was a mere formality, it was a new experience to Caroline. What a first day!

"As you know, I'm Constable Caroline Clarke from City Central command. Because you were the driver involved in a major rail incident, I now require you to take a breath test under the Rail Safety Act and the Crimes Act. Please count into the mouthpiece until I tell you to stop.", Caroline explained.

The driver counted out loud, pausing between each number. "1 ... 2 ... 3 .... 4 ... . 5 .... 6 .... 7 ..."

A MOMENT IN TIME by Eric Brook

The machine let out a loud beep. "You can stop now", Caroline instructed. Looking at the machine, the driver's reading was zero. That was one less complication.

"Thanks. You passed. I'll get a brief statement from you now if that's ok." The driver started to explain her story.

She was coming into the platform at low speed and reached the arrival end of the platform at around 25 kilometres per hour. Near the arrival end of the platform, a man was standing on the platform and suddenly, he leapt off the platform and the driver tried to stop the train. The driver hit the man with the train doing about 15 kilometres per hour and stopped the train. She let the train guard know about the situation and then made an emergency call to her controller.

Caroline wrote all of this down and thought that it was lucky that the train was going so slow. Getting the driver to sign her notebook, Caroline would call the driver in a few days to get a full statement at City Central. Caroline and Sabrina thanked the driver for her help and wished her well. The railway manager led the driver off the platform.

Towards the centre of the platform, a bigger crowd was gathering to watch the rescue. Leila went to the office in the centre of the platform and asked to make an announcement over the Public Address System. This was unusual but the large crowd was getting in the way of people waiting to go home. They were also dangerously close to the edge of the platform as well as the crime scene tape. After a quick lesson in how the particular microphone worked from the station staff "push the button down and hold it", Leila made an announcement in her most authoritative police voice.

"Ladies and gentlemen, this is the Police. If you are not travelling, please leave the platform now. If you are travelling, please catch the first possible train. Do not gather in the centre of the platform. This message is for your safety."

While it was obvious to Sabrina and Caroline that there was nothing that the train driver could have done to avoid the incident and that the man underneath the train put himself in that position, they still needed to investigate further. They merely could not take the train driver's word as the complete investigation. Sabrina told Caroline to go and find Leila and see if there were any witnesses to the incident.

Sabrina would work on getting some camera footage. Sabrina was used to working with CityRail to get video footage as the Police were often called to railway stations to deal with incidents.

A MOMENT IN TIME by Eric Brook

Sabrina picked up her mobile phone and made a call to the Rail Management Centre to see if she could view some footage. She did not want Caroline to see the footage just yet as the probationary constable was already dealing with a lot on her first day. After speaking to the Supervisor of the Security section of the Rail Management Centre, Sabrina decided to go there directly and assess the footage for herself.

After letting Nicole what she was doing and what she needed done on the phone, Sabrina left the platform and headed across to the other side of the station. She had made the trip on a few occasions. Normally it was not worthwhile making the trip personally but she needed a decision to see if she needed the Forensics section to attend pretty quickly. After all, once the man was released, CityRail would want to resume services quickly. Across the centre of the city, all the city stations were very busy, busier than normal.

Sabrina was met at the unmarked door by the Security Supervisor. Overall, they were dressed very similarly despite the fact that they had different employers. They were both government employees doing a similar job. In the lift to the Rail Management Centre, Sabrina asked the question she did not really want to ask but knew that she had to. "So how is it looking? How bad is the footage? What happened?"

A MOMENT IN TIME by Eric Brook

"Well, we have the footage saved from the platform just before the time of the incident. One of the operators is going back at the moment to see how long the man has been hanging around for. At the moment, we don't think that it involves any foul play. You know how it is, we have to work backwards." The supervisor clicked his card onto the card reader and the door opened. "I've got one of my best operators on the case. He likes this sort of thing."

Sabrina could see many camera images on the large monitors in front of her. "At the moment, we are concentrating on this incident and how it is affecting the whole City Circle line. As you can see, the Underground is pretty full, more than usual." Sabrina could see live footage from Central. She could see that the rescue effect was continuing. Leila and Caroline were talking to people, hopefully witnesses. Nicole was watching the rescue effort intently from platform 18 with the fire brigade. Sabrina could see all that and she was not even on the platform.

She thought it would be pretty cool if she could see and hear what her officers could see and hear just like on a Channel 10 TV show called Rush. They were a fictional Special Operations Group and they were highly trained, highly tooled up and highly wired for sound and vision.

"Sabrina, meet Peter. He'll look after you. If you need anything, let me know."

A MOMENT IN TIME by Eric Brook

"Hi, Peter. What have you got for me?", Sabrina asked.

Working feverishly with his keyboard and mouse, Peter found the footage that he thought Sabrina was looking for.

"Well, Sabrina, he comes onto the platform just before 5pm from the Devonshire Street end. He paces around a bit and is on the platform for about 5 minutes. A bit later, he decides to jump off the platform and the train hits him. He wasn't pushed or chased." Peter plays the footage. It is never easy to watch the footage but it had to be done. Sabrina watches intently, trying to assess what the man was thinking in the minutes before, if anything.

She knew that some people hung around for a while before deciding to try to kill themselves but others got straight to the station and jumped right away.

"At that time of day", Peter continued, "those two platforms are quite busy as you can see. Several trains on both platforms come and go while he is there but for some reason, the train that he jumped in front of was going a lot slower than the rest of them. It appears as though the slowest train got him. He is still alive, isn't he?".

A MOMENT IN TIME by Eric Brook

Peter knew the answer to the question but asked it anyway. "If he jumped in front of any of the other trains that went faster, he might be dead by now. Note that he did jump from the arrival end of the platform. If he didn't do that, the driver would have had a hope and may have been able to stop."

In her own mind, Sabrina could now see that there was no other people that were involved. She would need the footage but in her mind, it was not worth getting the crime scene Police out here, rushing through the city traffic. She asked Peter for a form to gain access to the footage. While she was filling in the paperwork, she called Nicole.

Because of the live camera images, she could see Nicole answer the phone. "Nic, it's Sab. I'm up here with the security guys. I've seen some footage. He was on the platform for about 5 minutes before he decided to jump. Looks like he picked the slowest possible train to jump in front of. I don't think it is worth getting the DNA Nerds down here for this. Grab what pics you can and I'll be down in a second." Speaking on a mobile phone enabled Sabrina to speak a little freer than she would over the radio.

Sabrina then made a similar phone call to the radio operators at the Sydney Police Centre. "Hello, radio. It's City 14 here. Just to let you know, there's no suspicious circumstances here at Central. I've had a look at the footage, the guy's jumped with no help from anyone else. The Ambos will have the guy out soon. There's no need for our Rescue or Crime Scene."

Back on platform 16, Leila and Caroline were trying to find witnesses. Sure, they had a statement from the train driver. The train guard did not see anything. When the train hit the person, the guard's carriage was close to arriving onto the platform. Many people who may have seen the incident, none of them were making themselves known to the policewomen. Maybe they did not want to get involved, maybe they thought that the cameras would see what had to be seen. Maybe they thought that what the train driver saw would have been enough. Many people wanted to see the rescue effort but no one wanted to own up and say "we saw it."

Nicole and the rescue teams had soon discovered that the best way to access the man under the train was not to be on platform 17 but from platform 18. There was no trains running past platform 18 and there was no platform on that side of the train. Nicole had the station's exhibit camera and took a variety of photos. Occasionally she would take a call from Sabrina or the radio room. The rescue workers were working really hard to get the man out of the train. Nicole did not want to be the female paramedic who was under the train talking to the man and treating his injuries.

A MOMENT IN TIME by Eric Brook

When she arrived, the man was screaming a lot but over time, his screaming reduced. Nicole did not know if that meant that the paramedic gave him drugs or not. Hopefully he was not in too much pain.

Nicole wondered what could be so bad that the man thought that the best option was to jump in front of a train. Was it selfishness? Was it a call for help? Was the fact that the train was going slowly the only reason he was still alive? At this stage, Nicole had no idea about the extent of the man's injuries. She did not know if the paramedics knew, either. It was difficult to assess the man's condition properly while he was under the train. There was not a lot Nicole could do at the moment. All she could do was wait.

The fire brigade and the paramedics had their hands full, though. Nicole's appearance there kept the media and the general public back at a safe distance. With Nicole's experience, she knew that the man did not have a lot of time. She had been there at Central for about 45 minutes. She also knew that the rescuers were working hard after difficult circumstances.

On this occasion, there was a good result - well as good as there could be under the circumstances. The rescue teams were sliding the man from under the train on a spine board. The man was in a lot of pain on the back of the spine board. The paramedics had left a stretcher on the platform. There was no use trying to lift the man and the heavy stretcher from the tracks onto the platform. It was easier to put the man on the spine board. The spine board was a precaution. It was easier to lift the man and the spine board onto the platform.

On the opposite platform, Leila and Caroline were still having no luck with the witnesses. Most people were more worried about going home. After walking up and down the platform, they went over to where Nicole was standing. It was good for all three of them to be able to see the man be lifted up onto the platform. He was in no state to tell anyone what happened. Nicole had a telephone conversation with Sabrina to tell her that the man had been freed. With his condition, the man could not talk at the moment. There was no reason for the police to go with the man in the Ambulance or to the hospital. They could get all the information they needed from calling the hospital.

Having seen the video evidence, Sabrina thought that no crime had been committed and that no one else was involved. Believe it or not, it was not a crime to jump in front of a train. Nor was it an offence to disrupt the city or to have up to 15 emergency workers involved in a rescue. Nor would the man be given a bill to recover the costs involved. When he was physically better, he would also have to be mentally assessed. The priority for the moment was for the paramedics to get the man to the hospital.

A MOMENT IN TIME by Eric Brook

With all that had happened, the last task that Caroline and Leila had to do was to roll up all the crime scene tape. Sabrina was really anal about re-using the tape. It was almost as if Sabrina was paying for the tape herself, Caroline thought. With arms full of crime scene tape, the three officers return to their car, ready for the next job. Sabrina would get started on the paperwork from the station. If the man's condition changed (especially if it changed for the worse), the hospital would call Sabrina.

Nicole reached for her portable radio. "City 36, back on from Central station." City 36 were ready for their next job. There always was a next job......

Chapter 11 - Katrina to the Rescue!

5.10pm Thursday 01 April 2010

Zooming up the ramp, Richard "Chicago" Crawford was driving Pumper 1. He was very surprised to see a tram crawling up the ramp. He could not see it at the intersection but as he climbed further up the ramp, he saw it looming rather large through his windscreen.

"WHAT THE FFUU"

"CHICAGO!", Renee yelled. Renee did not yell at work often and especially not at her senior driver.

Renee and Richard yelled at once, somewhat drowning each other out. He lifted his right foot off the accelerator and brushed the brake, trying to warn Scott behind him in the Rescue. Renee blipped the siren. BLIP BLIP BLIP.

"No use doing that, Reno!", Chicago said. "We can't get past him. There's no way to get past him and he can't swerve."

A MOMENT IN TIME by Eric Brook

"Well, I didn't want Scotty and Kat imprints in the back of the Pumper, Rich!", Renee explained. He nodded. She looked in the mirror. Her Rescue truck was ok and following them up the ramp.

"Sydney Comms, Pumper 1 & Rescue 1 code 3", Renee said over the radio.

The two trucks followed the tram turning to the right. The tram stopped at the station seemingly unaware at what was going behind it. The two fire trucks parked off the tram tracks. "Alright, one of you come with me. I don't care who. The rest of you, stay with Chicago. We might need you to bring some stuff to us.",

Renee instructed the crew. Renee, Katrina, Scotty and Troy left the trucks and headed over towards platform 16. Scott had a trauma kit and Troy grabbed a fire extinguisher, just in case. Walking through the main concourse, many passengers were moving around the station. Troy almost walked into several people, all girls, co-incidentally. "Eyes back in your head and on the job, T!", Renee scolded him.

"Sydney Comms calling Pumper 1, message."

A MOMENT IN TIME by Eric Brook

Renee's radio came to life. "Pumper 1, from the Ambos, the best access to the train is via platform 18. They are waiting for you. Power is cut, train is secured."

"Pumper 1, power cut, train secured, heading to platform 18", Renee repeated the message to confirm it.

There were many people rushing around the station. On the suburban concourse level, the team could see an Ambulance motorcycle shut down near the stairs leading to platform 18. "Wouldn't mind riding that!", T chuckled. Renee shook her head.

"What, ride the bike or the rider?", Scotty said as he punched T in the arm.

"BOYS!"

Renee did not have to say any more. Climbing the stairs, the crew could hear the screams of the man under the train. It was not a nice sound to hear.

"Ready, Kat?", Renee asked.

"Ready as I'll ever be, Renee!"

A MOMENT IN TIME by Eric Brook

Kat breathed deeply. At the top of the stairs, the train looked strange with the front of the train on the platform and the back half not. The sign on front of the train above the front windows kept flashing in bright orange letters "Liverpool via Bankstown."

"T, go to platform 17 and see what you can see there.", Renee ordered. She walked up to the Ambulance Supervisor who she knew slightly by being at other jobs. "G'day, Keith. What have we got?"

"G'day, Renee. Guy jumped in front of the train. He's under the second carriage there. It's a tight squeeze under there, stuffed if I know how he managed that!"

"Do we know if he is alive? How bad is he?", Renee asked, as if somehow she could not hear his loud, chilling screams. Keith explained that a paramedic was talking to the man from a distance but had not been under the train yet. Looking at the train, Renee thought for a few seconds. "We are going to need airbags. No one is going under that train until we put airbags in and lift it."

Renee turned her radio to another channel. "Chicago, got your ears on, Firemanground?" Each truck had a main channel that they used to talk to Comms and a separate channel (known as a Fireground channel) to talk amongst themselves. She did not want to walk back to the truck if she did not need to. They did not need to talk directly to

A MOMENT IN TIME by Eric Brook

Comms on this channel. The channel was officially called a tactical channel where they often talked about what was happening with the incident, especially if the incident was over a wide area.

"Yo, Reno, wassup?", Richard answered on his radio while sitting in his truck, well out of Renee's line of sight.

"Rich, grab Shawno and get him and someone else to grab an airbag pack and two small airbags. I'll send T over to show them the way back here, ok? Got that?"

"Roger, Reno!"

Meanwhile, Keith and his paramedic was having a mid track meeting. The paramedic wanted to get under the train before the airbags were in place. Upon hearing this, Renee asserted "no way, Keith! The airbags have to go in." Keith told her that the train was stable and not derailed. The paramedic's plan was to climb under the train and medicate the man while the airbags were going in. The paramedic said she needed another pair of hands, Katrina's hands in particular.

Scott and Renee put their heads together in thought. "I've got no dramas with it but we should involve Katrina in this discussion. After all, she's the one going under it, not me." Scott said. "It's her first big rescue. She'll be fine. Ask her."

Renee walked over to Katrina who was looking at the front of the train. "Hey Kat, can you please go under the train? The paramedic needs a hand. I can understand if you say no. We are getting airbags but the medic wants to see the patient and she can't wait."

"Sure, Boss!" Katrina said. "That's why I went to Rescue school!"

"Be careful under there, Kat. Keep your ears and eyes open.", Renee instructed in trainer mode. "I'll be right here as will Scotty. The airbags are coming. Keep the radio on, if you need anything, sing out!"

Renee switched her radio back to the main channel.

"Sydney Comms, Pumper 1, Blue."

"Pumper 1."

A MOMENT IN TIME by Eric Brook

"Pumper 1, train versus pedestrian as per print out. Male patient alive. Rescue 1 and Ambos assisting in recovery. No further assistance expected at this stage.", Renee asserted over the radio. It was important for Renee to let Comms know as soon as possible if she needed extra assistance.

Renee grabbed some supplies that the paramedic asked for and placed them on the backboard. "Good luck, Kat. Take it easy under there. It's not pretty. Don't forget your gloves.", Renee instructed.

Laying down on the ground, Katrina looked under the train. It was going to be a tight squeeze. Maybe she will need to get used to it as the smaller of the two rescue operators in the platoon. Worming her way over the rail, Katrina would have preferred not to have slid in over the rough rocks. Then again, she thought, if the paramedic could do it, she could.

The torch attached to her shirt helped to lit up the scene somewhat. She could see bits of body and some blood over the rocks. After a couple of minutes of stomach sliding, Katrina met up with Natalie the paramedic. Somehow, Katrina earned the nickname of "Rescue Chick" from Natalie.

A MOMENT IN TIME by Eric Brook

Working together, they immobilised Steve, the patient. Katrina wondered how Steve managed to fit under the limited room available. Looking over Steve quickly, Katrina saw that he was missing an arm and a leg. She hid her squeamishness from Natalie and Steve well. She needed to, the last thing that everyone needed was Katrina adding vomit to the blood and body tissues already under the train. She was glad that Natalie was doing the majority of the hands on work. This soon changed though.

Discreetly as she could under the circumstances, Natalie asked Katrina to bag Steve's missing body parts. Sternly whispering back, Katrina was shocked. "You want me to do what!" Natalie explained that it was important to bag up the parts in different bags so there was every chance that they could be re-attached at the hospital. Resigning herself to the task, Katrina knew exactly what she had to do. She was hoping that Steve could not see his missing limbs.

No wonder Renee warned her to be careful. "How you doing under there, Kat?", Renee asked over the radio.

"Not bad, considering. It's not pretty under here."

That was an understatement from the rookie Rescue operator.

A MOMENT IN TIME by Eric Brook

While Katrina was under the train, Renee, Scott, Troy & Shawn were busy putting the airbags in place. Guided by the railway training they had received earlier and the railway's own fire team that had arrived a few minutes before, the team placed an airbag either side of the wheels of the train on the side closest to them. The bags were deflated and were attached to an air compressor with hoses. The air compressor was wheeled onto the platform by Shawn and Troy. It was too big to lift onto the tracks and there was no real need to do so.

When she was confident that the bags were in the right position, Renee radioed Katrina. "Ok, Kat, we are going to lift now. Ready?"

"Ready. I could do with some extra room under here."

Renee signalled to Shawno who was standing on the platform next to the compressor. It was a noisy machine. Even so, Shawno still had to warn some people to move away. The compressor started much like a lawn mower did. It was very loud. The patient's screams had quietened down by this point but even at the height of his screams, the machine was still louder. Slowly, the two airbags started to grow in size. It started growing wide first and then it started to grow taller.

A MOMENT IN TIME by Eric Brook

Located either side of the wheels, it took a few moments to raise to the floor level of the train. By this stage, a lot of air was being pumped into the bags. Renee warned Katrina that she should notice the bag rising soon.

"Can't come soon enough, Boss!", Katrina said over the radio. "We need to get the patient out soon!"

At long last, the people not under the train noticed the train starting to rise slowly. Care needed to be taken because there was no airbags on the other side of the train. With the train about 50 centimetres above the rail, Renee asked Katrina if they had enough room to get the patient out.

"That's a great improvement, boss. A bit more would be nice though! I'll slide the haz bag out first and then we'll bring Steve with us", Renee's radio squeaked with Katrina's higher than normal voice.

When the bio-waste bags came out from under the train, Renee's breath was taken away. She'd been at City of Sydney for several years. Normally in situations where people got hit by trains, it was Renee's experience that the person had died by the time she arrived. This was the first time that she could remember being involved in a rescue under a train where the patient was alive.

A MOMENT IN TIME by Eric Brook

Handling the bags with the arm and leg inside was not something Renee had thought of. She handed the bags to one of the paramedics who was standing by for safe keeping.

"Ok, Renee! We are coming out now. Have the medics waiting."

If Katrina had trouble getting under the train, she was about to have even more trouble getting out. She was still lying on her front. Her legs were pointing out towards Renee and she needed to wiggle out. Just to make things harder, she was at the feet .... oops ... foot of Steve. She was slowly dragging him out from under the train while he was strapped to the spine board. Natalie was pushing slightly at the head of the board.

"Pumper 1, sitrep (situation report) from Central. Patient is about to be released. Further message to follow."

Katrina was surprised how quiet Steve was. The main thing that could be heard on the way out of the train was the beep beep beep of the heart monitor. Katrina did not know what drugs Natalie had given Steve, nor was she expected to. Whatever it was, it was working a treat, Katrina thought. She had been lucky so far in life as she had no major injuries or illnesses and had not had any deaths in her immediate family.

A MOMENT IN TIME by Eric Brook

While she had been stationed at Lidcombe, she had not had a lot to do with trains despite the fact that the fire station was across the road from the train station. The night of the railway station was the exception rather than the rule.

Soon enough, Katrina eased herself out from under the train. Not long after, the harsh sunlight hit Steve and then Natalie the paramedic. "Great job, you two!", said Renee with a touch of glee in her voice. She had some idea how difficult it was for both women under the train. Katrina stretched herself after being cramped under the train. It felt great to be able to stand up rather than lying down on the uneven rocks.

Had the incident been at an underground station, the majority of tracks are situated on concrete floors which would have been a little easier for Katrina. Still, the little discomforting niggling pain that Katrina was feeling at that minute was nothing compared to what patient Steve was feeling. He was now about start his trip to the hospital in the back of an ambulance.

Even though he would be in good hands if he made it to the hospital alive, she knew that his life was going to change dramatically. While the blood and the gore affected her slightly at the time, thankfully she did not vomit in front of the patient.

A MOMENT IN TIME by Eric Brook

"Renee, I need to freshen up before I get back in the truck. Can you spare me a minute?", Katrina asked.

"No worries, Kat. Go back to the truck when you are done. Scott will pack up the airbags. Take your time.", Renee gave her a sly wink as she said this.

Renee had some idea why Katrina needed to freshen up. Renee had to do the same herself early in her career. It was a natural reaction to what was an awful smell. The smell could take a while to leave a person's nostrils, too.

"Sydney Comms, Pumper 1, green."

"Pumper 1, pass your stop message.", the voice at the other end of Renee's radio answered.

"Pumper 1, from Central station as per previous sitreps. Male patient released by Rescue and Ambos. Patient about to be conveyed to RPA by Ambulance. Making up now. The railway blokes are doing the wash down.", Renee reported.

"1759. Channel clear."

A MOMENT IN TIME by Eric Brook

Katrina took the lift to the lower level of the station. It was lucky for her that the lift was not the high speed lifts that were used at Sydney Tower and other high rise buildings otherwise she might have lost her lunch. Sedately, the lift gently lowered her to the ground level. She walked fast to the female toilets that were nearby.

Holding back the vomit that she had been wanting to get rid of for the last 30 minutes, Katrina found an empty cubicle at the end of the row. She placed her helmet on the hook behind the door and closed it. Confident that she was out of sight of the general public, she relaxed and let the vomit out of her body and into the toilet bowl. It was not pretty and not ladylike but then again, neither was the last 30 minutes.

It was lucky that Central station had toilets that were so close to where she was. For that five minutes at least, Katrina was Ms Joanne Citizen. As much as she did not want to do what she had just done while on scene, she did not want to do that at the fire station, either.

She did not want her platoon to think she was weak. While she thought that most rescue operators did not like blood and guts, they did not show it publicly. Flushing the vomit away, Katrina placed the toilet seat down and took off one of her work boots. She then took off her sweaty navy blue sock and briefly placed it near her nose, hoping to get rid of the near death smell. Breathing in deeply, she preferred her own smell compared to patient Steve's. She had certainly worked up a sweat underneath the train.

While she could not do much about the gear she was wearing until she could get back to the station, her own smell was relatively nice. Putting her sock and boot back on, Katrina left the cubicle. As most normal people would do after throwing up, she rinsed her mouth out, washed her face a little and then left the toilet with little thought. Walking back to the fire engine, Katrina felt a lot better. She eased herself back through the crowds and soon made it back to the truck where Chicago, Pumper 1's driver, was waiting.

"Tough call, Kat?", Chicago asked. He loved to mentor the new people to the platoon. Sometimes he led by example but he saw the need for some words of encouragement. "I heard you got the guy out. Good job."

"Yeah. It wasn't pretty. Tight fit under there. Can't wait to have a shower!", Katrina replied. "The quicker we get out of here, the quicker we can go home. Are we on overtime, Chicago?"

"When Reno put in the stop, the OT meter started ticking. If you are so concerned, what are you doing here? Those airbags don't put themselves back, you know."

A MOMENT IN TIME by Eric Brook

"I had to visit the little girl's room. Reno must have thought it about time that T and O did some work for a change. Scotty too. They should be back soon."

"Reckon he'll live?"

"Dunno. I was shocked at how he has made it this far. His life is screwed. Lost an arm and a leg, you know. Poor bloke."

In the meantime, the job at the platform was not quite complete. Talking with the railway fire officer, the railway boys had agreed with Renee to do what was blandly called "the wash down." This meant using a high pressure hose to wash the bottom of the train, the tracks and the rails. The last thing people waited to see when waiting for a train was parts of someone on the tracks. With the railway fire officer near the wheels, Shawno slowly started to deflate the airbags. It was very important to lower the airbags very slowly, mostly not to damage the train.

The two fire services had trained together for this sort of eventuality. While Shawno was not a rescue operator, he was expected to be able to help out in a situation just like this. Soon enough, the train was back on the rails. With that minor milestone reached, Shawno and Troy could remove the airbags and start to roll them up. Disconnecting the air hoses, Renee thankfully turned the air compressor off. Everyone on the platform was thankful about that, Renee guessed. She sure was!

Rolling up the airbags into their carry bags pushed out some more air. As long as the airbags fit in the carry bags, that was good. With the airbags secured after a couple of minutes effort, Troy and Shawno carried the bags away back to the truck. Scott wheeled the compressor and Renee carried the fire extinguisher which thankfully did not need to be used.

Throwing Katrina's trauma bag on her back, Renee and the team left the platform. The only emergency service Renee could see still on the platform was the railway's own fire service who surprisingly agreed to the wash down. It must have been the famous Renee Wagner charm.

"Ok, guys. Let's go home. Can't keep the night shift without a pair of trucks, can we?", Renee laughed.

It was nearly home time and it could not come soon enough for the day shift of City of Sydney's Pumper and Rescue. The Flyer and Bronto crews were probably halfway home by now as they were still at the station.

"Home, thanks Chicago!", Renee laughed.

Chapter 12 - Natalie To The Rescue!

5.10pm Thursday 01 April 2010

Sliding into her jumpsuit and leather jacket, Natalie quickly went to the garage and jumped on her bike. Turning the key, the bike roared into life. Natalie revved the bike and turned on the lights and sirens. Behind her in the Supervisor's station wagon was Keith along with the Chronicles of EMS crew. An Ambulance was also on the way from another part of the city.

The helmet camera that Natalie was wearing would give you a great feeling for speed. Every time Natalie's head moved, the camera moved too. All of the traffic decisions were hers alone. She had no second pair of eyes to help her through. She was quicker than Keith though.

Natalie checked her right as she turned left onto Broadway. Weaving her way through the traffic, frequent intersections and heavy traffic tested her abilities and reflexes. She needed to slow down for some of the intersections where she did not have the right of way. Unfortunately, the Ambulance Service's vehicles did not have the ability to change the traffic lights but somehow, a late running bus did. Now was not a good time to think about that, though.

A MOMENT IN TIME by Eric Brook

Intersections with traffic lights were trouble if there was red lights. The motorcycle was handy in this situation. The bike had greater acceleration than the station wagon that Keith was driving and almost double that of a regular ambulance. Unlike a larger vehicle, the bike could get through in between the parked cars.

The important intersection of George Street, Pitt Street and Broadway was fast approaching. In some way, one direction of traffic would probably be going. The best Natalie could ask for would be for the pedestrians to be crossing. At some of the city intersections, the lights allowed the pedestrians to cross all at once. Luckily for her, Natalie managed to time her run perfectly and traffic was going in her direction. Leaning to the right, Natalie turned towards Pitt Street but turned sharper into a road leading to the station. She was almost there.

With a last spurt of speed, Natalie arrived at the station entrance. Repeating something she had done earlier in the afternoon, she turned the siren off but kept the lights flashing. She kept the engine revving high as she dodged pedestrians in all directions.

In a case of dumb luck, Natalie spied that a side security gate was left open near platform 3. "Why not!", she yelled to herself under her breath. "Wittoh medic, let's do it!"

A MOMENT IN TIME by Eric Brook

Turning to the right and then straight through the gate, there were a lot less passengers on this side of the building. There was not a constant flow of passengers as not all the platforms were being used. The platforms and the path moved to the right so Natalie turned right and then quickly to the left.

Central was an old station and there were corners and passageways everywhere. Passing a newsagent, Natalie decided to keep going. Most of the motorcycle medics would be off their bikes and running but not her. There was an escalator to the left and empty stairs to the right.

Bump.

Bump.

Bump.

Bump.

Bump.

Bump.

Bump.

Bump.

Bump.

A MOMENT IN TIME by Eric Brook

Slowly and carefully, Natalie rode her motorcycle down the stairs. Passengers on the escalators were stunned. Of course, no one dare say anything.

Bump.

Bump.

Bump.

Bump.

Bump.

Bump.

Having passed that challenge, the final part of the journey was easy in comparison. She had been around Central station many times and Natalie knew she had to take the right hand passage.

Arriving at the stairs up to platform 18, Natalie shut her bike down. She took out her trauma kit and heart monitor and replaced them with her helmet and leather jacket. Going up the stairs two at a time, swarms of people were in Natalie's way. After all, it was the height of peak hour.

"Paramedics, coming through! Excuse me, paramedics coming through!", Natalie shouted at the stair full of passengers. "Sydney, Bike 1 on scene. Sitrep to follow".

http://www.amomentintimenovel.com

Arriving on platform 18, Natalie could see the train. She could see that the train was half on platform 17 and half off. She could also hear screaming from under the train. She could not see any other emergency services on the platform. Her plan may have worked. The plan was to go to platform 18 so there was more room to work. There was not a lot of room to work between the train and platform 17. There was a lot of room between the train and platform 18. Natalie spoke on the radio again.

"Sydney, Bike 1. Confirmed train versus human accident on platform 17. Patient is still alive. No other services on site. Best access via platform 18 for us and rescue. Need you to confirm trains stopped and power off, platforms 17 & 18 at Central."

While Natalie wanted to jump on the tracks, they could have still been active. She went to near where the screams were coming from, 2 carriages from the front of the train. Placing her supplies on the ground, the paramedic laid down on her front on platform 18, facing the train. She might not be able to touch the man under the train yet but she could still get started talking to him until the power was off and the trains were stopped.

"Hey mate, can you hear me?", Natalie yelled. "My name is Natalie and I'm a paramedic. We will get you out. Can you hear me?"

A MOMENT IN TIME by Eric Brook

The man screamed loudly. Sure, it was not a reply worthy of a dinner party but it was better than silence at this point. At the very least, Natalie knew the man was breathing, awake and alive. She wanted to keep it that way.

A crowd gathered around Natalie. "Unless you are a doctor or can help me, move along people, nothing to see here!", Natalie yelled.

The Communications Centre called Natalie on the radio. "Sydney calling Bike 1." Hopefully this call would mean Natalie could go onto the tracks.

"Bike 1, Sydney."

"Bike 1, the trains are stopped and the power is off as you asked. Rescue is not far off. How's the patient?"

"Sydney, the male patient is stuck under the second carriage. I can hear him but I can't see him at the moment. I'm going in for a closer look now."

Natalie eased herself down onto the tracks like a person would ease themselves into a pool. Now standing on the track, she could not reach her gear.

A MOMENT IN TIME by Eric Brook

"Excuse me, could someone please pass me my gear?",
Natalie asked no one in particular. Soon enough, two
people handed Natalie's bag down to her.

Grabbing her bag, Natalie walked towards the screaming
man. She followed the screams and placed her bags onto
the rocks. Natalie knelt down and looked underneath the
train. She could see the man for the first time. Not
expecting the man to be alive, it was a bonus that he was
still alive. He was not out of the woods yet. "Hey mate,
there you are! Where are you hurting?", Natalie asked.

"Oh man! I'm sore all over. HELP ME!"

"We'll get you out of this, mate. Don't you worry about
that! I'm here and more help is coming. You are in good
hands."

Natalie looked up and could see Keith, the Chronicles of
EMS crew and two more paramedics. The two
paramedics leapt onto the tracks. She walked over to
Keith who was standing on the platform. Her head barely
reached platform level. Unless Keith crouched, Natalie
had a great view of his shoes. He crouched, not wanting
to get onto the tracks unless he could help it.

"Ok, Nat, what have you got?", Keith asked.

A MOMENT IN TIME by Eric Brook

As he asked that question, the Fire Brigade's officers had also arrived. Keith looked down the track trying to possible think of something that Natalie had not considered or that she had forgotten about.

"Well, the guy is under this carriage here. It's a tight squeeze under there. He's in a lot of pain. He needs pain relief, quickly. I think I can reach him but it isn't good down there."

Keith and the leader of the Fire Brigade worked on a plan. They figured that they needed to lift the train slightly to allow someone to get underneath the train to assess the man. Then they could try to slide him out. That was the best thing to try. They could not do a proper assessment on him at the moment from where they were. They could not even see the man.

Natalie called Keith to get onto the track. The Fire Brigade officer joined them. This way, they could talk easier. Keith explained what the plan was. "We are going to put a couple of airbags under the train. That will give us more room to assess him."

"We can't wait that long!", Natalie said through gritted teeth not wanting the whole of Central station to hear her. "The firies aren't even set up yet! I'm not waiting until they decide to man up. This man needs pain relief!".

A MOMENT IN TIME by Eric Brook

Keith's body language was closed and not to Natalie's liking. "Damm it, Keith! I'll throw you under a train and see how you like it! All I'm saying is to medicate him!"

Natalie was fighting on behalf of her patient. She did not care that the Chronicles crew was filming over Keith's shoulder. This was part of the job, trying to do what is the best for the patient. In this case, her patient needed pain relief and he needed it now, not in 10 minutes time.

"How exactly do you propose to do that, Natalie? How are you going to reach him? How are you going to relieve his pain? Will you even fit?", Keith asked with a hint of despair in his lowered voice.

"You might be 6 foot 4", Natalie looked up at his face, "but you won't get under there. Rick over there hasn't got a hope unless the train's a mile off the ground. And Tim doesn't know what day it is."

"So you are going to do this all yourself? You are going to get under the train and assess him and drug him all by yourself?", Keith asked. "What if he codes under there? Then what? You going to drag himself yourself?"

Natalie looked at the emergency workers on site. She had already said that none of her paramedical colleagues could get under there. She looked wider to the firefighters standing around. Not even the Chronicles of EMS guys could fit under there even if they could assist.

Natalie and Keith were still talking closely so no one else could hear them. "We are wasting time. That rescue chick can fit under. I'll take her with me." Natalie's last words was not a question or a polite request. It was a statement.

"Fine. I'll speak to the O-I-C." Keith said. Apart from the fact that she was not a paramedic, the "rescue chick" as Natalie called her was a similar size to Natalie. Keith knew he was running out of time. He knew Natalie would try and do what she wanted anyway. Already, Natalie was on the ground, talking to the man. Keith went to see the leader of the Fire Brigade.

Meanwhile, Natalie was calling out to the man. "I'm coming to help you, mate! I'm Natalie and I'm an Ambo. What's your name?"

In between the screams, the man said his name was Steve. "Alright, Steve. I'm coming in. Can you see me?" Steve screamed and Natalie did not know if that was a yes or no answer to the question but she did not really care. At least he was talking and if he was talking, he was breathing. If he was breathing, he was not dead.
Natalie was now under the train. There was not a lot of room under there. Somehow, the bottom of the train was greasy. Natalie was sliding the best she could with the

uneven rocks, avoiding rubbish that people had thrown onto the tracks. As she got closer, she was also avoiding Steve's blood and body tissue. "Steve, I'm coming!" Steve groaned. She slid along the ground like a snake. It was lucky that she did not wear her leather jacket under there. "Nearly there, Steve. Keep still, mate. The pain will be gone soon."

After a couple of minutes, Natalie reached Steve. "Hey, Steve. Good to see you. I'm going to kill your pain and then we'll lift the train up a bit and get you out." Steve groaned. "Lie still, mate. I need to have a look at you."

The body tissue that Natalie met on the way to Steve was the tip of the iceberg. It was pretty dark under the train but even so, Natalie could see that Steve had lost his right arm and leg. No wonder he was groaning. Natalie reached for her radio.

"Keith, I could use a good pair of ...... um I need some help under here!", she whispered into the radio. She did not know for certain if Steve knew that he now was missing an arm or a leg, hence her pause. "My patient's name is Steve. I need as much morph as I can get. We need to get him out but he needs pain relief NOW." She empathised the word now. "Get Rescue Chick under here with some morph, a C collar and a backboard."

"Copy, Nat. Anything else?"

A MOMENT IN TIME by Eric Brook

"Tell Rescue Chick to be careful."

Keith went into Natalie's trauma bag and got a C collar, a space blanket while Tim retrieved a needle loaded with morphine from his kit. He put that into a smaller bag. He also got a backboard off the stretcher that Rick and Tim brought up with them.

"Here you go", Keith said to the Fire Brigade Rescue Operator named Katrina. "Be careful. If she gives you trouble, let me know."

"I thought the patient was male?", Katrina asked.

"He is. His name is Steve. Princess Natalie is waiting and she doesn't like that. Get going."

Katrina placed the backboard onto the ground and placed the supplies on top of the backboard. Getting onto the ground, Katrina eased herself onto the ground. "Natalie! I'm coming!"

A few minutes later, Katrina introduced herself to Natalie and Steve. "You took your sweet arse time, Rescue Chick!", Natalie said sarcastically. It was true, even though she knew Katrina was only following orders from her officer.

A MOMENT IN TIME by Eric Brook

On the platform, the Chronicles of EMS team were watching intently. "Do you have trains like this up your way, Mark?", Justin asked. Mark looked at the train. There were long distance trains but not a commuter service such as the one that continued to go on in the background despite this incident.

"Nothing like this! I can't believe these two women, they are incredible! I don't see any guys under that train!", Mark observed.

Meanwhile, Katrina was under the train. It was her first time under a train. She thought that Natalie must have spent half her life under there, she looked that comfortable. "Here's your stuff. What do you need me to do?", Katrina asked.

Natalie reached for the bag. She saw the morphine needle in a protective cover. She also grabbed the space blanket and the C collar. Despite everything, Natalie was not comfortable but having some supplies and an extra pair of hands would come in handy.

"I need you to hold his neck still and I'll collar him.", Natalie told Katrina. Speaking to Steve, she told him the plan. "Steve, meet Katrina. She is going to put a special collar on your neck to keep it still. Then we are going to give you some drugs then work on getting you out of here."

A MOMENT IN TIME by Eric Brook

Katrina put her hands on the upper half of Steve's head. Natalie put the collar on Steve's neck like she had done many times before to other patients. But this was the first time she had been under a 45 tonne train carriage, though. Doing up the collar, Natalie asked him if he was ready for the drugs. Obviously that was a silly question.

Natalie reached into her bag and grabbed the needle. Meanwhile, Katrina remained at Steve's head. Finding the one hand that he still had attached, Natalie put a cannula into the top of Steve's hand and then injected the morphine. It would work quickly, Natalie knew and Katrina hoped. In a minute or so, Steve was a lot quieter. The morphine had worked, for now.

"Keith", Natalie spoke into her radio. "I need my heart monitor. Morphine is on board. I need a bio bag or three, too. I'll send Rescue.... um .... Katrina out to get it."

"Natalie, I'll be fine. Just slide the board out and he'll put the stuff on it and slide it back." Katrina asserted. "Work smarter, not harder."
"Good thinking, Rescue Kat! When the stuff gets back, we need to bag the bits up. In the meantime, cover him up with the blanket. Do you think we can board him now?"

"Let's not risk it. Let them raise the train a bit." As Katrina spoke, she covered Steve up with the lightweight space blanket. "How you doing, Steve?"

Steve groaned but not as loud as before. Katrina slid the backboard out to Keith and soon after, he slid the board back with the heart monitor on it. Natalie got the monitor out of the bag and started attaching the pads to Steve's chest. Soon, Natalie could see exactly what Steve's heart was doing. She could see that his heart beat was below average but OK under the circumstances.

"Keith, how's the lifting of that train going?", Natalie asked. Keith told her in reply that the airbags were nearly ready to go. Raising the train with the airbags had to be really carefully done. The compressor was a purpose built model that was highly rated but it could still take some time to fill the airbags first then gradually raise the train.

Confident that Steve was too drugged to care what she was saying, Natalie started to relay Steve's condition to her base to relay that to the hospital. "Steve's a man in his mid twenties. He was hit by a train at an unknown speed and is currently underneath the train. He has lost his right arm and leg, left arm badly severed at the wrist. Heart rate is 80 over 50. GCS of 3 with one dose of morphine on board. Extreme blood loss is evident. No loss of conciousness since paramedic arrival. Patient immobilised by C-collar only due to space constraints. Awaiting Rescue to lift the train."

Switching radio channels, Natalie spoke to Keith. "He's losing heaps of blood. Rescue Kat is grabbing the limbs and tissue. Do you want me to give him blood and O2 here?"

A MOMENT IN TIME by Eric Brook

"Won't be long, Nat. Rescue are getting the bags ready now. Doesn't help that they are a Rescue Op short, you know! I'll let you know when we are lifting the train. Keep an eye on him. We'll hydrate when we get him out. Until we get him fully immobilised, keep him as comfortable as you can. And look after yourselves too!", Keith replied.

"Where else am I going to go? Idaho City?", Natalie snapped back. Katrina laughed at that Natalieism. Natalie smiled at Katrina. "Ya know, I could use a partner like you, Rescue Kat."

"I'll leave the blood and guts to you, Natalie. I like putting the wet stuff on the red stuff. Chopping up cars is pretty good, too.", Katrina said.

"Didn't see you earlier at Broadway. You would have some cutting done. Car versus bus. Have you filled those bags up yet?", Natalie enquired.

"Yep. Want me to send them out?"

"Sure."

"Keith, we are going to slide out the bio. Ready?"

A MOMENT IN TIME by Eric Brook

Upon his answer, Katrina slid the backboard out with Steve's arm and leg in separate bags. There was a slim chance they could re-attach the limbs back onto Steve's body. Soon enough, the empty board slid back. "Ok, ladies, the train is going up now. Tell me when to stop.", Keith explained.

Slowly, the train began to rise and the wheels left the rails. Katrina could see two airbags holding the train up. Placing the backboard next to Steve, Katrina went to Steve's feet and Natalie was near Steve's upper body. When the train was half a metre off the ground, Natalie told Keith to stop lifting the train. The train stopped moving.

Before moving Steve and immobilising him fully, Natalie wanted to medicate him again. Thankfully, Keith had sent along some extra morphine knowing that one dose was not enough. Natalie injected Steve with another dose of morphine, hoping that moving him would not cause any extra pain.

Natalie was now working well with Katrina. That was a nice surprise for both women. "Ok, Rescue Kat. Let's get Steve here onto the backboard. Roll him onto his left side. On 3."

A MOMENT IN TIME by Eric Brook

"1"

"2"

"3"

On hearing the number 3, the two women rolled Steve onto his left side. Sliding the spine board underneath him, they lowered Steve onto the board. Where Steve's right arm used to be, Natalie placed the heart monitor onto the board. "Let's go, Rescue Kat. We'll slide him out. You first."

It was not easy to slide both Steve out along with themselves at the same time. They inched their way out from underneath the train. Reaching the rail, Katrina stopped and eased herself over the rail. Natalie was right, no one else there would have fit. Finally, the bright sunlight and the ability to stand up vertically was a great relief to Natalie.

Two firemen lifted Steve onto the platform and then Rick and Tim lifted the backboard onto the stretcher. Padding some voids and tying the backboard to the stretcher, Rick gave Steve some fluid via the cannula which Natalie had inserted earlier.

A MOMENT IN TIME by Eric Brook

In what seemed like 2 hours but what was in reality closer to 25 minutes since they were under the train, Natalie and Katrina stood up. They were covered in sweat, grease and blood. They could both use a shower back at their respective stations.

"Good job, Rescue Kat. Think about what I said. See you next time. Call me at the station when you get back if you want to come out for a drink after work. My shout. Got a couple of guys you should meet." Natalie said as she helped Katrina to her feet. Natalie pointed to Mark and Justin on the platform and waved coyly. They were not shy about waving back.

"Thanks, Ambo Nat! I think I'll take you up on that offer for tonight!", Katrina replied.

"There won't be a next time!", Keith said sternly to Natalie. "I want to see you in my office before you go home. Go back to the station and clean yourself up, again. You are now out of service!" It was not very often that Keith forcibly removed a resource from service, especially a rapid response unit.

As Tim and Rick raised the stretcher and wheeled the lucky-to-be-alive Steve away along with Natalie's heart monitor, Katrina's space blanket and the bag of body parts, Natalie walked along the track towards the end of the platform, kicking the occasional drink can along the ground as she walked. She did not see or care about the crowd of people on the platform but she knew they were there.

She felt like screaming but knew she could not at that point. She could not understand why Keith seemed to be mad at her. She got there quickly, which was her job. She got the patient pain relief, which was her job. She stabilised the patient, which was her job. She got the patient out, which was her job.

She did not see Keith, Tim or Rick underneath the train treating Steve. It was her and Rescue Kat underneath the train who were greasy, smelly and covered in Steve's blood. Keith, Tim and Rick's uniforms were as clean as they were when they graduated from paramedic school.

Maybe that's why Keith was mad, Natalie thought. She was the bike medic whose bike spent half the shift parked because the rest of the Ambulance Service could not do their jobs, she thought.

Climbing up the ladder at the end of the platform, Natalie was physically and emotionally spent. She pushed the button for the lift. When it arrived, she went inside. As it lowered towards the concourse level, Natalie shed tears quietly. The first one was for the man who died in the toilets earlier. The second was for the driver who died at Broadway. The third was for Steve.

Chapter 13 - Goodnight, A Platoon!

6.15pm Thursday 01 April 2010

Back at the City of Sydney Fire Station, all of the trucks were back in their bays ready for the next call. The majority of the day crew had left for the day and the night crew were settling in for their shifts, checking their trucks.

While the outgoing shift might say "the trucks are sweet", it was important for the incoming shift to check anyway. There was a check list that the driver and the officer usually checked the truck together. Often the checks were easy, especially if there had not been any jobs where hoses were used.

On the far side of the station upstairs, the female showers were hot and steamy. Renee liked to go home feeling fresh, especially if she had just been on a job and was going home. She normally did not shower between jobs - the last thing she wanted was to be in the middle of a shower and the bells drop. But now she was not on the clock, she could take her time as the night shift Station Officer had taken charge. Renee was sweaty but not as sweaty as Katrina was in the next shower.

A MOMENT IN TIME by Eric Brook

While she was a new Rescue operator, Katrina had come through with flying colours today. Train rescues were difficult at the best of time. It was made even more difficult when the patient was alive. If the patient had died, there is not a major rush to extract them.

Depending on the situation, the body may even be left in-situ until crime scene or crash investigation police attended and documented the site. There were things that happened that afternoon that would not have happened if it was a body retrieval.

Katrina hoped that she would not be living inside various confined spaces while her rescue partner Scott would be standing around watching. As she learned today, being small could have some advantages. It would be up to Katrina (possibly with Renee's help) to make sure that Scott did his fair share.

Katrina wanted to scrub really hard and to wash that death right out of her hair. Sure, Steve had not died but the smell was similar. It was a smell that she would have to get used to, especially if the patient did not make it. In the living stakes, she got lucky today. This sort of rescue was the type of rescue Katrina wanted to do. It was not always the sort of rescue that made the last story of the night on the news because she rescued a cat from a drain. In fact, the night shift might have seen her on TV already.

A MOMENT IN TIME by Eric Brook

To both women, the hot water was heaven. Each drop hit their naked bodies and worked like a bolt of electricity, recharging their batteries. It was like grabbing a power-up in a video game. Hopefully the shower might help them both relax. Katrina might even need a massage to help with aches and pains. She was lying under that train in awkward and unusual positions for a relatively long time.

The two women were showering in separate cubicles but were able to talk to each other. They could not see each other, though. "So Kat, how do you think you went today?", Renee informally asked through the steam. She did not know if she would get an answer. It was not normal for both women to shower at the same time. Normally, Renee would be doing some paperwork at the end of the shift. She still needed to do her report about the Central job but she decided to have a shower first.

"I was surprised that he was still alive. I enjoyed working with Natalie. Bit sore, though!", Katrina answered while turning her shower off. Renee wanted to stay under the hot water for a bit longer so she kept her shower running. Even though she was no longer on the clock, Katrina was superstitious about being in the shower for too long and being sent on a call mid shower.

A MOMENT IN TIME by Eric Brook

"It's not an easy job, Kat. If you need to talk, you have my number. There's also the Employee Assistance Program. You might be ok now but it can hit you later. What are you planning on doing on tonight?" Renee asked. Their stretch of night shifts started in just under 24 hours time.

Even though there are beds at the station and they were allowed to sleep between calls, both women knew that it was important to assume that sleep was not possible overnight at the station due to their workload. They also knew that they would not be able to go straight to sleep even though they had been at work for 12 hours. Even though the last job was not an easy one, it had been a pretty quiet day overall by City of Sydney's standards.

"Natalie the Ambo invited me out to some drinks tonight. There's a couple of foreign paramedics in town she wants me to meet. They were at the Central job. The one in the blue was pretty hot."

This was the first time that Renee had heard Katrina talk about a member of the opposite sex in that manner. While they were both women, Renee and Katrina had so far kept their working relationship on a professional level. Renee was eager to ensure that sexual tension did not exist between the platoon. "Go and unwind, Kat. You've earned it. See you tomorrow night, yeah?"

A MOMENT IN TIME by Eric Brook

"No worries, Renee! Will do!", Katrina replied while getting dressed into a different set of clothes. She liked to have a couple of sets of casual clothes in her locker in case she decided to go out after work. It was not ideal to go out between two consecutive day shifts. Consecutive night shifts were worse depending on the night's work. She never had her work uniform on display on the way to or from work.

Renee had mentioned to Katrina that it was a good idea to have a shower before leaving the station at the end of the shift no matter what. Renee always felt better after the end of shift shower and Katrina soon got into this habit also. Katrina did not worry about this at her previous station as she lived close by. Now she was about 20 minutes away on the train with a 7 minute walk away from the train station.

Katrina sprayed some perfume onto herself and looked into the mirror of the female locker room. Unusually for her at work, she was wearing a dress. Also, her freshly washed hair was not in its normal ponytail but let out naturally. You would not think that an hour before, Katrina was under a train helping to rescue a man's life.

The hot water was still bouncing off Renee's shoulders and running down her toned body when the station's alarms went off. The Pumper and Flyer were being called. Out of habit, Renee took this as a sign to turn the shower off even though she was no longer on duty. If she was on duty, Renee rarely showered. She did not want to quickly towel down and get dressed and then rush downstairs.

Unlike many of Sydney's fire stations, City of Sydney still had a fireman's pole to quickly get to the ground floor. Partly in order to prevent the need for a pole, many stations were single level.

In the female locker room, Katrina also heard the alarm. Even if she was on duty, she was not going on that call anyway because it was not a job for the Rescue. She had quickly discovered that not every call was for her. Reaching into her locker, she grabbed her handbag and then closed her locker. As the nights in April were still warm, Katrina wore a dress without needing a jacket. The pink dress suited her complexion and was a nice change from the normal navy blue that she regularly wore at work. The dress was complemented with black knee high boots.

If you did not know any better, you would swear Katrina was on a date. Fully dressed again, she went to the fireman's pole and slid down it even though she was wearing a dress. She quietly said "woo hoo" as she slid down the pole.

Luckily for Katrina, the remaining members of the platoon were watching TV. Renee was still getting dressed so she did not see it either. Heading to the front door to the station, Katrina pulled her mobile phone out from her handbag and sent a text message. She wrote: "See you soon. Rescue Kat."

Because daylight saving was still in effect, there was still daylight even though it was well after 7pm. It was a nice night for a walk as it was still warm without being uncomfortable outside. Walking across to George Street, Katrina blended in with the myriad of locals and tourists walking around the cinema strip. The lights of the surrounding buildings were on but because the sun was still out, the lights did not seem to be on full brightness.

There was so much noise that was being funnelled down the alley of buildings. Most of the noise was due to the many cars, trucks and buses driving down the street. Occasionally there would be a siren competing with the rest of the noise. There was rarely a quiet moment in the centre of the city where someone could hear the birds singing.

Katrina was enjoying the walk south towards Central station. Normally she would go out for drinks closer to the fire station because there was a variety of bars and clubs nearby. Tonight was an exception because Natalie the Ambo invited Katrina out for a drink.

With Katrina out of the station, Renee was the final member of A Platoon in the station for the day. As the

A MOMENT IN TIME by Eric Brook

Station Officer, she believed she should be the first person in and the last person out on the shift. Unlike Katrina, Renee was going home to watch some TV and then go to bed. She was feeling sleepy after her long shower. But first, Renee had some paperwork to do.

Settling in to her chair, Renee started to type. Most of the information had been always filled in by Comms. Renee only had one paragraph to type:

"On arrival, unknown male was trapped under the train. Unknown male released by Rescue 1 & Paramedics by using 2 airbags to lift the train. Unknown male suffered a leg & arm amputation. Transported by Ambulance to RPA. Condition of unknown male unknown at time of this report."

Keying in her details, Renee saved her report and printed out a copy. It seemed wrong to Renee for here to sum up the the rescue in one paragraph. Closing down her computer for the final time that day, Renee said a quiet prayer for Steve, the unknown male under the train.

Chapter 14 – Leila Cruises For Chinese

6.15pm Thursday 01 April 2010

Across the city, 3 women were cruising the streets looking
for trouble. Or maybe, trouble will find them. It always
does, especially when the car they were in had blue and
white checkers on the side. Finding trouble came easily to
the trio of policewomen sitting inside the police car.

Driving through the Chinatown area of the Sydney CBD
area, it was very different to Central station which was
their last job. If you did not know any better, you would
think you were in down town Beijing rather than Sydney.
Leila was sitting in the passenger's seat in the police car.
She lowered the electric window halfway to smell the
aroma of the Chinese food that filled the air. "Feeling
hungry?", Leila asked no one in particular. No one
answered in a simple one word answer as she expected.

Nicole was driving the police car slowly through the
traffic. "So Speedy, where did you learn to run like that?
They wouldn't have done it like that at the Academy.",
Nicole said while continuing to watch the road ahead.

Listening to the conversation but also thinking of the
smell of the Chinese food all around her, Leila chimed in.

A MOMENT IN TIME by Eric Brook

"Yeah, you left us for dead! I think I know who will be the queen of foot pursuits will be around here!"

"I did athletics since I was a kid", Caroline explained. "I got to state level but running doesn't pay the bills unless you are Olympic level in the top few percent."

"Just be careful, Constable Dash. You don't want to be first there and first in an ambulance.", Nicole warned. "It might have been ok today but if it's stacks on and there's 1 of you and 50 of them – comprende?"

"Comprende", Caroline said begrudgingly, knowing that Nicole was more experienced and more importantly, correct. Nicole had seen too many cops running into a hostile and violent situation while vastly out-numbered and getting badly bashed as a result.

As Nicole explained, this was exactly what happened to the last new officer who was at City Central. A fractured skull was the result of that situation. The new officer had ignored instructions from his workmates and ran into the middle of an angry mob. He was set upon and was still away from work from the resulted injuries. Protests and unruly mobs were common in the city area.

"So what a first job for you, Caroline! I can't believe the guy was alive! No way I'd want to be an Ambo", Nicole observed. "Wow. Those two chicks under that train were amazing. There's no way in hell I'd do that!"

"Poor train driver. Hope she is going to be ok. What hope did she have?", Caroline said.

"Don't forget the support available, Dash.", Leila said helpfully. "After my shooting, they were really helpful." Nicole knew the story but obviously, Caroline did not. Leila continued the story for Caroline's benefit. "We got called to a hold up alarm at the Commonwealth Bank opposite Central on Elizabeth Street."

She had told the story so many times during the investigation and counselling sessions that it was almost second nature to her. She did not tell the story often but there was a point to retelling it this time – to help educate Caroline.

"It's Surry Hills' area but we beat them to the job as it turned out. They could argue that it was a borderline job but we were close by. It was a double beeper so we radioed up and ran hot to the job. We expected it to be a false alarm like most of them are. But we ran hot just in case it wasn't. We beat Surry Hills easily."

Leila cleared her throat and continued. Caroline was on the edge of her seat. "The crooks were coming out as I was heading in. There was three of them, dressed just like you see on any bank robbery movie. One of 'em was tooled up and aimed at me so I unloaded my clip into him. It was him or me. My former partner Andrew didn't have his mind on the job and it was nearly a turkey shoot. I didn't wanna be that turkey."

Her tone of voice changed slightly. "I wanted to put a cap in Andrew's ass after that and they transferred him out. After that, the Surry Hills truck just rocked up casual as we are driving now. My speed that day nearly saw me full of lead. So keep what Nic said in the back of your head."

"Holy crap, Leila! Glad you made it!", Caroline said. Her respect for Leila just went up a notch. Leila might be small but Caroline now knew she could handle her weapon. Leila must have been reading Caroline's mind. "I might be small but I go alright when things go pear shaped. It was him or me and I'm glad it was him. I didn't miss, either. The other two guys did not argue with us after that and surrendered on the spot. It all happened so quick."

A part of Caroline wanted to give Leila a hug. There was obviously more to the aftermath than Leila wanted to share now. There was the post-incident drug and alcohol test. There was the investigation into the incident where with the benefit of hindsight, it was easy to analyse Leila's thoughts and actions in minute detail. After a few months off duty, Leila was officially cleared and was rewarded with a bravery commendation. In investigation was very stressful for Leila. However it turned out that she was the only blue uniform that was stressed about the investigation and she was in the right. She believed that not enough was done to her former partner. For a while after the incident, she was not allowed to be on active duty.

While the investigation continued, Leila had many sleepless nights as she doubted her actions. It took her a long time for her not to feel guilty. She did still feel anger to her former partner, Andrew. It was lucky that neither of the police officers were shot. Andrew got careless and lazy and was ill-prepared to act. Indeed even after killing one of the robbers, it was left to Leila to arrest the other two offenders with the assistance of the bank's security guard. Andrew froze and was useless. Somehow, he still had a job.

"So if you need to talk about today, talk to us first if you want to. The shrinks mean well but often have no idea what we go through.", Nicole offered. "It's ok if that job freaked you out. I hate railway jobs."

"Thanks, guys. I think I'll be ok. It's not like I saw the guy or anything", Caroline explained.

Leila thought it would be a good idea to change the subject. "Oh man, that Chinese smells good!" Leila was getting hungrier by the minute. She loved Chinese food, not that you would know it by looking at her slim figure. Nicole enjoyed teasing Leila from time to time as she continued to drive the car around the Chinatown precinct. Leila needed a distraction. Leila needed food. Caroline needed food. Caroline needed her first arrest on her first shift to keep up with her friend Megan.

Typing on the keyboard in front of her, Leila asked the in car computer to check the police records of the blue Subaru Impreza WRX in front of her. While a small number of Highway Patrol cars had inbuilt number plate recognition, City 36 did not. She could see that the car had one person in the car, the driver. Nicole heard the keys of the computer and knew that Leila was after some action, possibly for Caroline's benefit. After a short pause, the result of Leila's check came back.

"Nic, that Rex is stolen. Taken last night in the Cross. Wanna pull him over?"

"Let radio know. We'll follow him for a moment then wheel him over", suggested Nicole.

Leila reached for the car's radio. "Radio, City 36."

"Go ahead, City 36."

A MOMENT IN TIME by Eric Brook

"City 36 following a confirmed outstanding Suburu WRX, Echo Romeo Kilo 4-6-9."

"Copy, City 36. Your location?"

"City 36, we are southbound on Sussex Street near Goulburn Street."

In case something happened, Nicole wanted to make sure that the radio operators and nearby units knew where they were. When pulling the vehicle over, it was possible that the car would refuse to pull over. Looking at the traffic ahead, the car had a commuter bus in front of it. The intersection with Goulburn Street was fast approaching. Suddenly, the bus stopped at the traffic lights, trapping the car.

"Go, go, go!" Nicole said to Leila and Caroline. Leila knew what Nicole was thinking and quickly left the car. Caroline soon followed. Nicole turned on the roof lights and blipped the siren quickly on and off. Leila un-holstered her gun and Caroline did the same. Leila pointed to Caroline, indicating for her to go to the passenger's side of the car.

"POLICE! GET OUT OF THE CAR! GET OUT NOW!" shouted Leila and Caroline in unison. Their guns were drawn and aimed towards the driver. The driver opened the door slowly. "PUT YOUR HANDS UP!" The driver complied. If he was unarmed, he did not have much choice. The policewomen could not assume that he would simply give up without a fight. Desperate people do strange things sometimes to avoid being arrested.

"GET DOWN ON THE GROUND!"

Again, the driver complied. He now had three women aiming guns at him as Nicole had got out of the car also. Leila was directly in line with the driver who was now on the ground, face down. Nicole rushed over and yelled at the man to put his hands behind his back. Nicole leapt onto the man and handcuffed him. With the driver in custody, Leila and Caroline checked the car for another person. After a quick check, Leila was confident there was no other person to deal with and re-holstered her gun.

"What did I do?", the handcuffed man asked Nicole. He was starting to wiggle around. Leila moved behind the man and crouched down, holding his legs. They had worked together for long enough that Leila did not need to wait to be told that Nicole might need a hand. Other sirens could be heard in the background.

"You are under arrest for driving a stolen car. You are not obliged to say or do anything unless you choose to do so. Anything you say or do may be taken down and used in evidence against you. Do you understand?"

The man nodded. Nicole did not want to release her hold on the man because he was easier to control that way. She looked at Caroline. "Call it in, Dash! We need a Truck and 14 here."

Caroline pushed the press to talk button on her radio. "City 36. One in custody. Nil outstanding (this meant that they were not after any further offenders). We require a truck and City 14 at the corner of Sussex and ..... um"

"Goulburn", Leila quickly filled in Caroline's mental block for her.

"Sussex and Goulburn, radio."

"Copy, City 36."

On George Street near the Town Hall, City 16 heard Caroline's call and told the radio operator that they were going to assist. Sabrina also heard the call and headed across town from the station. It was not long before City 16 arrived, parking in front of where Nicole and Leila still had the prisoner lying on the ground handcuffed. By this stage, a small crowd of pedestrians had gathered to watch from a safe distance.

A MOMENT IN TIME by Eric Brook

Traffic was slow as they moved around the police car and took a few moments to look at was going on as they passed by. A man with a large digital camera was moving around the intersection taking lots of photos. Most likely, he was from one of the city's major newspapers.

City 16's crew of Dave and Colin were the stereotypical old school policemen. They were tall and strong and were great to have on a caged truck. They took no nonsense from the crooks. Colin spoke first.

"Afternoon, 36. What do we have here?" He was very careful not to use the officer's name around the offender.

Truth be told, the offender was probably enjoying being held down by the two fit policewomen. That was about to end. The man knew that there was no point struggling. Colin grabbed the man by the shoulders and both female officers released their holds on him. Dave added his weight and helped the man to his feet.

"Stolen vehicle", Leila said. "He's been cautioned already. Hasn't been searched yet."

With the man now standing up, Colin and Dave held the man strongly. Dave gave Nicole a pair of handcuffs to replace the pair that was tightly around the man's wrists. Nicole patted the man down and searched his pockets.

A MOMENT IN TIME by Eric Brook

She did not worry about the nicety of a male officer patting down a male offender. Luckily, Nicole did not find any large weapons like a gun which was a load off her mind.

Continuing her search, Nicole found a small pocket knife in one pocket of his jacket and a small bag of white powder in his front pants pocket. This meant that he was up for at least three charges, driving a stolen car, being in possession of a knife and being in possession of drugs. At this stage, they did not know the man's name or his past history.

Meanwhile, Leila and Caroline were searching the car. They were unaware of what Nicole had found on the man at this stage. Wearing gloves, they were careful not to disturb anything or leave their own fingerprints. They were looking for anything that might be able to be used in evidence.

The car needed to be towed away for safekeeping and fingerprinting prior to returning the car to its rightful owner. After a few minutes, Leila was happy that she had searched the car and called the station to organising a tow truck to remove the vehicle. It would be taken to a secure holding yard and would be examined in minute detail by Forensics.

A MOMENT IN TIME by Eric Brook

The forensic examination would take a lot longer than the mere minutes that Caroline and Leila had spent checking the car. Unlike some other types of crime, it was not important to fully examine the car where it was stopped. The crime had not started there but is where 3 of Sydney's Finest had stopped it.

With the prisoner searched, Dave and Colin marched the prisoner into the back of their truck to take him back to City Central. He would be processed by Rowley, the shift's Custody Manager. The man would be placed into a cell while a lawyer was organised for him. That would also given time for City 36 to return to the station and get started on the pre-interview paperwork.

Then, the man would be interviewed about being in the vehicle. Did he steal the vehicle himself? What plans did he have for the vehicle? Did he act alone or did he have some help? If he only drove the vehicle but did not steal it, it might mean a difference in the time that the man could spend in jail. The forensic police would be able to tell how the car was stolen. Someone would also need to confer with the police who originally took the report of the vehicle being stolen. The location of the theft might have some useful evidence for the police.

With the prisoner safely in the back of the truck, Nicole handed Dave the knife and the white powder inside a couple of sealed zip lock bags. They would be booked up with the prisoner. "Thanks, guys!", Nicole said as Dave and Colin climbed into their vehicle for the short trip back to City Central. There was no need to rush back to the station under lights and sirens.

"That's one more bad guy off the street", Nicole quietly said to herself.

"City 16 back on, returning with 1 on board", Colin said on the radio from the front of his truck as he left the scene. He blipped his siren quickly as a way of giving 36 a salute, a tribute, thumbs up for a job well done. Colin and Dave would hand the prisoner over to the Custody Manager and then return to the streets to answer more radio calls. They were pleased with 36's catch and more pleased that they did not have to do 36's paperwork.

As City 16 left, City 14 arrived. The way it was going this afternoon, the supervisor might as well have placed herself on the crew of City 36. Sabrina parked behind Nicole's car, leaving her roof lights on as well. With the prisoner on the way back to the station, the crew of City 36 could talk more freely and compare notes. Sabrina wanted to know what had happened and what needed to be done.

"Good job, guys!", Sabrina congratulated her junior officers. "How did you find the car?"

A MOMENT IN TIME by Eric Brook

Caroline was beaming with pride. She had played her part in a good arrest and now felt like things were for real and that all the hard times at the Academy were worth it.

"We were behind it in Chinatown and a hunch led me to do a transport on the car. I'm not sure what it was but a WRX could always be worth a look" Leila explained. "I checked it on the MDT and it came up as stolen. It was taken from the Cross last night. We are just waiting for the rostered tow now."

Nicole continued "We arrested the driver and I found a knife and some dope on him. Thankfully we managed to stop him before he took off. Looks like that car could go quite hard in the right hands..."

"Like yours?", Leila interjected with a laugh. "Maybe Tom will let you put some police stickers on it."

"Ha ha, Constable Quick Draw McGraw.", Nicole laughed back. Caroline seemingly did not get the joke. Suddenly, a light bulb went off in Nicole's brain.

"Do you reckon the owner would mind if I drove it back to their house for them?" Sabrina knew that Nicole knew the procedure and she was joking.

A MOMENT IN TIME by Eric Brook

"Why don't you guys head back? It doesn't take three of you plus me to wait for a tow. I'll wait for it", Sabrina offered. Sabrina knew that City 36 would be busy with the prisoner for a while and would be off patrol for about 4 hours. Nicole thought that was a good idea. She walked back to her car. Caroline and Leila followed.

Sabrina moved her car to be directly behind the stolen car. While she waited for the tow truck, Sabrina would take some photos of the car and some of the contents of the car for evidence. It was handy to have images of where the vehicle was stopped. Having as much evidence as possible in addition to the statement that City 36 would later extract from the offender was vital in order to secure a conviction.

Returning to their car, Nicole once again sat in the driver's seat. Leila motioned for Caroline to sit in the front passenger's seat. For the first time, Caroline called radio from the front seat of City 36.

"City 36 back on from Goulburn Street and returning to the station. 16 took the prisoner back and 14 is awaiting the tow."

Nicole started the engine of the car. Caroline certainly had a story to tell her friend and fellow probie Megan. She had just been involved in the arrest of an offender at gunpoint with a stolen car, a weapon and some drugs. It was certainly a lot better than Megoo's shoplifter at Manly this morning. Caroline tapped out a short message to her friend.

"CI36, stolen car. Check the news. Moo."

Once inside the police car, Leila removed her mobile phone from her pocket. "Who wants Chinese? My shout! A good arrest deserves some good food, I reckon. Paperwork's far better with Chinese. Welcome to Central, Caroline."

Chapter 15 – Judy Wants Out

5.30pm Thursday 01 April 2010

Judy walked through the peak hour crowds heading up the stairs to the platform. The passengers heading in that direction were very eager to get home after a hard day in the office. At this time of the afternoon, many more people were going up the stairs rather than leaving the station like Judy wanted to.

She squeezed her way down the stairs. At this point, she wished that she was not wearing the uniform that she was wearing. Neither did she have anything to cover the uniform with. The best she could do for the moment was to take her orange safety vest off and put it into her bag. Some drivers had a plain jacket that they put on as soon as they left the train. Sydney in early April was usually not jacket weather, though.

Reaching the bottom of the stairs, Judy saw a paramedic motor cycle parked. She presumed the paramedic was working on the guy that she had just hit with the train. Apart from the fact that she was busy dealing with the police, she did not watch the rescue effort. She was not expected to supervise the emergency services but she would be available to assist in terms of train matters if required.

A MOMENT IN TIME by Eric Brook

Turning left, Judy was being rapidly overtaken by many people heading longer distances home on intercity trains. The passengers heading in that direction towards the trains were the hardcore commuters. Rather than spending a few minutes on the trains that Judy drove, the majority the passengers were on the train for between 1 and 3 hours in each direction as the costs of living in Sydney increased. Depending on the person, they used the train as a mobile office, a mobile bed (albeit with difficulty) or a mobile library. If they missed the train by a narrow margin, there was at least a 30 minute wait, often longer. None of this mattered to Judy after seeing the man use her train as a mobile killing machine.

She had one more task to do, organise her own taxi home. The manager had not done this for her, merely handing her a Cabcharge docket. If the taxi had been organised, she did not know about it. This was not a surprise, though. Sometimes, Judy needed to catch a taxi as part of her normal day to travel between depots and other locations. This was especially the case late at night or early in the morning. At times, there were screw ups with planned taxis so a screw up with an unplanned one at the middle of the afternoon peak hour was no surprise.

Judy entered a door than many members of the public did not even know existed. It was a door in plain view which was busy with train crew arriving and departing. Inside the large foyer, it was similar to an information desk at a bank. One side was for drivers and the other half was for guards. The counters were the equivalent of

A MOMENT IN TIME by Eric Brook

Judy's sign on room. At her depot, they didn't have separate people looking after the separate job classifications. As this was not her depot, she felt like a visitor. She did not know either man being the counters. Moving to the driver's counter on the right hand side of the room, the man was not busy. At this time, crew did not sign on because of the time of the day. The timetable dictated that the maximum number of crews were on their trains during the peak hours. The man was doing a Sudoku in the newspaper.

Judy dropped her work bag noisily, not caring if that thud attracted the man's attention or not. If the thud of the dropped bag did not attract his attention, the growling female voice did as a mobile phone rang from floor level.

"Now's not a great time for this!"

Thinking that the gruff female voice was for him, the man lifted his eyes from his puzzle that he was working on. "Can I help you?", he stammered.

"I'm the driver of 711 run. Has a taxi been booked for me?" Without looking down at his list of crew sign on times and taxi bookings, he shook his head. He could not directly see his list even if he wanted to as he had it covered with his newspaper. He did, though, look at his watch.

A MOMENT IN TIME by Eric Brook

"It's 5.30 in the afternoon. Haven't you heard of a train?", he mockingly said, eyes returning to his newspaper. Not for the first time this afternoon, Judy shook her head.

Also not for the first time that afternoon, she muttered "First day on the job, is it?" Becoming clearer in her tone "You've got your head so deep into that newspaper that you wouldn't know if a train was up your arse and I blew the horn."

The centre's supervisor came rushing over to see what was going on. This sort of outburst was uncommon. It was clearly made so people could hear it. There was another driver off to the side, texting on a mobile phone. "What's going here, driver?", the supervisor asked Judy.

"This muppet behind the desk hasn't even checked to see if a taxi has been ordered for me. I'm guessing that if he had a migraine, he'd be in the first available limo. He's too busy reading his newspaper."

"I'm guessing you are the driver from the fatality before. Lucky you came over because we didn't know where you wanted to go. Grab a form and we'll book it now for you."

In typical fashion, things could not happen unless there was paperwork involved, even if the two people concerned were right next to each other. Judy knew what the taxi booking form looked like. A few simple questions and answers was enough to get the job done. She walked to a bookshelf and saw many various forms.

There seemingly was a form for everything! Reading several forms briefly, Judy found the form she needed. Taking the form to a nearby bench, she filled in the required details. Many things needed paperwork including the upcoming taxi trip. She would have many forms to fill in over the next few days.

While filling in the form that a monkey-riding elephant could have designed in 2 minutes, Judy's mobile phone buzzed. Retrieving it from her pocket, she saw an unwanted text message from her ex-boyfriend. That was the last thing she needed at that point. He was also a driver and may have heard about the fatality. While she was tempted not to read the message, she did anyway.

OH: "You've got your head so deep into that newspaper that you wouldn't know if a train was up your arse and I blew the horn!"

"That bastard!" she exclaimed. She had not taken notice of him but her ex-boyfriend Matt had obviously overheard her conversation and quoted it back to her.

A MOMENT IN TIME by Eric Brook

Returning her attention to the form, a few quickly written words and numbers was all that was needed. Noticing that the supervisor still at the desk, she handed the form back to him. Seemingly undisturbed by Judy's outburst, the counter jockey returned to his puzzle.

"Thanks. I'll call it through myself for you. Go wait at the taxi rank and the cab will be there soon."

"That would be great. Thanks."

Judy picked up her bag and followed a passageway that led to the outside. Going this way, she did not need to go through the ticket barriers. The sun was still out and the amount of people had reduced dramatically while she had been inside the building. Turning left, the wide open spaces of the main concourse had seen many people over the years. As she walked from one end to the other, Judy reflected on the changes she had seen in this area during her time working for the railway. The basic structure of the area was the same but subtle changes were noticeable if you knew where to look.

Her demeanour had improved slightly walking through the terminal. Her face was still showing a scowl though. It prompted a couple of the local homeless people to give Judy a wide berth. Normally, the same homeless people would not hesitate to ask everyone, railway workers included, for money and cigarettes. Not today.

A MOMENT IN TIME by Eric Brook

Arriving at the taxi rank, there were several taxis waiting. There was a steady turnover of taxis from different companies. Even though she was waiting, she had to wait for an allocated taxi from the company that had the contract. Most of the taxis were white but there was no requirement to do so, unlike the yellow taxis of Melbourne and New York and the black cabs of London.

"A holiday would be good right now!", Judy said to the young uniformed flight attendant standing next to her in the queue. The lady in the red coat smiled.

"I've just got back from Perth. It's a lovely city." Because of the nature of their work, flight attendants worked various routes often staying in different cities each night. To many people, flight attendants always always looked so pretty and glamorous. Judy felt neither at that moment in time.

"You don't know the half of it", Judy said.

A taxi driver was calling her name but because of his Indian accent, it sounded different to her. "Duty, Duty", the turbaned man called out while looking in her general direction.

Saying goodbye to the flight attendant, Judy moved towards the door of the taxi and opened it. When she was seated and seat belted, the driver drove away from the kerb. "Sorry I'm late. It's been murder on the roads this afternoon."

"It's been murder on the train this afternoon, too."

Chapter 16 – Natalie's Shout

6.15pm Thursday 01 April 2010

While Renee was helpful with her rookie rescue operator, across town at the city's main Ambulance station, there was a storm in progress instead of a relaxing shower. Ambulance supervisor Keith was very unhappy with his paramedic, Natalie. Natalie was dirty, smelly, angry and hungry. Keith was simply angry. "Natalie, why do I bother to put you on the bike? It spends half the shift on a stand while you think you are still a paramedic."

"Well, I AM a paramedic." She stressed the word am. "If you want a fast bike rider, that's me. If you want an awesome ambo, that's me. If you want that combined, that's me. If you want someone fast for the stats and for them not to do anything when they get there, get a bike courier with a first aid certificate."

Keith started to talk but Natalie interrupted him. "Back at the bus crash, I asked you if you wanted me to go back into service when the troops arrived. But no, you said to keep working on the patient. So I did."

Keith shook his head and tried to get a word in but Natalie was too angry. "At Central, you could have pulled me out at any time. I didn't see you size up the situation. I didn't see you under the train."

A MOMENT IN TIME by Eric Brook

Keith interrupted her back."I'm a supervisor. I don't do initial size ups. You do that and I agreed with how you decided to set that up. Don't you worry, I would have pulled you up on site if your plan wasn't good. Most of us would have gone where the cops did. I don't go under trains. I don't treat patients. That's your job."

"So don't bloody hang me out to dry for doing my job! I didn't see Rick or Tim under there. I didn't see the other Rescue guy under there. I didn't see any of those other firies under there! It was just me and Rescue Kat. I seriously don't see the problem here, Keith! We arrived quickly. We sized up. We got a plan in action. We got to work with the firies. I assessed and treated the patient. We got him out, alive. We didn't get injured. If we got the same call tomorrow, I'd do the same. It's been a long day, I'm pissed off and I think it's my shout at the pub. Coming?"

Keith stood still, slightly stunned. He was well aware of the effects of grief and knew that Natalie had a bad day. She had seen 2 deaths and two major traumatic cases since lunch time. For reasons only known to himself, Keith wanted to have that discussion with Natalie now. Perhaps with hindsight, he could have waited.

Natalie left the room without a further word. If she was a cartoon character, her face would be bright red and cartoon steam would be coming out of her ears. "Think about it, Natalie.", Keith said out loud but effectively he was talking to himself. It was not the last word on the subject either person would say.

The Chronicles of EMS team were sitting in the comfortable seats in front of the TV. Despite having the volume up, Mark and Justin could hear every word that was shouted. Mark shook his head. Both of them were stunned. They had watched Natalie in action. They had ridden around all day with Keith. "I hope that wasn't for our benefit!", Mark whispered to Justin. "To me, it's bang out of order! Natalie did a good job today. Let's go get a pint."

Justin sighed. That's all he needed to do. Changing the subject, he asked "Do they even sell pints here, man?"

Natalie stormed through the female locker room door, shoulder first. If the door was made out of newspaper, it would have been a ball of paper by the time Natalie made it to the shower. Knowing the room was empty, she stomped towards the shower. Stopping at her full length locker, she opened the door and grabbed a towel. Sitting on a bench, Natalie was the only female on shift who was back at the station. Undoing her work boots and removing her socks. Her tiny feet were very happy to be free of the heavy books.

Stripping out of her uniform, Natalie left her clothes on the floor and did not worry about covering her body. As there were no female supervisors at the station, she felt like the female locker room was a management-free oasis. Striding to the shower, the sweat had to go. Natalie waited for the water to heat up before standing underneath the nozzle. That was slightly ironic because she was already hot. A warm shower was often a lot better than a cold one, though.

Mark and Justin had not moved from the rec room. They hoped that Natalie would feel better after a shower. Sometimes after work, all someone might need is a change of clothes, some perfume or deodorant and they were good to go. Mark & Justin were quite happy to put a plain jacket over their uniforms tonight but Natalie really needed a shower. It had been a long day for her. It would be good for everyone to finish work for the day. The rec room chairs were really comfortable so waiting for Natalie was not an ordeal for the two men. "Oh man, this chair's comfortable. It's better than the chairs at my station!", Justin lamented.

"Better than your station chairs? Bugger that! These chairs are better than the ones in my lounge room! The only way they could be better if they vibrated!", Mark counter-attacked jovially.

Mark did not see the remote control in Justin's hand which he strangely pointed at the chair Mark was sitting in. There was a long buzzing noise and a vibration that took the Englishman by surprise.

A MOMENT IN TIME by Eric Brook

"What the ......?"

"No one told you about the vibrating chair?"

"No, lad, they didn't! Turn it up, please!"

Several minutes later, the door to the female locker room opened. There was a woman standing there with long hair and a little black dress. Mark was happily sitting on his vibrating chair but Justin turned his head around to face the door. "Wow, Nat! Is that the new uniform?"

"Are you two blokes ready to get on the cans or what?", Natalie asked her overseas guests. They looked puzzled.

Looking her in the eye, it was obvious that she was happy to be out of the uniform and going out for the night. "Nat, you've got very nice cans", the Englishman said.

Had that statement have been made by an Australian man, he might have got yelled at. In her current mood, she might have slapped the guy in question. However, this was Mark speaking. He did not get yelled at or slapped. The Australianism confused both men."

"No, man! She means going dancing, right?"

A MOMENT IN TIME by Eric Brook

"No, you two! 'On the cans' means to have a drink, usually at a bar."

"Ohhhhhhhhhh!" both men said in unison.

Mark rose out of his chair & Justin followed. Still not entirely at home with the station layout, they let Natalie led the way. "Let's go, boys!"

The trio walked down a hallway that Natalie knew well. It was a shorter way to the street. Opening a door, the artificial light was soon replaced by the final rays of sunlight for the night. Next week, things would be different as Sydney left summer time. Leading the way towards the city, Natalie placed her hands on each of her hips. Justin & Mark took this as a sign to link arms with Natalie.

"So, do you guys need to get changed or anything?", Natalie asked.

"Nope, we're good", Justin replied. "Let's get something to eat. Know somewhere good, Nat?"

"My local's pretty good. You should be able to find something you like."

A MOMENT IN TIME by Eric Brook

Continuing the walk to the hotel, Natalie's phone beeped. It was a text message from Rescue Kat. They were going to meet up at the hotel. The different emergency services did not usually socialise together but today was different. Today, it felt like Katrina & Natalie were in the same team. Natalie's fingers zoomed across the keyboard, returning Katrina's message.

"How far's the pub, Nat? Back home in England, there's almost a pub on every corner! Certainly makes a pub crawl easier!" Justin must have had a confused look on his face because Mark continued to speak without a pause.

"Oh that's right, you'd call it bar hopping." The two men had stayed together on the road together for the Chronicles project that they were used to translating between American English and British English as the situation dictated. Laughter filled the air. Adding Natalie to the mix confused things further. Some things were still confusing, though.

"Have you both heard of the Circle Line pub crawl?"

Again, there was no pause in Mark's speech.

"There's over 20 stops on the tube line ... ok, Justin, subway .... and you get off at each stop & have a drink.

A MOMENT IN TIME by Eric Brook

Apart from getting totally maggotted, the aim is to get around the whole loop and get back to the original station and pub. Often, they'd end up in the back of an ambulance or a police van."

The smell in the air changed from fresh air to stale beer and tobacco. The inside of pubs in the modern day pub was very pleasant due to an indoor smoking ban. It was great for people who didn't smoke and for those who did, they didn't have much choice. The trio walked through a side door of the hotel and went straight to the bar. Natalie did not go to the bar every night but she went there often enough that some of the staff knew her by name. Often, she drunk alone. Tonight, she had company and so she was going to take advantage of this.

After a busy day, the international trio of paramedics were very hungry. Unlike many jobs, it did matter if a paramedic was unavailable because they were getting something to eat. They often needed to eat when they could, knowing that they could be interrupted at any time for a call. Knowing a good place to eat that was quick at preparing food was important. Spending 10 minutes or longer waiting for food to be cooked was not an option. However, they were now off duty so they could take their time to choose something to eat and to eat it. There was zero chance of getting an interruption tonight because they were now off duty.

While they were waiting for Katrina to arrive, there was some chitchat while sitting on the comfortable lounges that was becoming a frequent sight in some hotels in the city. The lounges were a welcome relief, especially for Natalie because of the harder seat on the motorcycle compared to the ambulance.

According to the agreement at the station, Natalie had to buy the first round of drinks because she was spotted on TV first. Mark was very surprised to find that the beer was cold. This was his first taste of Australian beer and his first drink and social opportunity in the country. He felt right at home because in some ways, Australia was just like England to him, except for the beer.

After a few minutes of quiet drinking, Mark and Justin had to buy the next two rounds because they were also on TV today. The hotel was filling up with patrons taking advantage of the long weekend which had effectively now commenced. The noise levels were increasing by the minute as the room filled with people. Conversations between different groups blended together, especially when passers-by worked out that Mark and Justin had accents. There were large screen TVs located around the room showing a variety of sports. Somehow, a horse race caught Natalie's attention.

"Oh look! An ambulance!"

A MOMENT IN TIME by Eric Brook

Looking up, an ambulance could be seen trailing the horses in case a jockey fell off their horse. The horse tracks were long but the horses were not doing continuous laps so it was better for the ambulance to follow the horses. The sun was setting in Sydney but the vision of the screen showed the track to be in bright sunshine. Due to the time difference, the horse race was live from the west coast of Australia.

"Oh look, Mark! They are wearing green jumpsuits!", Justin laughed. Mark's green coloured uniforms was a running joke between the two men. Mark laughed also.

After three drinks, it was time to start the shouting cycle again. They had not seen a news program since returning from the Central job and were discussing if they should just continue in the order that they started. After a few minutes of joking banter, the decision was made with the arrival of Katrina.

"Hey, Katrina! It's nice to see you!" Natalie stood up and hugged her new friend. Justin and Mark stood up as well.

"I'd like you to meet my overseas visitors. Justin's here from San Francisco and Mark's from England. They are paramedics back home and they are here to see how we work. They were at Central earlier checking us out."

A MOMENT IN TIME by Eric Brook

"Nice to meet you, Katrina!" Mark smiled as Justin spoke.

"Are you hungry?" Natalie handed Katrina a menu.

"I'm starving! I haven't eaten for ages!"

"What do you want to drink, Kat?", Natalie asked.

Looking in the direction of the bar, Katrina knew that she wanted to have a drink but did not know what.

"Hmmmm. I dunno. How about an American Paramedic On The Rocks?" Katrina laughed at her own joke and Natalie laughed as well. Justin (the only American paramedic in the group) was somewhat stunned. Katrina looked directly into Justin's eyes. "How about Sex On The Beach, Justin?"

Justin did not get flustered easy but on this occasion, he did. He looked Katrina up and down in her dress and smiled. He was stunned, though. "That sounds good but we've only just met, Katrina. Shouldn't I buy you a drink first?"

Mark spoke up on behalf of the group. "Who thinks that it is Katrina's shout? If you do, raise your hand." Justin raised his hand straight away, closely followed by Mark and Natalie. The 3 paramedics clearly out-voted her and decided that it was her shout at the bar for the fourth round.

"Batter up, Katrina!", Justin exclaimed as if he was at a baseball game back home.

"Okie dokie! Did you see me on TV or something?", Katrina chuckled. Laughter filled the room. If they did not laugh, they would cry.

Chapter 17 – Steve's Struggle

6.20pm Thursday 01 April 2010

The Ambulance's lights finally could be switched off now that it was safely at the hospital. Throughout the trip, Rick had made sure that he did an assessment on Steve's condition as best he could, considering the amount of blood he had lost. The trauma team would have their hands full. A complete arm amputation and a leg amputation at the thigh - "how the hell was he not dead?", Rick thought. His training told him that this guy should be dead.

Tim left the driver's seat and went to the rear to help Rick. With all the wheels of the trolley on the ground, the medics started to wheel Steve's stretcher into the hospital. This was a well rehearsed and often completed skill, doing a moving patient handover to the hospital staff. Rick began his speech like handover.

The trauma team were waiting at the front door of the Ambulance entry having been pre-warned by the Comms Centre. Rick gave a quick handover. Steve was still in a critical condition. He needed fluids and he needed blood, fast. He needed a switched on team which is exactly what he had.

A MOMENT IN TIME by Eric Brook

"This is Steve", Rick began. "Hit by a train about 5pm, arm & leg amputation. Lost a lot of blood, unconscious for most of it. Under the train for about 20 minutes. Morph by 3, oxygen, fluids."

"Resus 1!", Dr Lisa Brenning raised her voice, instructing the team about where to go. Wheeling Steve into the Resuscitation Room, the team carefully lifted him from the ambulance stretcher to the hospital bed. The Resus bays (as they were called for short) had all the the equipment needed for rapid treatment of the most critical of patients. In this hospital, there were 4 similar bays. On a good night, the resus bays were empty. On a bad night, all 4 bays were full and then some. Lisa and the rest of the team were very experienced in handling the busy nights, usually Wednesday to Sundays.

Being close to the inner city, they were experienced with incidents happening on trains and stations. Trips, falls, assaults and overdoses were common. People jumping in front of trains usually resulted in a one way trip to the mortuary. But for Steve, his time had not yet come. Lisa and her team were determined to keep it that way.

With their patient now safely in the hospital, the paramedics were now clear to return to work. That was one good thing about a category 1 patient, the hospital usually took them in straight away. With lower category patients, the paramedics often had to wait with the patient until the handover was conducted. Patients and their relatives wrongly believed that an ambulance ride was a passport to jumping the queue into the emergency treatment beds. They would not believe that they did not get immediate treatment. Steve needed immediate treatment and would get it regardless if the patient came in via ambulance or someone drove them.

In Resus 1, a nurse named Jen connected the hospital's heart monitor, a drip, a bag of blood and placed an oxygen mask on Steve's face. "Steve, we are going to look after you the best we can." Another nurse cut Steve's clothing off his battered body. For the first time since the accident, Steve's amputations were plainly visible. His missing parts had been retrieved by the on-site paramedics. A specialist surgeon was assessing the body parts in another room.

Even though the surgeon had possession of Steve's arm and leg, he did not know if it was worth attaching them at this stage. The important thing at this time was to try to stabilise Steve. They needed to find the bleeding and stop it. There was only so much that the bandages that Natalie put on at the scene could do.

As quick as the blood was flowing in, it was coming out. "People, we need to find this blood loss and stop it, fast", Lisa said. Her mind was now fully on the job. The earlier death that she had to deal with seemed like such a long time ago even though it was only a few hours ago.

A MOMENT IN TIME by Eric Brook

Looking up at the monitor, Lisa did not like what she could see. She was not surprised, though.

She wondered if it was worth letting Steve live at all. While artificial arms and legs were better than ever, he had a long recovery and rehabilitation in front of him. If she was questioning her profession before, she was questioning it harder now. As much as it was her job to help save Steve's life, his quality of life was not great right now. According to her protocols, Steve being alive was a good thing. She might not personally agree, especially after today.

It was time to give Steve some more morphine. If the team was going to work on him in his current condition, he deserved to be pain free. Nurse Jen measured the dose and pumped it into Steve's seemingly lifeless body. Lisa was privately disgusted at this point but she knew it was her job to help keep Steve alive even it was rapidly becoming something she did not want to do. She thought that somewhere, Steve must have friends and family who care for him and should not see him like this. Between the police and the hospital staff, someone would have to tell his family.

"Would we treat a dog like this?", Lisa said out loud to no one in particular. The trauma team were looking at her in shock. Lisa did not normally talk like this. Looking down at Steve, she again thought out loud. "What made you decide that jumping in front of a train was a good idea, huh?"

A MOMENT IN TIME by Eric Brook

If Steve ever woke up, several people would be interested in his answer. Lisa talking broke the silence that the team had been working in. Lisa squeezed Steve's remaining hand. "You've fought hard, mate." She was hoping he would squeeze her hand back even though she knew that he was so full of morphine that he did not know where he was.

The heart monitor changed tone. It had slowed down since his arrival into the Emergency Department. This was a concern. The heart rhythms on the screen had changed shape. This was a concern, too. Had the paramedics been too slow to get Steve to the hospital? Was the morphine wearing off and straining Steve's heart? Had he lost too much blood? There were so many questions going through Lisa's brain. She did not have time to process each thought separately, she did not have time.

Things were not good for Steve. His heart had changed rhythm and not for the best. The stress and trauma combined with the major blood loss was stressing Steve's heart. If the team was to keep Steve alive, they needed drastic action right at that moment. Lisa needed to shock Steve's heart. Looking down at the pads on his chest, she quietly said to him "Sorry mate." and then said to the room "Shocking! Clear!"

A MOMENT IN TIME by Eric Brook

The whole team stood back from Steve. They needed to do this for their own safety. Another doctor pressed a button on the machine at Lisa's command. The machine delivered an electric shock to Steve's chest. That afternoon, his life and the life of everyone who worked hard to save him on the scene, in the ambulance and in the hospital had changed forever.

To live or not to live, that was the question.

His heart rate was dangerously low. "We are using so much blood! 9 bags so far!", Jen explained. It was her job to make sure that the blood was flowing into Steve. The paramedics did not carry blood products with them so they could not have started that process. Despite the pressure bandages, an hour had passed where blood was coming out but no blood was being pumped in.

In an attempt to catch up, Jen was pumping blood into Steve using two bags of blood at once. "I will need some more blood soon!"

The heart monitor showed some improvement in the terms of heart rate. Lisa squinted as she looked at the heart monitor mounted on the wall. She wanted to see if the rhythm had improved. It was not unconceivable that another shock would be needed. Sometimes, a second burst of electricity might be needed. "Shocking again! Clear!" Once again, Lisa shocked Steve's heart.

A MOMENT IN TIME by Eric Brook

"C'mon, Steve! Don't give up now!". Lisa was alternating between wanting him to live or die. It was an awful feeling that she never dare tell a patient. Looking over at the heart monitor again, Lisa had a worried look on her face. Against the odds, Steve was showing a lot of fight. Surprisingly, Steve's heart rate was improving. It was either because he was going to get better or he was about to die. Lisa did not know which way it was going to go.

"Oh my god!" Jen squealed. This was unlike her. "Oh my god!", she repeated. Taking her eyes off the monitor, Lisa's eyes moved to the closed eyes of her patient. She squeezed his hand. The whole team was looking towards Steve. The brightly lit room was deathly silent.

Jen's squeal led the entire team to look at Steve's monitor. They knew her well enough to know that she did not lose her professional control. Professional nurses did not squeal, professional nurses did not cry out or scream.

Against the odds, Steve's condition was improving. With the forces involved in the impact, it was a credit to everyone concerned that Steve was still alive. The wrong move at the wrong time could have resulted in major consequences such as paralysis or death. Death was always on the cards in this situation. All of the team knew what it was like to lose a patient. Despite their experience and the support available, it never got easier.

http://www.amomentintimenovel.com

A MOMENT IN TIME by Eric Brook

Breaking the silence in the room, Lisa cleared her throat being speaking. "Steve! Welcome back! Do you know where you are?", Lisa asked. On this occasion, Lisa did know the patient's name. That was not always the case.

She moved her pretty face next to his. His face was bloody as no one was worried about his appearance just yet. The expression on her face changed from fear and concern to happiness, only if it was to be short lived. For the first time since he was screaming at Central, Steve spoke.

In a low, croaky voice, he did not know where he was. His eyes opened slightly, squinting against the harsh light of the hospital room. Looking deeply into Steve's eyes, There was a tear running down Lisa's face. The tear fell from Lisa's face and landed on Steve's bloody face. Because of the tube down his throat, it was hard for him to talk.

"Me ..... me Steve?"

A MOMENT IN TIME by Eric Brook

ACKNOWLEDGEMENTS

http://www.amomentintimenovel.com

A MOMENT IN TIME by Eric Brook

This journey of writing A Moment In Time was a very interesting one as a first time novelist. There are several people that I would like to thank for their inspiration, support and assistance, even if they did not know about it at the time.

Kenn Crawford, RE Chambliss, Scott Sigler

When I came up with the concept of A Moment In Time, these authors inspired me in different ways.

Kenn's debut novel Dead Hunt was about to commence as a podiobook. I did not know Kenn at the time that he sent an email looking for voice talent. Kenm did not know me apart from the fact that I was an Australian podcaster. Dead Hunt was already written but Kenn has big plans for me in Dead Hunt II which he is writing. I voiced the role of Wade in the podiobook version. Kenn was very patient and supportive with me in my first voice role.

Through Kenn, I met RE Chambliss. Renee narrated Dead Hunt and also her debut novel Dreaming of Deliverance. It was when I was listening to Renee narrating her story while I was driving a train that I came up with the idea for A Moment In Time. Again, Renee has been a good source of support.

http://www.amomentintimenovel.com

A MOMENT IN TIME by Eric Brook

A couple of days prior to starting on A Moment In Time, I was lucky to be able to hear a reading then hang out with Scott Sigler. Arguably the most successful person to use podcasting as a way of building an audience and distributing his work, the evening I spent with Scott Sigler was inspirational. I got an insight into his dedication, drive and passion. Even while flying many miles from home, Scott was busy writing. He was writing, working with his audience and running a promotion in addition to what he was actually in Australia to do. He was also having a lot of fun at the same time.

Judy, my mum

Even though I dedicated the book to her in the front of the book, my mum Judy is the most important thing in my life. She is always supportive, loving and caring. Apart from myself, she is also my biggest critic on occasions that I need it. She has gone from knowing nothing about computers, the internet and podcasting in 2009 to being very passionate about the medium. In many ways, this book and Channel Erk would not happen without her.

My Writing Nook

Speaking of this book possibly not happening, My Writing Nook made it so much easier for me. I am writing this part of the dedication at Central railway station in between my trains. Earlier, I wrote while sitting as a passenger on a train travelling through the inner western suburbs. This illustrates in part how handy My Writing Nook (and by extension my iPhone) was for this book. Almost totally written on the iPhone, it was great to be able to write when and where the mood struck using a device I would have with me anyway. Without it - who knows?

Caroline, Nicole, Leila, Judy, Renee, Katrina, Natalie & Lisa

These names are not just random names plucked out of thin air for my major characters. They are the names of real people that I know. Some of the characters' actions are based on those of the real life person. Apart from anything else, it was so much easier to visualise what the characters were doing if they took the form of a familiar person. Out of all the major characters, Natalie's character is the closest to her real personality as real life Natalie (aka Ms Paramedic online) is an American paramedic. Thanks for alpha-reading the book, Ms P!

http://www.amomentintimenovel.com

A MOMENT IN TIME by Eric Brook

Mark Glencorse & Justin Schorr (Chronicles of EMS)

A massive thank you to Mark and Justin for allowing me to use their likeness and much of their online personas in A Moment In Time. As is written in the book, Mark and Justin are paramedics in their respective countries and are the public image of the Chronicles of EMS project. While the guys might not make it to Australia in the flesh anytime soon, they were here in spirit thanks to me. Thanks to Justin for alpha-reading the book in advance. Thanks Mark for trusting me enough to write the book and your character the way I did.

Thorium Girl

Thorium Girl did an outstanding job with the cover! I had an idea in mind for the cover and she came through for me, far exceeding my expectations. I could not have done what she did with it over many hours of work. Thanks for your ongoing friendship, support and guidance TG. You rock!

Megan

The only regret about A Moment In Time that I have is that I did not meet Megan sooner. Meeting her a lot earlier would have been awesome. Since telling her about the project in the very final stages, she has been very supportive. She was very helpful with her critical (she calls it pedantic) red editing pen. In addition, she has agreed to narrate the podcast version which you can hear in 2011. I wanted an Australian female voice around the age of the characters and when I first heard her narrating voice, I was blown away. Thanks, Megan!

Aimee Maree

I love Aimee Maree's passion and she has become a close friend. The amount of passion she has for anything she talks about was inspiring for me while writing this book. During her recent European trip, ahe was spreading the word about the book, mainly about the tech that I used to write A Moment In Time. I am looking forward to seeing Europe in 2011 with her, it will be an interesting trip!

A MOMENT IN TIME by Eric Brook

Channel Erk, Writing, Social Networking & Podcasting Communities

There have been so many people that have assisted me since I started podcasting in 2007. Some of them have had characters named after them in this book. Many people have shown a lot of support and friendship to me. Some of these people I have met in person, some I have not. There are too many people to mention here but thank you, everyone.

Three podcasts have been very handy listening while writing A Moment In Time.

These are:

- I Should Be Writing
- Dead Robots Society
- Sydney Writers' Centre

In their own ways, each podcast has helped me learn more about writing. Thank you to Mur, Terry, Justin, Ryan & Valerie for their efforts in producing such excellent writing podcasts. I am well aware of how much effort goes into podcasting but you have all allowed me to look into what needs to go into writing. All three shows are excellent resources with personal stories, helpful suggestions and inspiring interviews.

THANK YOU!

http://www.amomentintimenovel.com